PRAISE FOR SAMANTHA M. BAILEY

A Friend in the Dark

"Suspenseful, twisty, and addictive. *A Friend in the Dark* is smartly written and deliciously chilling. I couldn't put it down. This is Bailey at her best! I paused an episode of *Below Deck: Down Under* to finish this book. That's how invested I was."

—Jeneva Rose, *New York Times* bestselling author of *The Perfect Marriage*

"Wow! Chilling, riveting . . . and page-turningly edgy. The oh-so-talented Samantha M. Bailey has created a twisted (and steamy!) world of power, passion, and vulnerability. This seductive thriller with its deep understanding of psychological trauma and the heavy secrets of the past is brave, original, and haunting. Fans of Gillian Flynn and Lisa Unger will cheer this must-read author."

—Hank Phillippi Ryan, *USA Today* bestselling author of *The House Guest*

"Samantha M. Bailey never disappoints! *A Friend in the Dark* is one of the most intriguing and surprising books I've read in a while. You think you know where it's headed . . . but you don't. This thriller shocked me to the very end."

—Samantha Downing, internationally bestselling author of *My Lovely Wife*

T0036380

"With *A Friend in the Dark*, Samantha M. Bailey has crafted what's destined to be one of the most binge-worthy, buzzed about thrillers of the year. Wholly propulsive with twist after mind-blowing twist, richly layered characters, and an intricate plot, Bailey is at the top of her game and delivers not only a spine-tingling thriller but also a potent examination of the complexity of female desire and the terrifying, dark side of online relationships. *A Friend in the Dark* will have you glued from its first page to its explosive conclusion. An absolute masterpiece from the master of suspense!"

—May Cobb, award-winning author of *A Likeable Woman* and *The Hunting Wives*

"A tautly written story of twists, deception, and long-simmering desire, *A Friend in the Dark* is a thriller that consumed me from start to end. Samantha M. Bailey is a master of surprise endings and complex antagonists, and each chapter of this story flew by. Do not miss this one!"

—Elle Marr, Amazon Charts bestselling author of *The Family Bones*

"A sexy treat of a thriller loaded with twists and hairpin turns! Fans of Colleen Hoover should love *A Friend in the Dark*. It will keep you guessing and up way too late."

—Daniel Kalla, bestselling author of *Fit to Die*

"When you sit down with a Samantha M. Bailey novel, you expect to be nailed to your seat for the duration. *A Friend in the Dark* does that and so much more: this electrifying, layered, and psychologically acute thriller examines female desire, marriage, and motherhood while sweeping you off on a twisty ride all the way to its visceral, explosive finale. Bailey expertly crafts dark history and human foibles into an addictive narrative cocktail. Welcome to your next book hangover."

—Damyanti Biswas, bestselling author of the Blue Mumbai series

"*A Friend in the Dark*, by Samantha M. Bailey, is a knockout punch of a thriller. This wild ride starts with a marriage in freefall, then twists through a series of escalating and creepy turns before careening to a stunning conclusion. I read this one in a day and so will you."

—Darby Kane, internationally bestselling author of *Pretty Little Wife* and *The Engagement Party*

"Several lives burdened with tangled histories of desire, fear, cruelty, revenge, and murder are on a collision course until they intersect brilliantly in Samantha M. Bailey's *A Friend in the Dark*. Eden Miller finds herself suddenly without her husband, at war with her daughter, at a crossroads she never anticipated when, vulnerable and eager for attention, a long-ago flame reenters her life, igniting a forgotten passion. This is a sexy, dark, and twisty tale from a master of the genre. Highly recommended!"

—Jon Lindstrom, author of *Hollywood Hustle*, and four-time Emmy-nominated actor and award-winning filmmaker

"Clever, sexy, and compulsively readable, *A Friend in the Dark* is a pulse-pounding thriller with one jaw-dropping twist after another. Samantha M. Bailey has created a compelling cast of characters, a dark and layered mystery, and an insightful look at marriage, motherhood, and female identity."

—Robyn Harding, bestselling author of *The Drowning Woman*

"Savage secrets and desires collide in Samantha M. Bailey's *A Friend in the Dark*. Bailey is a master of misdirection, spinning twists and building tension until there's nothing to do but race to the knockout finish. *A Friend in the Dark* is a fierce, gutsy thriller, and Bailey is unstoppable."

—Tessa Wegert, author of *The Kind to Kill*

"Samantha M. Bailey's *A Friend in the Dark* simmers with palpable desire and twists that'll have readers gasping. Just when you think you know the direction of her story, you get knocked sideways with twist after jaw-dropping twist. This is a must-read for any thriller lover!"

—Heather Levy, Anthony-nominated author of
Walking Through Needles

"Sexy, fast-paced, and deliciously twisty, *A Friend in the Dark* is Samantha M. Bailey at her suspenseful best. An unpredictable thrill ride that packs an emotional wallop, readers will be hard pressed to stop turning pages until they reach the spine-tingling conclusion. A compelling, addictive must-read."

—Laurie Elizabeth Flynn, bestselling author of
The Girls Are All So Nice Here

"This sexy, heart-pounding thriller is everything a reader craves. Brilliant plotting and misdirection and mind games will have you flipping pages at warp speed. With twists and turns galore throughout, this is a one-sit read that will leave you shocked. A compelling look at fantasy versus reality, *A Friend in the Dark* is sure to stand out as a fan favorite of 2024."

—Jaime Lynn Hendricks, bestselling author of *I Didn't Do It*

Watch Out for Her

"Yet again, one of our most beloved thriller writers brings us a story with the heart of a family drama and the pulse of an edge-of-your-seat spine chiller. Filled with foreboding from the very first page, this one will keep you up all night—and have you checking the locks!"

—Marissa Stapley, *New York Times* bestselling author of
Reese's Book Club Pick *Lucky*

"Shows that Bailey is no one-book wonder. It's as tightly plotted and skillfully written as her first, with a great backstory to carry it off . . . Bailey builds the suspense here with excellent pacing and clues that drop at exactly the right times. This is a great book to take on that summer holiday or the cottage weekend when all you have to do is chill, eat, and read."

—*The Globe and Mail*

"Bailey is a strong writer who keeps the reader turning pages . . . A cautionary tale about the fine line between diligence and obsession and the dangers of doing the wrong things for what we believe are the right reasons."

—*Toronto Star*

"A cleverly written, twisty, and brilliantly creepy thriller. With compelling characters intertwined with obsession, lies, simmering menace, and secrets at its heart, this is a page-turner that drew me in and kept me hooked. A real must-read!"

—Karen Hamilton, internationally bestselling author of *The Perfect Girlfriend*

"A tense and claustrophobic thriller in which Bailey makes you question whether the heart of a family is a place of safety or danger. Paranoia, obsession, and secrets ensure a twisty read."

—Gilly Macmillan, *New York Times* bestselling author of *What She Knew*

"Creepy, surprising, and relentlessly tense, *Watch Out for Her* is so much more than a thriller; it's an unflinching exploration of the roles we allow women to fill. With dark secrets and cliff-hangers galore, this thrill ride will keep you up long past your bedtime. I couldn't put it down."

—Andrea Bartz, *New York Times* bestselling author of Reese's Book Club Pick *We Were Never Here*

"A hair-raising, suspenseful page-turner [that] will have one watching their back wherever they go, but what really gets to the novel's heart is the unexpected and chilling ending . . . The narrative is so well written and joined together it flows effortlessly."

—*The New York Journal of Books*

"Samantha M. Bailey's latest thriller is as propulsive as her sizzling debut. Two troubled women enter into a complex relationship that could shatter not only their lives but also the lives of everyone they touch. A page-turner in the most literal sense of the word—I could not put this book down until the final shocking twist."

—Robyn Harding, bestselling author of *The Perfect Family*

"An irresistible story about what happens when we take our obsessions too far. Propulsive, electrifying, and sinister, I could not tear myself away from the narrators, two women each hiding dark secrets from their families. Bailey's assured prose delivers as enthralling a tale as her stellar debut."

—Stephanie Wrobel, bestselling author of *This Might Hurt* and *Darling Rose Gold*

"Addictive and relentlessly twisty . . . Nobody else writes a propulsive, family-centered mystery quite like this: Bailey is queen of the domestic thriller for a reason. *Watch Out for Her* masterfully deals with the shifting power of obsession and the secrets we keep from our loved ones . . . and ourselves."

—Laurie Elizabeth Flynn, bestselling author of *The Girls Are All So Nice Here*

"A compulsive and chilling exploration of trust, obsession, and voyeurism, Samantha M. Bailey knocks it out of the park with this intricately plotted domestic thriller. With dark secrets and surprising twists, this one's sure to be a new favorite!"

—Christina McDonald, *USA Today* bestselling author of
Do No Harm

"Wow! Relentlessly tense and incredibly twisty—*Watch Out for Her* proves the amazing Samantha M. Bailey is the queen of family suspense. With authentic emotion and complex and heartbreaking relationships, Bailey shows her brilliance in revealing the destructive power of love and the intensity of the need to belong. I flew through the cinematic pages, riveted and completely immersed in this propulsive and original thriller. Everyone will be talking about this—do not miss it!"

—Hank Phillippi Ryan, *USA Today* bestselling author of
Her Perfect Life

"An addictive read from start to finish, Samantha M. Bailey's talent and skill are on full display in this well-crafted domestic thriller. *Watch Out for Her* will have you second-guessing everyone you meet and rooting for characters you don't trust—and there is nothing more fun than that. Absolutely riveting."

—Jennifer Hillier, bestselling author of *Little Secrets* and
the award-winning *Jar of Hearts*

"This insanely addictive, utterly propulsive, and unbelievably tense thriller will consume you. With intoxicating, scalpel-sharp prose and gasp-worthy twists, Bailey has crafted a fresh and deeply unsettling take on obsession and voyeurism. Reading *Watch Out for Her* is like pulling a pin from a hand grenade and waiting for it to detonate. This is destined to become the most talked-about, explosive thriller of the year."

—May Cobb, author of *The Hunting Wives*

"A deep dive into a world of secrets, where no one is who you think they are and everyone has something to hide. Bailey's deft hand at ratcheting tension makes this an exquisite read. It will suck you in, and you'll love every moment of it!"

—Amina Akhtar, author of *Kismet* and *#FashionVictim*

Woman on the Edge

"A debut that's tough to resist."

—*Toronto Star*

"A remarkable thriller."

—*Morning Live*

"One woman's struggles with motherhood and another's desperate desire to be a mother collide in this explosive debut. *Woman on the Edge* is a white-knuckle read that welcomes a bright new talent to the world of psychological suspense."

—Mary Kubica, *New York Times* bestselling author of *The Good Girl*

"This is the page-turner you've been looking for! Bailey's writing is gripping and emotionally resonant at once, and her debut novel, perfect for fans of Lisa Jewell and Kimberly Belle, will keep you on the edge of your seat until the final sentence."

—Marissa Stapley, *New York Times* bestselling author of
Reese's Book Club Pick *Lucky*

"A fast-paced, twisty roller-coaster ride in which a desperate widow, a guilt-ridden new mother, and the secrets of the past collide—with a baby's life hanging in the balance . . . I couldn't race to the end quickly enough! An exciting, binge-worthy debut."

—Kristin Harmel, bestselling author of *The Winemaker's Wife* and
The Room on Rue Amélie

"Begins with a bang and takes the reader on a tense, emotional journey of love, betrayal, and loss and straight into the heart of a mother willing to do anything to protect her child. Infused with riveting, hold-your-breath suspense, this masterful debut needs to be your next binge read. A knockout page-turner."

—Heather Gudenkauf, *New York Times* bestselling author of
The Weight of Silence and *Before She Was Found*

"Exhilarating and evocative . . . *Woman on the Edge* had me gripped. This book effortlessly ticks all the boxes: wonderful world-building, realistic characters, and a gripping plot that made me keep flipping the pages. It's about obsession and madness, motherhood and trauma. This is a debut you'll want to slip straight to the top of your to-read pile!"

—Christina McDonald, *USA Today* bestselling author of
The Night Olivia Fell

"With the narrative acceleration of a runaway train, *Woman on the Edge* kept me at the edge of my seat for its entire zigzagging ride; I had to remind myself to breathe. Bailey's confident prose and dark satire enrich the ingenious plot, and her authentic characters—whether damaged, yearning, or downright diabolical—make this compulsory reading for fans of suspense. An exceptional debut!"

—Sonja Yoerg, *Washington Post* bestselling author of *True Places*

A
FRIEND
IN THE
DARK

OTHER TITLES BY SAMANTHA M. BAILEY

Woman on the Edge

Watch Out for Her

A

FRIEND

IN THE

DARK

SAMANTHA
M. BAILEY

THOMAS & MERCER

This is a work of fiction. Names, characters, organizations, places, events, and incidents are either products of the author's imagination or are used fictitiously. Otherwise, any resemblance to actual persons, living or dead, is purely coincidental.

Text copyright © 2024 by Samantha M. Bailey
All rights reserved.

No part of this book may be reproduced, or stored in a retrieval system, or transmitted in any form or by any means, electronic, mechanical, photocopying, recording, or otherwise, without express written permission of the publisher.

Published by Thomas & Mercer, Seattle

www.apub.com

Amazon, the Amazon logo, and Thomas & Mercer are trademarks of Amazon.com, Inc., or its affiliates.

ISBN-13: 9781662513541 (paperback)
ISBN-13: 9781662513558 (digital)

Cover design by Mumtaz Mustafa
Cover image: © Jupiterimages / Getty Images

Printed in the United States of America

For my Beach Babes—Josie Brown, Eileen Goudge, Francine LaSala, Meredith Schorr, Jen Tucker, Julie Valerie—through all the ups, downs, and in-betweens, it's always us.

Every time I hear your name
Floodgates open, blood it rains
I can see where I went wrong
But you can't leave while I'm not strong

"Run & Hide" by the Watchmen
Lyrics by Joey Serlin

PROLOGUE

The back of my head slams against the wall with a ferocious crack. The pain is excruciating, but I can't give into it. My attacker's hands move from my shoulders down to the strings of my damp hoodie, twisting them around my neck until I'm choking.

My phone in my hand drops to the wooden floor. Blinding sheets of black slide across my vision until everything, even the lights flickering in the creepy chandelier hanging from the ceiling in the entryway, goes dark. I'm about to pass out.

I want to kick, to punch, to scream, but I know that no one who can save me will hear me. No one even knows where I am.

I bite my tongue until I taste blood. I need to stay conscious, because if I close my eyes, my life will end right here. Bitter, salty tears roll down my cheeks and into my mouth. They might be the last thing I ever taste.

And it's all my fault.

The pressure on my throat eases. I sink into a heap by the front door, but there's no way I can escape.

My eyes won't stay open any longer.

I've made a deadly mistake.

PART ONE

EDEN

CHAPTER ONE

I'm sick of being the good girl.

But I don't know who I'm supposed to be. I'm no longer a wife, since Dave asked me for a divorce six weeks ago in the parking lot at the University of Michigan, our alma mater, mere minutes after we'd said goodbye to Ava for the start of her freshman year. And with no child to care for at home anymore, I don't feel like much of a mother.

I'm in agony, and I can't tell if it's from heartburn or heartache. Instead of making a wish, eating red-velvet cheesecake, and opening meaningful gifts, I'm alone and drunk on my forty-fifth birthday in my pitch-dark living room, with only an empty bottle of prosecco and my phone for company.

The sparkling wine was a gift from Jenna and Natalie, my closest girlfriends since we met at U-M in sophomore year. I'd burst into tears in the middle of an introductory psychology class because I'd received a C on our midterm. They'd taken me outside and hugged me until I stopped crying. The three of us couldn't have been more different: Jenna, loud and unfiltered; Natalie, self-assured and protective; and sensible, agreeable me, who never wanted to disappoint anyone, especially my parents, both professors, who I knew would be furious that I'd almost flunked an exam.

Even though my parents passed away two years ago, I still don't want to disappoint them. My broken family is the first thing I've ever actually failed at, and a hug from Jenna and Natalie can't make it better.

They tried to drag me out tonight to celebrate, but I don't want them to see me like this—a miserable, pathetic mess of a woman who should be in the prime of her life.

I don't deserve to feel this bad. I'm not the one who tore our family to shreds. I didn't see the end of us coming at all.

"I'm not who you need me to be, Eden. I'm so sorry. You deserve better," Dave whispered raggedly in that parking lot as we stood between our cars, which only a few hours earlier we'd packed up with Ava's things, following his carefully designed guide of what should go where. Dave's been the most efficient packer since we moved from Ann Arbor to Grosse Pointe twenty-three years ago.

The bedding and all Ava's clothes were stuffed in my blue Camry. In Dave's gray Range Rover went Ava's guitar, books, and posters, and of course, our daughter drove with her father. Even an hour alone with her mother was apparently too much for Ava. Twenty years of marriage was clearly enough for Dave, who, like his daughter, seems to think I have standards that are too high for everyone to meet.

I was blindsided. The man in front of me was a stranger and not the person who'd been my rock and best friend for almost a quarter of a century. The only certainty I'd had in life was Dave.

"Is this about your dad?" I ventured, desperately hoping, once again, that Dave would let down the wall he'd constructed around himself since March, when his father, Chuck, died suddenly of a massive stroke while playing squash at our local private club.

I expected him to finally break down in my waiting arms, but like it had every time I'd tried getting through to him since Chuck's death, Dave's face shuttered, locking me out of his private turmoil. "It's about me."

And without another word or a chance for me to respond, Dave opened the door of his car and slid inside. I saw his shoulders shake as he drove away, and I knew he must have been keeping it all in until Ava was safely in her new home. It took a good half hour before I could drive to our silent house; I felt ill from the shock and rejection. I still do.

I had assumed Dave and I would be together forever, like we'd promised. Divorce was never an option for me. For Dave, it seems to be the only option. And I don't understand what I did wrong or how the man who once blushed and stammered every time he spoke to me could give me up without a fight.

I rub my breastbone, where the gnawing ache of grief never goes away, and shiver at the haunting shadows in the living room from the gnarled branches of the sugar maple tree outside the window. Every creak and moan of this big house is so loud when I'm alone.

My phone pings with a new Facebook notification. It's almost midnight, so I've given up on a message or call from Dave, who appears to have forgotten it's my birthday. All I got from Ava was a quick HBD text a few hours ago, which took me a moment to figure out means "happy birthday." Apparently, I don't matter enough for a full sentence.

My head throbs from more alcohol than I've consumed since my early twenties, and my middle-aged eyes burn from reading my screen with no light. Reaching over, I flick on the silver floor lamp and look at the notification. It's a new post on my page from Natalie, who's tagged me in a photo.

You look exactly the same as in college! Love you!

I laugh sadly at the picture of me and Jenna sitting on the Diag with a crowd of people. It's from senior homecoming. Jenna does look exactly the same, with her long, thick, pin-straight strawberry blonde hair streaming over her shoulders, but she no longer wears crop tops or has a diamond pierced into her navel. I don't look the same at all.

I'm in yoga pants and a long-sleeved black shirt that I'm sure she and Natalie told me to wear; I knew nothing about fashion then and am only marginally more stylish now. And though my fine blonde hair doesn't hang limply anymore, thanks to layers, this Eden is prettier than I ever felt I was. She was also flush with the radiant glow of youth and hope that's disappeared with age and responsibility. This naive Eden had no idea that close to the end of that year she'd meet Dave Miller, a nerdy law student in wire-rimmed glasses who awkwardly flirted with her by telling terrible jokes. Two decades later he would smash her life into pieces.

I don't want to think about Dave right now. He's cut me out of his life as though he's simply snipped us in half, while I feel like he's stabbed me in the heart with the scissors.

I like the post and bring the screen closer, hit by a wave of nostalgia as I carefully examine the photo. I remember this day so well. It changed senior year for me. My whole life, actually.

Natalie's behind the camera, as she always was back then. She snapped me and Jenna sitting on the grass with a crowd of students, right in front of the stage set up at the far end of the Diag, where the Screaming Demons, the hottest band on campus at the time, were playing. Natalie had captured Jenna's wicked laugh as she caught me staring hungrily at the shirtless drummer who was clashing the cymbals so hard that sweat dripped down his tattooed biceps.

When Natalie sat down to join us, Jenna said to her, "Our Eden has a thing for bad boy drummers like Justin Ward. I had no idea."

Neither did I. But the moment I laid eyes on Justin, I was a goner. Not even Jenna's warning that he was a player who'd hit on her in a bar a few weeks earlier could deter me.

I had no clue Justin was in my contemporary English literature course, which topped out at two hundred people, until a week after the concert. As I was heading out of class, I overheard our professor suggesting Justin get a tutor to help him write essays or he might fail the course.

Usually shy, I offered right then and there. And for the rest of senior year, Justin was the object of my every inexperienced sexual and romantic fantasy. I wasn't allowed to date in high school, and I'd only kissed two boys in college. But for an hour twice a week in a secluded carrel at Shapiro Library, I sat beside Justin Ward, aching to trace the colorful ink on his sinewy forearms while he chewed on a pen, wrestling with getting his thoughts onto paper. I struggled with how to flirt, never having done it before in my life. But I was hopeful that he liked me, too, when after our final tutoring session together, he invited me to a graduation party at a frat house. It was the last time we ever spoke.

All these years later, I can still vividly recall awkwardly standing by myself in the hallway of the Sigma Chi house, my ankles chafing in my new cherry red Doc Martens—which Jenna had made me buy when she realized I was going to the party whether she liked it or not. The aggressive beat of Rage Against the Machine shook the floors while I searched for Justin among the crowd of already-wasted students. Self-conscious, I debated leaving, when through the smoky haze, he strode toward me. It was like something out of a movie. He handed me a red Solo cup filled with a foul-smelling alcohol and playfully tugged a strand of my hair. I was so out of my element that I downed half that cup in one nervous gulp. Almost instantly, I felt like I'd lost total control of myself, overcome by the alcohol, the music, the crowd, and most importantly, Justin.

I didn't care that we were in full view of everyone. All I cared about was the overwhelming desire and excitement coursing through me. After nearly a year of sitting next to him, imagining what his lips would feel like against mine, his skin under my fingers, I couldn't wait any longer. I crushed my mouth against his, ran my hands over his chest, arms—any part of him that I could reach. The only reason I didn't lose my virginity to him right there against the wall is because as he slid his hand under my denim skirt and his fingers pushed aside my underwear, I felt a burn in my throat and the undeniable churn in my stomach.

I ran from him, straight upstairs to a bathroom. That was the end of us before we began. It was Dave who found me passed out in the hallway and took me home.

Justin was the first man I ever loved, the first person to destroy my heart, though I'm not sure he ever knew that. Until the day I saw him on that stage at homecoming, my focus had been school. I'd been raised to believe that achievements took precedence over emotions. I didn't know how to handle my all-consuming love for Justin—or my unbearable pain when he ghosted me after that frat party.

Of course I've checked him out online over the last twenty-three years, but I always stopped myself from reaching out. There was no point in dredging up the past. He'd made his decision to let me go when he didn't respond to a single call after that night. A couple of months later, I moved on with Dave, who loved me more than anyone had and made it clear that I was the only woman for him. Now he doesn't want me either.

I'm sure Jenna and Natalie would be shocked that I'm even contemplating reaching out to Justin considering how much I'd cried after the party. If they were here, they'd take my phone away from me, just like they begged me to stop leaving him messages and held me back from showing up at the house he shared with his band. They sat me down with a bowl of mint-chocolate-chip ice cream—our cure-all then—and gently explained that if Justin were interested, he'd find me. He never did.

Sighing, I curl into the corner of the beige linen couch, where until six months ago, Dave would lean against the arm, my head in his lap, as we read whatever books we'd chosen for each other that month. Books were our initial connection—we'd met when he'd come into the off-campus store, the Book Nook, where I worked in college. After Chuck's funeral, the cozy spot on the couch became cold and uncomfortable as Dave and I sat on opposite ends, silently watching reruns of *The Office*, neither of us feeling like reading much anymore.

I type Justin's name into the Facebook search bar. His page pops up, and I immediately navigate to his photos.

"Jesus," I say out loud, sitting up straighter. The first picture is of Justin in a fitted gray Henley and jeans that hang low on his hips, standing on a construction site, the same mischievous glint in his mesmerizing green eyes, and the thick, messy, dark hair I once ran my fingers through. He still makes me feel like a thousand butterflies are flapping their wings in my stomach.

I've barely been touched in months, so it's no wonder this photo of Justin sets my whole body on fire. Dave has spent the last half year rebuffing my every advance, claiming stress and fatigue. I saw the circles under his eyes and the almost manic energy he poured into taking on more pro bono cases at the corporate law firm he's helmed for fifteen years and hosting barbecues and brunches for his staff of ten while I made sure the food was perfect, the bar was fully stocked, and Ava was as charming as possible, when she was actually around. Dave seemed to be doing everything he could not to be alone with me.

No matter what I did, everyone got his attention but me. Eventually I gave up trying because feeling unwanted is worse than no intimacy at all.

I'm lonely. It's not Dave who I miss, necessarily, because it's hard to miss someone who's been emotionally absent for months. But I do long for the comfort and security of my family all together in this house, which has been unbearably quiet without Ava slamming her bedroom door and Dave trudging heavily upstairs.

What do I have to lose by sending a friend request? I hover over the Add Friend button, close my eyes, and press it.

Not even three seconds later, I have a new notification.

Justin Ward accepted your friend request.

Oh my God. My heart crashes against my chest and my hands shake. "Get it together, Eden," I say aloud, because I can.

It's just a casual connection on social media. We're both adults now, presumably more mature, who both happen to be awake at midnight on a Friday. I wonder if Justin's still a musician; if he still stays up all hours performing or jamming with friends. If he just got home, saw my request, and simply clicked Accept.

I should go to bed like the responsible adult I am. Usually I'm asleep by 10:00 p.m. at the latest, even on weekends. I've got an open house tomorrow morning, and I cannot be hung over. Sylvie Greenwood, the elegant, whip-smart owner of Greenwood Realty, where I've been a Realtor for three years, is in her midsixties and wants to bring me in as a partner. I can only do that if I have the cash to invest—and if I show up on time and sober. But I don't move from the couch. I want to send Justin a message. I have so much to ask him.

I never got the closure I wanted. Maybe the way forward is by going backward. Or I'm a glutton for punishment. Either way, I can't stop myself. I rap my knuckles against my palm, running ten different sentences through my head. Finally, I type:

Eden: Long time! I can hold my alcohol better now. 😉

This is obviously a lie, because after I press the blue arrow, I burp. I don't know how to playfully banter. That's more Ava's domain. I immediately want to undo the lame message. I toss the phone onto the couch and put my head in my hands. I'm such an idiot. He might not even remember me.

Ping.

I snatch up my phone.

Justin: Eden Hoffman. This is a blast from the past!

My heart rate speeds up. I'm already sweating. What should I say? I keep it simple.

Eden: My friend, Natalie, posted a shot of your band on my wall, so you came to mind. How have you been all these years?

Justin: That's a lot of years to catch up on. Up and down, like everyone, I guess. It's great to hear from you.

Eden: Do you still play the drums?

Justin: Sadly, no. Shoulder injury. A toolbox fell on me at a site a few years ago. I miss playing. It's like I lost a part of myself.

I'm sad for him. Oh, how many shows I went to in seedy dive bars once I started tutoring him just to watch his band play. Only seeing him an hour twice a week wasn't enough for me. I'd beg Jenna and Natalie to come, then make them lurk in the shadows with me at the very back tables so Justin wouldn't spot me salivating over him.

Eden: You were a fantastic musician. I'm sorry. I always wanted a passion like that.

Justin: Do you like working in real estate?

My pulse spikes. He clearly checked me out too. But I blow out a breath to calm down. I don't want to seem like I'm still the insecure girl who was obsessed with him, even though I feel like her right now.

Eden: I do. I love it. But I've never had a talent or hobby that drives me like music did for you.

I had taken on so many roles in high school: volunteer at the local homeless shelter, president of the social justice committee, reporter for the school newspaper. Of course, all this extra work was forced on me by my parents so I could be "well rounded" for my college applications. And then once I was in college, all the extracurriculars fell away so I could focus on my studies. Getting pregnant with Ava at twenty-seven set me on the path I felt destined for: becoming a mother and a wife. Yet here I am at forty-five, with no real purpose.

Justin: I used to get so nervous before a show. I don't miss that.

A flash of one of our conversations in the library carrel comes back to me. He told me that every time before he went onstage, he was sure that this would be the moment everyone found out he wasn't good enough. His unguarded admission lasted only a few seconds, but I saw through his dimpled smile.

> Eden: I have a daughter who's studying music. I don't know if she's ever nervous before a show. She doesn't tell me much. She just started freshman year at U-M.

> Justin: Hard to believe you now have a daughter in college. And at U-M. Full circle. How old is Ava?

> Eden: Seventeen going on twelve going on thirty-five.

It's not until I send my response that I realize he knows Ava's name. I upload photos of Ava but can't tag her. Even if I could, she'd never want us socially connected online in any way. She won't even follow me back on Instagram.

There's a loud knock. I jump. It's just a branch banging against the window, but I don't want to be in the living room by myself. Even with the curtains drawn and everything locked up, I feel exposed and vulnerable. But I also don't want to stop talking to Justin. With the phone glued to my hand, I head to the kitchen, turn on the lights, and grab an Advil and a glass of water. But it's more depressing to see spotless counters and no plates covered in crumbs and icing to scrape off and load into the dishwasher.

I lean against the counter and respond.

> Eden: How did you know my daughter's name?

> Justin: It's on one of her baby photos you uploaded.

14

I rear back from the screen. Is this the same guy who never finished a single book on our syllabus? I'm amazed he would investigate my pictures so thoroughly. I don't know what to say next, how to keep the conversation going. But the kitchen, where I insisted on sitting down at the table together for dinners at least twice a week, even when it was clear that neither Dave nor Ava wanted to be there, isn't the place to do it.

On the way back to the living room, I stop in the hall, where across from the stairs hang our family photos in a collage. I linger on the last one Dave had put up before he'd left me. It's a picture of Ava onstage at her high school graduation, where she strummed the guitar that's like her appendage. Her long, silky golden brown hair with purple streaks flows over her small shoulders, and she sports her half smile—the one I both love and loathe in equal measure because it frustrates me with its ambivalence. It's the smile that proves I did something right by raising such a fierce, confident young woman. Yet it's also a smirk that feels like it's aimed directly at me for never being the mother she wants me to be.

Under the lights, her skirt is transparent, as I'd known it would be.

"Is that what you're wearing?" I asked before we left the house that evening. I thought it was too risqué for a high school performance, but the second the words were out, I wished I'd kept my mouth shut.

Ava's jaw tensed. "I can wear whatever I want. Don't shame me."

"I wasn't trying to. I just thought maybe for the photos and your teachers . . ." I stopped talking.

Dave shrugged. "I think it's fine. She's expressing herself."

If Chuck had been at Ava's graduation, I'm sure Dave would have been the one to gently suggest that Ava change into something that wasn't see-through, because her grandfather certainly would have balked. With his mother, Marsha, in a care facility for dementia, Dave only had his father left to impress. But with Chuck gone, Dave did nothing when Ava stole bottles of our alcohol or racked up obscenely high charges on our credit card at Sephora. I had to be the one who took away her phone and easy access to our money. I just didn't want our daughter to make mistakes she'd regret.

Leaving my family behind, I consider going upstairs, but it feels uncomfortable to talk to Justin in the bed I shared with Dave, even though it's all mine now. So, I flop back on the couch and pull the white microfiber blanket around my legs for comfort.

Thinking about Ava and the mistakes I made the last time I saw Justin heightens my worry for her, away on her own at college, not understanding the devastating consequences when limitless alcohol is available. That frat party had long-lasting repercussions. My friend—everyone's friend—Tyler Yates, vanished from the Sigma Chi house sometime during the night. He was reported missing the next afternoon, and by that evening, posters with his surfer-boy shaggy blond hair and sweet smile were plastered across campus. He's never been found.

> Eden: Ava starting at U-M makes me think a lot about Tyler. I saw you at his vigil.

I stood in the twilight, in the crowd of hundreds of sobbing students, faculty—every person whom Tyler Yates's kindness touched—still hopeful for any evidence or leads about where he could possibly be. Even now sometimes when I hear leaves crunch, I think of the dry grass crackling under my feet while Jenna, Natalie, and I huddled together, crying, each of us holding a candle.

> Justin: I could have used a friend that night at the vigil.

> Eden: You were with his parents. I didn't know you and Tyler knew each other.

> Justin: We went to high school together. Our moms are friends. Were you friends with him?

Eden: We worked together at the Book Nook on South State
Street. But Tyler was nice to everyone.

I'd met Tyler in junior year when I'd gotten the job at the small used
bookstore. We bonded over how much we both loved smelling the pages
of the novels as we sorted and shelved them. I still feel the loss of such
a vibrant person and think of Tyler whenever I smell almonds, which
is what the scent of old books has always reminded me of. Now they
remind me of Dave, too, whom I never imagined losing.

I push away thoughts of Dave and focus on the only person I'll talk
to before my birthday ends.

Justin: I think a lot about the what ifs of that night. What if I'd
talked to Tyler instead of smoking a bong with my band? Could
I have stopped him from disappearing?

Eden: I wish I'd never gotten so drunk. I'd never lost control of
myself like I did with you that night. Everything that happened,
honestly, was so unlike me. I blacked out.

The next day, I thought I remembered hearing Tyler say my
name while I was sick in the bathroom, but the police said I was
too drunk to make a reliable account. I felt awful about that.

Justin: I feel awful that I didn't know you were sick. I thought
you were rejecting me. That maybe I did something to hurt you.
To me, you were the one who got away.

I almost drop my phone. Could the entire trajectory of my life
have been different if rather than Dave taking me home, I'd have spent
the night with Justin? Would Justin and I have been eating breakfast
together a few days later? Instead, I was being questioned by the police
while Natalie and Jenna waited outside the interrogation room for me,

racked with guilt because neither of them had come to the party with me and I'd been there alone. Would Tyler be with his family, maybe married with children? I can't answer any of it.

I'm not sure what I'm hoping to accomplish by contemplating that. But I like pretending I can have a do-over, go back to the twenty-two-year-old with her whole future ahead of her instead of the woman whose life is half over.

> Eden: So why didn't you reach out to me after the party? You didn't even call me back. That did hurt me.
>
> Justin: I wanted to. I was afraid to talk to you.
>
> Eden: Well, I definitely didn't reject you. But that's in the past, I guess.
>
> Justin: Your photos are nice. You've grown up.

Does he mean I look older? Quickly, I click back to my page, scrolling through the photos to see how I might look to him now compared to the young woman I was. My eyes, a mud brown with flecks of yellow in the sun, are deep set; my skin isn't as smooth as it was, of course, and there are lines fanning out at the corners of my eyes. In every photo, my clothes are tailored pantsuits, button-up shirts, loose T-shirts, and elastic-waist pants—the outfits of a working mom. I realize how utterly drab they are. How much of myself I've hidden underneath them.

> Eden: Like what you see?

I send the message before I can change my mind. No response. I've gone too far, and I want to unsend it. I don't even talk like this. But it's exciting to be someone different, cool, flirtatious, a little reckless—if only for tonight. It's like I'm the person I wish I could have been with him years ago. The person perhaps both Dave and Ava wish I were.

Justin: Definitely. Has your life turned out like you wanted it to, Eden?

I'm so surprised by his question that the sob I've tightly held back all night breaks free. I don't know how to answer. But I need to talk to someone, and maybe it's best it's a person who doesn't know me anymore, whom I'll likely never speak to again. And this conversation doesn't feel real, almost like I'm talking into a void.

Eden: Not exactly. I'm recently separated.

Justin: Me too.

A confusing mix of relief and sadness flows through me. It's odd we're in the same place in our lives, yet I wouldn't want anyone else to face the same crushing shock I do when I wake up every morning and realize over and over that my marriage has ended and my life is my own now. To some people, that might be exhilarating. To me, the endless possibilities are terrifying. I've always had a checklist: receive a college degree, get married, have a child, build a home, be settled. It soothed me in its predictability; Dave soothed me by being my trusted partner in the chaos of life. Not knowing what comes next makes me feel adrift.

I clearly don't know where to begin, since I'm drunk-messaging my former college crush in the middle of the night.

Justin: It's hard to be all alone, isn't it?

An unexpected cry releases from my mouth. He's succinctly described exactly how I feel. And I have no one else to talk to about it. Of course, Jenna and Natalie support me. The moment I texted them after I'd gotten home from leaving Ava at U-M and Dave leaving me, they showed up at my door, bearing food and wine, offering to move in—whatever I needed to get through the next little while. I wanted to be alone with my misery, embarrassed that the perfect life I'd created wasn't so perfect after all. Jenna, a pediatrician with her own practice, is a happy single mother to her ten-year-old son, Ryder; Natalie is the in-house accountant for a marketing company and has three strapping boys she's raised with a firm but loving hand and a husband who adores her. Only I have failed at love. And there's no method to help me succeed because I don't know what the expectations are now.

Eden: Yes. I'm lonely.

Justin: Well, now I don't feel so lonely anymore.

I draw in a sharp breath. His comment provokes a visceral reaction right in my core, awakening a part of me that's been paralyzed for months. But I question if Justin is being honest or if he's still a player, like Jenna always said he was.

I glance at the time on my phone. It's almost 1:00 a.m. While this has been intoxicating and weird and bittersweet, entirely different from my usual Friday night of watching whatever show Netflix chooses for me and falling asleep in front of the TV, this won't go anywhere beyond fun, flirty nostalgia.

Eden: I'd better get to bed.

Justin: Alone?

I swallow hard.

Eden: Yes.

Always, I don't write.

Justin: Sweet dreams, Eden. Happy Birthday.

I put my phone under the pillow so I don't respond. And I tuck the throw blanket around me to sleep on the couch. I don't want to break this bubble of happiness by going upstairs to my too-big king-size bed, brushing my teeth, getting into pajamas. I don't want to do anything but savor my conversation with Justin. I doubt he and I will message again. Still, I smile as I close my eyes.

I haven't felt this alive in a very long time.

CHAPTER TWO

I open my eyes. The living room is out of focus. When I run my tongue along my teeth, my mouth tastes like fur. I barely slept, because I replayed every word of my messages with Justin all night long as I pored through my memory like a lovesick teenager.

I pad to the kitchen, a ridiculous grin stretching my cheeks. I'm happy for the first time in six weeks, because of Justin. Longer, if I'm being honest. This morning I'm not going through the motions, trying so hard to pretend everything is okay. I'm wide awake. Even if Justin and I don't speak again, last night was like therapy, and I'm grateful.

Talking to Justin was easier than with Nancy, the therapist I went to twice about three months ago. I suggested couples counseling to Dave, but he refused, insisting that he just needed time to process the loss of his father, Ava leaving soon for college, and at forty-eight, his own mortality.

But frustrated and frightened by all the nights anxiously lying next to him, hoping for a kiss, touch, or whispered confidences that never came, I finally decided our lack of intimacy and connection had to be my fault. I couldn't talk to Jenna and Natalie about it. They love Dave, even though they're both angry with him for leaving me right when Ava was leaving home. It felt like a betrayal to talk about him with people who know us both.

Nancy explained that everyone grieves differently. When my mother passed away of congestive heart failure two years ago at eighty-four, two months after my father had died of liver failure, I cried, but not much changed in my daily life. My father, a quiet, cold man, and I didn't speak much, and my mother and I only had lunch three times a year. She'd regale me with her latest pieces published in academic journals and stories about the conferences where she and my father were still invited to be keynote speakers. She'd inquire about my life as though checking it off a list. I was a commitment, not a fulfillment, for her. Chuck's loss hit me harder. I wanted to discuss it with Dave, work through it together like we had every health scare, emergency room visit with Ava, her heartbreaks with friends, then girlfriends, and our job stresses. But he'd retreated into a shell.

Nancy suggested patience. So, I continued pretending everything was fine, grasping on to the only control I had by throwing myself into making endless lists for Ava to complete to get ready for college, which she ignored. I cooked Dave's favorite curry dishes, watched the action movies he loves that I hate. It was all useless, because we weren't talking or touching. I stopped seeing Nancy, and I definitely didn't want to go back to her after Dave asked me for a divorce, because there was nothing that I could do to fix us anymore.

While the coffee brews, I tap in my password—Ava's birthday. Ava rolls her eyes at my old-school ways when it comes to technology, but I don't want to use my fingerprints or face to unlock my phone. It feels creepy. I open the Messenger app to reread my conversation with Justin. I blink. There's an unread message from him.

Justin: Good morning, sunshine. I couldn't sleep. I thought about you all night. It was really good to talk to you again.

He sent it at 6:00 a.m.

I run my hand through my tangled hair, and my wedding ring—I haven't been ready to take it off yet—snags a few long, dirty-blonde strands.

I slide the ring down my finger and place it on the marble counter. It glints in the sunlight pouring through the window over the sink that faces the backyard.

My finger is bare for the first time since Dave put the ring on me twenty years ago. I took it off only when I was pregnant with Ava, because my fingers swelled like sausages and I was afraid it would cut off my circulation. There's a smooth band of skin a few shades lighter than the rest of my finger. I wonder how long that will take to fade. Whether I'd ever want another man to slide a different ring there.

"Slow your roll there, Eden." I laugh at myself. Why can't I be me and single? I don't need a plan. Or at least, after the high of last night, I want to be more spontaneous and live in the moment. I'm just not sure how.

I don't want to misinterpret Justin's early morning message and our late-night exchange of confidences as anything more than a reconnection with someone I used to know, but a part of me wants it to be more. The mere idea of having feelings for anyone other than Dave, but especially Justin Ward, overwhelms me, and I need caffeine to absorb it. I fill a cup and catch my pasty reflection in the small mirror attached to the side of the fridge. There are crease lines on my face from my pillow and deep bags under my eyes. I look awful. At least Justin didn't ask to FaceTime with me.

I turn to open the fridge door so I don't have to see myself anymore, and I grab the milk, pour it into my WORLD'S BEST MOM mug that Dave gave me for our twentieth anniversary in July—Mother's Day, sure, that would have made sense, but an anniversary? It was a gift that epitomized how he saw me: a nurturing caregiver, not a sexy, desirable woman he couldn't wait to come home to, like when Ava was little. Every day, Dave would rush through the door at 5:30 p.m. on the dot, wrap his arms around me, kiss me, no matter if I was covered in jelly or finger paint. I don't have a recent memory of Dave kissing me with more than a perfunctory peck.

Last night I felt desired.

But I'm not young anymore, and I have to be at my listing by 9:15 a.m. for the open house at 10:30 a.m. My job is the only thing I have holding me together. I've never led an open house on less than eight hours of sleep, especially not one as important as today's on Lakeside Drive, which could be my biggest sale yet. I need to sell this home.

I don't want alimony from Dave or his financial help at all. He asked for a divorce, not a separation, but as far as I know, he hasn't retained an attorney. Neither have I, because I'm not at all ready to face the legal end of us. I think it's fair that he continue to pay Ava's tuition for the time being. His lawyer's salary at his own firm meant that we've always been comfortable—my income felt like a bonus. I'd been a stay-at-home mother until Ava was in freshman year of high school and she didn't need me as much. Or it felt like that, anyway, so I decided to do something productive with my time and design skills. My parents paid my tuition and living expenses until I met and moved in with Dave. I've never truly been responsible for myself, and it's daunting.

Yet instead of showering and getting dressed, I sit at the kitchen table with my coffee, wondering what Dave would think about my surreal conversation with the drummer for the Screaming Demons, if he'd be jealous at all. If I want him to be jealous.

While of course Dave knew who Justin was, like everyone at U-M did, I don't think they ever crossed paths. Dave was in law school; Justin and I were undergrads. I know that Dave only came to the Sigma Chi party because of me. Tyler invited him. It was the last conversation Tyler and I ever had.

"Your boyfriend is here again," Tyler called out good naturedly the day before the party, like he did each time Dave walked into the Book Nook. Tyler and I were wearing our dorky blue vests with our name tags, always ready to help the students coming in looking for used textbooks, novels, or the pens and stationery that we kept by the cash register for quick purchases.

I never needed to help Dave—it seemed like he came in every time I was working, and he always knew what he wanted. Tyler loved to joke with us because there was clearly some kind of energy between me and Dave that he picked up on. Tyler was like that; he could sense things about people.

I liked Dave well enough as a friend, but I was fixated on Justin. I never corrected Tyler, because he was so sweet, and I didn't want to embarrass Dave. I figured if Dave liked me, he could ask me out and I'd say yes to a casual coffee.

As I was ringing up Dave's Post-its, Tyler came behind the counter. "Hey, you two, there's a party at my frat this Saturday night. You should both come." Then he winked at me.

I'd confessed to Tyler earlier that week that I had a crush on some-one. Clearly, he assumed it was Dave. He didn't know that Justin had already invited me to the party. I simply nodded. Dave adjusted his glasses, thanked Tyler, and tripped over the carpet on his way out of the bookstore.

Tyler had always been ready to have a good time, and I was glad, in a way, that he invited Dave that night too. In fact, I was lucky. Because of Dave, I got home safely. With Tyler disappearing that night, who knows what could have happened to me, considering how drunk and out of it I was.

I never told Dave about making out with Justin. Why would I? After Dave carried me down the stairs to his car and drove me to my apartment, he insisted on sleeping on the couch to make sure I was okay, even though Jenna and Natalie were both home. It endeared him to all of us, and he consoled me through the difficult weeks that fol-lowed with the investigation into Tyler's disappearance. He'd already passed the bar, so he stayed with me through the police interviews and held me when I cried. He assumed I was devastated over Tyler, which of course I was, but I was also heartbroken over Justin. When a month, then another went by with no phone call or any kind of communication from Justin, I finally saw Dave for who he was: a stable, kind, good-hearted man who I believed would never crush me. When Dave got a job as an associate attorney at a corporate law firm in Grosse Pointe, I moved with him, leaving the past in the past. Until now.

I open Messenger, about to write Justin back, when a memory pops up in my notifications. It's from a year ago, a gorgeous, crisp fall day, when Dave and I had convinced Ava to join us for a hike at Paint Creek Trail near Rochester. None of us are particularly sporty, but time together in the fresh air, only the three of us, seemed like the best way to reconnect after the busy start to her senior year of high school and our jobs.

I loved this photo because the brightly colored leaves stood out against the cloudless blue sky, our cheeks are rosy with health, and we look like a happy family. I think we still were then, because though I recall Ava complaining the whole time that her feet hurt, Dave and I had held hands as we always used to when we walked anywhere, and we'd even had sex when Ava went to sleep that night. It was gentle and tender, as it had been between me and Dave since the very first time we slept together, the night we lost our virginity to each other. I wasn't necessarily saving myself for marriage, like my mother told me nice girls should, but I definitely couldn't fathom anyone I didn't love inside me. Dave has always treated me like I'm made of glass. But maybe I'm not as delicate as he thinks I am.

I chew my lip, debating what tone to convey in my message to Justin. I go with breezy, casual.

Eden: Good morning. I had trouble sleeping, too.

Justin: I'm sorry if I'm the reason you couldn't sleep. You have an open house today.

I furrow my brow, scrolling through our messages once again to see if I told him about my listing. I didn't. I do post them on Instagram,

and my profile is public, though when I check, I see Justin hasn't fol-
lowed me there yet.

Eden: Are you always this attentive?

Justin: Only when I'm interested in someone.

Fear and excitement hit me at the same time. I have trouble believing anyone could want me when my husband so clearly didn't.

Eden: Do you chat with a lot of women online?

What if Justin does this all the time and I'm simply a new play-
thing? Tomorrow, he might not message me at all. It would devastate
me if someone else easily lets me go.

Justin: Not like this. You've always been important to me. And
when you lose someone you care about at a young age, it
makes you realize how short life is. We found each other again.
I don't want to waste time.

Eden: You mean you lost Tyler?

Justin: Yes. And then my drumming career. But if I'm making you
uneasy, we can stop talking.

Eden: No. I want to keep talking, but I feel guilty.

Justin: Why?

Eden: Because I wasn't the one who ended my marriage. I'm not
sure if I'm ready to move on.

Justin: Why feel sad if you don't have to?

He's right. I have nothing else, besides my job, making me happy right now.

Eden: I'm also scared.

Justin: You're safe, Eden. No one else is here but me and you. You can be free with me. What do you have to lose?

Eden: I'm afraid to get hurt again.

Justin: We always had a strong connection when we were young. Why not explore it as adults, if we can?

Whenever I've thought about Justin over the years, that kiss has always been at the forefront. But it's true that we had a connection. Now I vividly recall a winter afternoon, a storm raging outside, and us cozily tucked into our library carrel. Justin had snuck in hot chocolate with marshmallows for both of us—he seemed so young in that moment, a man sipping a children's drink. While he tapped a pen on the table like a drumstick, he told me that he was scared to fail, which was why he procrastinated on his essays. The youngest of four brothers, the only one who didn't play team sports and struggled in school, Justin wanted his mother to be proud of him. She didn't see his music career as an achievement, only a distraction that wouldn't put him ahead in life. In turn, I told him that being an only child put pressure on me to fulfill all my parents' expectations.

I've forgotten how easy it was to be myself with him. I miss having a man to talk to.

I should be getting ready for my open house; my phone is blowing up with reminders every ten minutes. I ignore them all because I don't want to leave this bubble.

Justin: Tell me something I don't know about you.

Eden: Sometimes I feel unlovable.

I close my eyes and click to send the message, trying not to care how pitiful that makes me sound. Because it's true.

Justin: I feel the same. It's difficult to feel good about yourself when the person you've given your life to treats you like you're nothing to them.

Tears well in my eyes, blurring the creamy-white walls in the kitchen, the first room that Dave and I renovated when I was four months pregnant with Ava.

Justin: For what it's worth, you've always meant something to me.

I'm exhausted from watching my every word, so I tell him what I've wanted to for over twenty years.

Eden: I was mad for you in college.

Justin: I love hearing that. Can I tell you something?

I bite my lip.

Eden: Please do.

Justin: I dreamed about you last night.

Eden: What did you dream?

Justin: That we didn't stop at the party. That we went to the back of my van.

I laugh. I fantasized many times about being with Justin in the back of his white van, the Screaming Demons logo emblazoned in red and orange on the side, a place where I was sure he had taken other girls. The whole band had groupies.

Eden: That's classy.

Justin: What I want to do to you isn't classy.

My hand twitches so hard my coffee spills all over the table and my skin. I leave the spill be and quickly wipe my hand on the sweatpants I'm still wearing from last night.

Justin: Do you want me to continue? Say no if you don't.

My face flames like I'm having a hot flash. I blow out a breath and type.

Eden: Continue.

Justin: I've thought about your soft skin many times. I'm turned on thinking about it.

My jaw drops. The humming of the fridge seems very loud. Is Justin *sexting* with me?

My head knows I should stop the outrageous turn this conversation has taken before I do something I'll regret; yet my body and heart can't resist Justin's provocative pull or the impulse to be someone else for a brief moment. Jenna hooks up with guys she meets on Tinder all the time, has no shame about no-strings sex. Is that who I'm going to be, now that I'm single? Is that what I want?

Justin: Will you touch yourself for me?

I've never done anything like this. The only visual I've really had of steamy sex is in books and movies.

And what if he shares or posts the messages? Screenshots are so easy to take—once Ava showed me what to do, I've used the feature regularly to help with listings. I don't know what Justin's true intentions are.

Justin: Don't overthink it.

How did he know I was analyzing every possible fallout?

Shouldn't I try it, at least once, in real life? No one has to know. And this is what I wanted from him in college. Take the lead and teach me all the things I was too scared to do. I lean back in the pale-yellow upholstered chair as the light pours into the kitchen from the backyard, and I see my next-door neighbor Tom whacking at the weeds on his lawn at 8:00 a.m. Our yard is already choked with weeds, because that was Dave's Saturday chore, and I haven't bothered to take it on myself.

As I reach over and close the blinds, I know a part of me wants to prove to Dave—and myself—that someone desires me. I know all this, but somehow, I still can't resist, no matter how stupid and risky this is.

And I'm angry. Angry that Dave wouldn't help me fix what went wrong in our relationship, that Ava dismisses me. Angry that they only see me as the nagging mother and wife with the schedules and checklists instead of the person who wants her daughter to reach her full potential and her husband to pay attention to her. I deserve more.

Eden: I'll touch myself for you.

I send the message, my heart banging against my ribs, lust pulsing through every nerve ending.

I've never gratified myself during the day. Only in bed late at night when Dave had a dinner meeting. And even then, with Ava right down the hall, it felt reprehensible, like something a mother shouldn't be doing or need to do.

Right when I'm about to go for it, my phone buzzes in my hand. Shit.

My heart in my throat, shame scalding my skin, I scramble to answer the call before it goes to voice mail. "Hello?"

"Mrs. Miller? This is Julia, the hall director at Bursley."

Am I still Mrs. Miller? I haven't thought about changing my name back to Hoffman. But that's not important right now, because anxiety clenches my stomach. Why is the director calling me on a Saturday at—I glance at the clock on the stove—8:15 a.m.?

I focus my full attention on Julia, who informs me that Ava was caught with three other girls in her dorm room last night, bottles of vodka strewn on the floor, music pumping from the speakers. Two broken ordinances: noise and alcohol. *My seventeen-year-old daughter was drinking.* Damn it, Ava.

"I'm sorry to hear about your, um, recent family difficulties. Ava seems to be struggling with it a bit," Julia continues. "She explained that she's maybe acting out to deal with it."

I slump. "Yes, it's been a hard time. I'll definitely speak to Ava. What are the consequences?"

"Well"—her voice is gentle—"I have to write her up as a first strike. But I won't put her on probation, because of the extenuating circumstances. Plus, Ava is like a mentor to other LGBTQIA+ students and always available to talk. She's a great person, and I don't want to penalize her too heavily for a first offense."

Tears prick my eyes. Ava *is* a great person. Maybe not to me very often, but her strength, sheer will, and unwavering conviction that her talent and brains make her invincible are inspiring. But even away at college, she's still trying to punish me by defying the rules, wanting me to feel guilty for the separation. It's her father she should be upset with, but I'd never say that to her.

I thank Julia, then stand up and grab a sponge to sop up the coffee from the table. I have to get it together. I call Dave. It goes straight to voice mail. For a moment, I wonder if he's with a woman. He's been adamant that there's no one else, and I shove the bizarre image away. What—or whom—Dave does has nothing to do with me. Knowing Dave, he's probably still asleep with Do Not Disturb enabled on his phone. Plus, there's someone else who seems to want me in ways Dave hasn't for a very long time.

I dial Ava's number. She doesn't pick up either. Of course she doesn't. But still light-headed from my conversation with Justin, I consider if perhaps I've been too hard on Ava, put too much pressure on her to be perfect, the way my parents did to me. My mother was forty-one when she had me; my father, forty-three. My parents were so busy striving to publish lest they perish that my needs were largely neglected. Have I ignored my daughter's real needs? Or coddled her so much that without me there to cushion her landing, she's unaware of how much trouble she can get into?

Yearning for the security from the family I created and once relied on, I walk upstairs to shower. Ava's room is to the right of the stairs. Her door is closed, as it always was even when she lived here. The moment I turn the knob, I'm hit with the cloying scent of her peach body spray still lingering in the air. I'd given her one of the vanilla candles that I use at my listings, but of course she didn't want it. Besides the fruity aroma, the room feels so empty without her guitar in the corner under the window, her desk covered in papers, and the graffiti-type posters and prints she tacked up all over the walls. My little girl is gone. And I don't know how to reach the almost-adult daughter I have.

I leave Ava's room, and while I shower, I remember what she said to me when Dave and I broke the news to her about us a week after she'd started at U-M. Though he'd asked for a divorce, it was *separation* he used when he sat on her dorm room bed, while I stood behind him, watching my baby girl crumple. She let Dave hug her, but when I tried, she said, "You've become really uptight since Grandpa died. I understand why Dad doesn't want to live with you anymore."

It shot me in the heart, because it was so unfair. I wanted to go back to the time when I'd burst out laughing during karaoke nights and Ava would cringe when Dave and I danced in the kitchen while making dinner. But one of us had to be the responsible parent who didn't let our daughter get away with everything. Dave had checked out.

So, it's fun I'm aiming for when instead of reaching in my drawer for my usual plain black bra and underwear, I take out the white tissue paper shoved at the back. I gently unwrap it to reveal the red lace push-up bra and thong I'd bought to surprise Dave with after we got home from dropping off Ava.

Instead, I came home to an empty house, and he drove to a condo he'd already rented without telling me. He'd secretly packed a suitcase of clothes—they'd been in the back of his car, and I'd never noticed, since he was in charge of packing.

I was embarrassed when I bought this lingerie, hiding it on the sales counter under a flannel pajama set, even though I knew the clerk would have to ring it up.

There's time to fix what's broken in me.

I slip on the bra and panties and look in the full-length mirror hanging next to the dresser. I like my curves, which suddenly seem sexy to me.

My phone pings.

Justin: Dave's a fool.

I whip around, immediately covering my breasts with my hands, as if he can see me through the phone. Then I roll my eyes. I'm so out of practice with dating—or whatever this is. While Justin's interest makes me apprehensive, it's also flattering.

I'm on a precipice. I can remain the lonely woman Dave has abandoned or leap into the unknown with a man who makes me feel like the sensual, vibrant, desirable woman I want to be.

I want to leap even if it scares me to death.

CHAPTER THREE

I lock the door behind me and get in my car to head to Lakeside Drive, a route I could normally do with my eyes closed. Today, though, once I'm on Charlevoix Avenue, I'm confusing left from right. All I can think about is Justin. As much as I want to be a different person, I can't stop my mind from jumbling with worry and dread that he's playing me. For what purpose, I have no idea. But I have a hard time believing I'm the only woman he's chatting with. He's too smooth and practiced at it. How quickly he moved us to sexting.

Maybe I'm not used to a man openly telling me what he wants from me. Dave and I were each other's firsts for almost everything, and it wasn't sex and passion that kept us together. It was our deep admiration, love, and commitment, until he threw that all away.

Justin could have scrolled through my page and intuited how thirsty I am for anyone to pay attention to me, a middle-aged mother in sensible clothes, one whose most exciting posts are fabulous chicken recipes and the latest book I read. Maybe I'm more insecure than I want to admit, because the second Justin opened the door to raunchy sexting, I raced through it.

I shiver, imagining him touching me, tasting me, and almost blow through a stop sign. Thank goodness no other cars are on the road. Once again, Justin Ward is consuming me. Even though I have doubts, I decide to ignore them, at least for now. I don't know if he's someone I can actually develop a real connection with as an adult, but the high of talking to him feels too good to stop. I don't want to come down, because if I do, I'm left with my desolate house and a hole in my heart that has only gotten bigger every day since Dave discarded our life together to seek out whatever it is he needs to find without me.

But I have a job to do, and I can't afford not to give it my all. "Focus," I berate myself as I stop in front of Pages, my favorite café / used bookstore on Kercheval Avenue to grab another coffee and peruse the shelves for a few minutes to get my bearings. I need to be in the kind of place that has always brought me peace, and I still have time to put my signs at the intersections along the way to Lakeside Drive.

I try to lose myself in the warm, cozy ambience of worn armchairs and dark wood shelves, lined with beautiful books, dog eared and full of history from previous readers' fingers touching the paper. I hear a girl's laugh and turn to the cash register, where a young woman in her early twenties shoves her male coworker's arm. And I'm hit with a rush of nostalgia and loss.

I didn't need a job at U-M; I wanted to work at the Book Nook. I was very close to Jenna and Natalie, but a natural introvert, I sometimes needed to be in a space that felt like it belonged only to me. And Tyler, during our four-hour shifts, was also only mine. We shared the cleaning, our snacks and meals, and made-up zany backstories about our customers. The first time Dave came in, Tyler whispered to me, "That guy is a spy for the CIA."

I laughed so hard that I snorted, and Dave looked over. He smiled, then looked away immediately. Tyler made it his mission to get us together after that. He saw a spark between us that I didn't pay much attention to until Justin was out of my life. And then, so was Tyler.

Tears fill my eyes. I don't want them to be red and swollen at my open house, so I shove away thoughts of Tyler and Dave and scan the shelves for a book to buy. My gaze lands on a battered copy of *The Unbearable Lightness of Being*. I pull my favorite Milan Kundera novel from the shelf, even though I still have mine from college. I flick through the yellowed pages, smoothing my fingers over the pencil notes in the margins. And I'm right back in my college memories, because the themes in this book were the topic of the last essay Justin and I worked on together.

By that point, I'd convinced myself he'd make a move if only I weren't such a sexless nerd. So, I borrowed one of Jenna's strappy little dresses, which came just above the knee on me, and twisted my hair in a claw clip, determined to make Justin ask me out on a date. It was a warm April afternoon, the sunniest day we'd had in months, so instead of in the library, we sat on the Diag.

"You look pretty," Justin said as he stretched out his long jean-clad legs on the grass.

I hung on to that compliment like a lifeline. And when he flashed his dimpled smile, I could barely focus with how desperate I was for him to give me any indication that he liked me as more than just his tutor and friend. He pulled the novel from his battered black backpack. "It was a good book."

"You read it?" I was surprised, because usually I'd have to give him the summary, and we'd cobble together a decent essay.

He laughed. "I watched the movie."

I giggled, though if it were anyone else, I'd be disappointed. "Do you identify with Tomas?"

Justin grinned, but I saw sadness flash across his face. "Because you think I sleep with a ton of girls?"

It is what I meant, but I didn't want to offend him in any way. "I meant is there power in sex for you?" My voice shook on the word *sex*.

He caught it. "Are you pure like Tereza?"

"I don't know about pure, but a virgin, yes." I felt slightly embarrassed after I admitted this, but for some reason I felt safe around him, and I hoped my honesty was attractive.

My eyes were glued to his long fingers as he ran them through his hair. "I think it's sweet that you're waiting. I'm not sure the girls I sleep with really care about me." His hand lightly brushed my arm.

"I'm waiting for love," I said, but what I really wanted to tell Justin was that I loved him.

He held my gaze. "Tereza was my favorite character. I'd bring her home to my mother."

Then he invited me to the Sigma Chi party.

Before the party, I analyzed that conversation with Jenna and Natalie to decipher his true feelings, as I did with every single moment that Justin and I spent together. As always, my two best friends humored me while shooting worried looks at each other—maybe they thought I didn't notice, but I did. They knew I was in love for the first time and how much it scared me.

They were both happy when I started dating Dave, because he was such a nice person and took care of me. When he picked me up from our apartment for a date, he'd bring flowers, chocolate, or a novel he thought I'd like, holding my hand as we went down the steps and opening the car door for me. Ava used to roll her eyes at Dave's gentle treatment of both his girls, telling him she could open her own damn door. But I loved feeling special.

Natalie was relieved my obsession with Justin had finally come to an end. She told me I wasn't wired to take on a bad boy. Jenna thought his charm was disingenuous, and she sensed a dark edginess in him that she didn't think I could handle.

Now I roll my eyes at my naivety. Justin must have been amused by my innocence, yet he never did take advantage of it.

I return the book to the shelf, buy a coffee that I don't need, and quickly leave the store, about to get in my car when something triggers a prickle on the back of my neck. I turn. I feel like someone is watching me. But there are only a few pedestrians, none of whom are looking at me. It's probably the lack of sleep, the sexting, and the book that are making me twitchy. But I'm tense as I start the car and drive away from the store, looking over my shoulder at each intersection that I stop at to prop up my signs.

I'm calmer when I pull up outside the stunning five-bedroom, four-bath Dutch Colonial I'm showing. After unlocking the powder blue front door, I go through all the rooms, grateful for Rebecca, my expert stager, who's created a modern rustic vibe with farmhouse-style tables and chairs, eclectic hanging-light installations, and soft white and gray rugs and pillows. I place my signature candles in the living and dining rooms, inhaling the rich, delicious scent of vanilla and nutmeg. But I'm not actually taking anything in. Justin is all I can think about.

As potential buyers and their Realtors file through the house, oohing and aahing over the floor-to-ceiling windows that overlook the lap pool in the immaculately designed backyard, the barn-style doors, and the exquisite wood paneling in vibrant red, yellow, and green on an accent wall in every room, my attention is on his tempting words, his emotional intelligence, and how he makes me want to constantly run my hands over my body. Not the angles and planes of only a mother, but of a sexual woman hungry to feel aroused.

While a trio of well-dressed agents from one of the largest brokerages in Grosse Pointe shows their clients the kitchen, remarkable with weathered wood beams and stone floors, I decide I have time to text Justin. I want what I'm feeling to be mutual, but my heart is still so vulnerable—how does anyone get over a marriage? How can I avoid getting hurt again?

Leaning against the distressed, dark wood island, I dig my nails into my palm, then type:

Eden: Are you being real with me?

Justin: Yes. Whatever this is between us is all I can think about.

Eden: Me too.

Justin: So, why don't we let ourselves fall into it?

Eden: Because I don't want to live in a fantasy.

Justin: I have every intention of making it a reality. But you need to trust me, Eden. You have to be real with me, too. I'm as vulnerable as you are.

One of the agents smiles at me as she and her client leave the kitchen. I wonder if she has a life full of color and intrigue, a secret that's hers alone. I like having something—someone—who belongs only to me. Justin's created a sizzling blaze under my skin, like my veins have been sliced open, exposed. I don't want to give that up. It makes everything difficult in my life seem easier. But I can't keep writing these messages. It's not enough for me.

Eden: I'm at my open house. Can we talk on the phone after? I'd feel more comfortable, and I want to hear your voice.

I see he's read my request, but my phone is silent. Did I move too fast? I never even dated anyone before Dave. I don't know how to do this. Finally, he's typing. I hold my breath.

Justin: I'll call you. What time works?

Eden: 2 pm. 313-555-7628.

Justin: Talk soon.

I put my phone back in my purse, thrumming with anticipation of how his voice will sound after all these years, what we'll actually say to each other. One of the two remaining agents in the kitchen fiddles with the collar of her blue button-down. And I decide to do something so perilous that if I don't do it right this second, I'll change my mind.

I leave the agents and their clients in the kitchen, sneak into the powder room off the front door, and lock it. Placing my phone on the white marble counter next to the vessel sink and angling it to get the best shot, I slip off my black blazer, undo my black silk blouse, and snap a photo of myself in the red lace bra. I'd kill Ava if she did what I'm about to, but I'm a grown woman, and it's only for one person's eyes.

I zoom in on the picture. I love how seductive I look—nothing like my usual self. I've never taken any kind of shot like this. I barely glance at my own breasts in the mirror at home. The rush is staggering.

I silence the voice in my head warning me how foolish this is, exhale a shaky breath, and share the photo with Justin through the Messenger app.

His response takes less than a second.

Justin: You're so damn hot.

No one has ever spoken to me like this. I think women are supposed to hit their sexual peak in their thirties, but I'm bubbling with what feels like true exuberance rather than faking it so everyone around me won't know I'm struggling. I quickly run water over my wrists to cool off, like I taught Ava to do when she was eight and upset when her then-best friend excluded her at recess. I'm unable to keep my grin at bay as I exit the bathroom. My phone pings again. I look at my screen.

Justin: I haven't wanted someone as much as I want you in a very long time. Hope you like this. I'm older than I was in college, of course.

He's in only a white towel wrapped around his trim waist. I gawk at his well-defined stomach, and heat shoots through me. His rich, dark waves are mussed and wet, and his arms are as strong and sinewy as I remember. On his left bicep, he has a new tattoo since college, the head of a griffin.

How could a man this hot want me? And his insecurity that he's not as youthful as he was when we first met tugs at me. It's that vulnerability I saw in him during our tutoring sessions: self-doubt I'm not sure anyone else recognized in him. I'm about to type back how much hotter he is now, when a husky female voice fills the hallway.

"This is a beautiful house."

I jump and immediately turn my screen face down. A tall brunette in fitted black trousers and a white sweater is in front of me. I hope my cheeks aren't as flushed as they feel. "The view from the balcony off the master is incredible. Have you gone upstairs?"

She shakes her head. "I just got here. I saw your sign and popped in for a peek." Her eyes travel to my chest, and smiling, she gestures with her fingers. "You might want to fix that."

I look down at myself. Jesus. My shirt is buttoned wrong, so the edge of my red bra is visible. Quickly, I turn away and redo the top three buttons, laughing nervously. "I left my house quickly."

She grins, her bright-blue eyes a striking contrast to her brown hair. "Happens to me all the time."

I smile back. "Thank you for telling me." I smooth my jacket, trying to appear professional, though inside I'm quaking. I can't believe I just sent a sexy selfie from the bathroom of my open house. Shame and a rush of dopamine hit me simultaneously. Maybe this is what being an addict feels like. I crave more.

I clear my throat to regain my equilibrium. "If you're interested, I'm Eden Mi—Hoffman." I shake her hand, trying out how my former name feels. It's definitely weird, but not as upsetting as I expected.

"Lila Cavanaugh. Nice to meet you." She glances at my pantsuit as though searching for a pocket. "Do you have a card I can take with me?"

I nod and lead her down the expansive hallway to the kitchen, where brochures about the house, neighborhood, and nearby schools are in a neat pile next to my business cards. I'm still trembling when I hand her one, but she doesn't seem to notice.

"Great." She tucks the card in her pants pocket and glances around the kitchen. "I'm going to look around, if that's okay. It's even nicer than it appears from the outside."

"Please go ahead. I'm here if you need anything."

"I'll let you know." She smiles again and exits the kitchen.

I blow out a breath, embarrassed to get caught not being as present and professional as I normally am. I don't even usually look at my phone when I'm at work. I'm happy when the last person exits the open house. I text Sylvie to let her know the showing went well and there was some genuine interest I'll follow up on tomorrow. I'll also order new business cards with my old-new last name. Taking that concrete step forward is jarring, but I can't hold on to what I've already lost. Dave wants a divorce, not even a trial separation, no matter what we told Ava. He doesn't want me back. He barely wants to talk, even if I'd be willing to work on us.

I have fifteen minutes to make it home for my call with Justin, but as I turn my key in the ignition, my phone rings.

My adrenaline spikes as a number with *734*, the Ann Arbor area code, flashes across the screen, and for a moment, I have trouble catching a breath.

"Hi," I answer after putting in my earbuds so his voice is closer to me, my own voice an octave lower than usual. I roll my eyes at how inane I'm acting.

"Hey. After seeing your photo, I couldn't wait any longer. Do you have time to talk now?"

I'm parked right outside my listing and should drive home before speaking to him, but I'm disoriented by the reality of his voice in my ears compared to the memory of what he sounded like twenty-something years ago. I remember his distinct low growl, yet his tone is gravellier now, even deeper, which makes me realize we're starting over and aren't young college students anymore. I need to separate the Justin I knew from the man I want to believe he's become. I want this escape from my sadness so much.

Tongue-tied, I turn off the car, not sure how to start. I clear my throat. "You sound different."

"*Different* good?"

"Yes. A man. Not a boy."

He laughs a deep rumble. "I forgot how sexy and sweet you sound."

I'm warm all over. No one's ever told me my voice is sexy. *Shrill* is what Dave has called it on occasion. *Shrieky* is how Ava describes it.

"What's sexy about my voice?"

"You sound innocent, but there's a mischievousness to it."

I laugh. "I don't know if mischievous is a part of me at all." But inside my car, where I drive to and from listings, grocery shopping, and appointments, I want to be exciting for once. "Maybe I can be, though."

"Oh yeah? How?"

My heart quivers as wildly as the leaves on the chokecherry tree on the front lawn of my listing. "I want to continue what we were doing this morning."

There's a pause before he asks, "Now, on the phone?"

I don't want to leave this spot and ruin the moment or give myself any time to overthink.

"Yes."

"What are you wearing?"

With a mix of embarrassed excitement, I answer Justin's question honestly, unsure of how far I want this conversation to go.

"A black pantsuit."

"When was the last time someone touched you?"

"Months." The tightly wound coil of misery inside me unwinds. I clamp my lips together so the relief of it won't fall from my lips. It's too much to release in a parked car outside the house I'm trying to sell. I also shouldn't be here talking to him like this, but there's no way I can stop now or I'll shut down and maybe never get the courage again. I turn the question back to Justin. "How about you?"

"Touched me how I want to be? Years. You're giving me something I've been missing for so long."

"So are you," I whisper, hesitant to let him inside my heart, my soul, me. "But I'm really nervous."

"I am too. This is new and different for me. But I've got you, Eden. Tell me what you want."

The cold air coming through my open window does nothing to smother the heat flaming my cheeks. What I want is for him to make me savage with lust, feel his hands and mouth all over me. I stifle the automatic giggle bubbling in my throat. I seriously don't know if I'm doing this all wrong. "I want to lose all control with you like I did in college."

His groan tells me it was the right thing to say. "Mmm. That sounds delicious. Unbutton your pants."

His demand tightens me with need, and I immediately obey. I need Justin to make me wild and uninhibited more than I remember wanting anything. I don't care that I'm technically still at work, that anyone could look out their window and see me. In fact, the danger of it turns me on even more. I want them to watch me. I lick my lips. "Okay, I've done it."

"You're safe with me. I want to unlock every part of you, Eden."

When Justin says my name, dots of sweat bead between my breasts. I'm fully aware that what I'm doing is wrong and illicit. It fuels my raw desire, so fierce that it wins out against any guilt or reason. I'm at his mercy, under a spell when I grab my bag from the passenger seat to put over my lap and slide down farther in my seat.

"Imagine I'm in the car with you. I slide my hand into your suit jacket."

I moan out loud at the same time I feel eyes on me. I glance out the passenger's side window. A woman at the house next door to my listing has appeared in her garden with a trowel. She darts her eyes toward my car before turning back around. She must have heard me. The fantasy of getting caught and the reality of it are different. I quickly close the window and duck farther down in my seat so she hopefully can't see me. There's no way for me to resist Justin. I'm too far gone.

"I rub my stubbled jaw over your skin. I suck on your bottom lip, and you open your mouth for my tongue to devour you. I want to taste every inch of you."

I'm almost hyperventilating. Dave and I *never* spoke to each other like this.

"Do you want more, Eden?"

"Yes," I whisper.

He chuckles softly and says things I've never even imagined a man saying to me.

"Please don't stop," I tell him, because this is the freest, most passionate I've ever felt, and I don't want it to end.

Justin continues his commands. It takes only ten seconds for waves of ecstasy to rock my whole body, and I vibrate, an odd sensation of delirium and discomfort coursing through me. I'm still pulsing when I hear a car door slam. I jump, and through my rearview mirror I see Dave striding toward me.

CHAPTER FOUR

"I have to go. I'll text you later," I say frantically to Justin, and then I pull my earbuds out and wipe my hand on a Kleenex in the console. My heart's beating so fast that I can't calm it before Dave knocks on my window.

I toss my bag on the passenger seat, open my door, and put a leg out to keep it from slamming shut. "What's going on? Why are you here?" I'm speaking too quickly and furtively look at my phone resting next to my bag, wondering if I missed Dave's call while I was getting myself off.

Dave bends and leans into the car, a cup from Beans, our favorite coffee shop in Grosse Pointe, in his hand. "I saw your missed call after Julia called me. So I called and texted you a bunch of times, then I checked your listing schedule online." He cocks his chin at the **FOR SALE** sign with my smiling, though pinched, face posted on the front lawn. "I wanted to catch you before you left. I thought we should go to Ann Arbor and talk with Ava together about what happened at the dorm."

My chest flutters painfully with panic over the terrible risk I've just taken. And it twinges at how casual Dave is with me, like I'm an acquaintance and not the woman he proposed to in Paris, his hands shaking as he slipped the ring onto my finger before I'd even said yes. I'm not sure how I feel about him anymore. I've been so hurt and angry, forcing myself to go numb so I won't collapse from the agony of losing my best friend. All I can muster right now is slight exasperation as I watch him put the cup on the roof of the car, then take off his glasses to clean them with the bottom of his light-blue long-sleeved shirt. It's such a familiar habit of his, and I'm glad I don't have to see him do it every five minutes anymore.

I step out of the car, peering down at myself. In my frenzy to hide my salacious actions from Dave, I only did up the top button on my pants and neglected to zip them. I button my suit jacket as fast as I can and tug down the bottom of the jacket, hoping Dave can't see my red underwear through the open fly.

He gets the cup from the top of my car and hands it to me. I don't need a third cup of coffee today, and irritation shoots through me when his eyes roam my face like he's assessing me. He squints. "You're all flushed. You sick?"

I touch my heated face. "Just a busy morning with my showing." I feel someone else's eyes on me. The neighbor is back outside, has stopped her planting, and is hooked on our every word. Did she know what I was doing in my car? What must she think of me? I don't care. Or don't want to, at least. People do wicked things all the time. This is the only time I've ever done anything that could be considered illegal. It's my new life, and I can't let it pass me by as though I'm in a coma, like I have for months.

"Can we talk at home?" I cough. "I mean, why don't you follow me back to the house?" I avoid his searching eyes, because whatever Dave's opinion is of me right now shouldn't matter. I don't belong to him anymore.

"Sure," he says, but he draws it out slowly.

His confused tone forces me to make eye contact. He's still looking at me carefully.

"What?"

He shifts from foot to foot. "You look good."

I scoff. "You just asked me if I was sick."

"On closer inspection, you seem . . . different."

I laugh out loud at the transformation my life has undergone in less than a day.

"Are you okay?" He pauses. "You're acting weird. Have you met someone?"

I look for any sign of jealousy or hurt, but his face is unreadable. This is not my Dave, whom I loved for almost half my life. That Dave had two moods: light and agreeable; tired and irritable. His feelings were always pretty easy to decipher, or so I believed. But he's pulled so far away from me that I question how long he might have been wearing a mask. If our issues are only about his grief. I don't know how to broach it, if I even want to right now, when I'm still on a high from my conversation with Justin. So, I simply ask, "Would you care if I have?"

"I want you to be happy."

"Are you happy, Dave?"

He just gives me a blank stare that I can't interpret, so I give up. "You look good too."

He does. He's cut his light-brown hair, so it's a bit spiky on top, and his hazel eyes are gold in the sun. But I'm not attracted to him like I am to Justin. I never wanted to tear Dave's clothes from his body and lick every inch of him.

Is that because our relationship was solid and safe, while with Justin, I was always on edge, anxious about what he truly felt about me? Or did our marriage run its course, and I refused to accept that until Dave forced my hand? I don't regret any of our years together, though. Without Dave, I wouldn't have Ava, and no matter how much she seems to dislike me a lot of the time, I love her more than anyone in the world.

Dave gets back into his car and tails me to Ivy Court, through the leafy, serene residential streets, past the middle school Ava attended and the field where she played soccer in elementary school—all these sights as familiar to me as Dave is unfamiliar in his cold distance.

After we both park, I grab the full cup of coffee to throw it away inside and walk up the four uneven steps to the porch—the ones we kept putting off getting fixed. It truly sinks in that he doesn't live here anymore.

"I'll change, and we can go. Sit for a minute." I point to the chair swing with the orange pillows, where I nursed Ava and where Dave and I waited for her when she broke curfew every weekend over the summer. When I insisted on accountability, I'd overhear Dave whisper, "I'll talk to your mother," pitting Ava against me so he would look like the good guy. Now that she's in college and Dave and I are no longer together, I'm not sure how we'll handle anything, where the boundaries lie.

He awkwardly does what I ask, pulling on his left ear, a nervous tic he's had since college, and gestures at the front door. "There's a package for you."

I look down. A pretty light-pink box with a white ribbon is propped against the doorframe. There's no card attached. I wonder if Jenna or Natalie left me another birthday present. I hide my smile. Because of the prosecco they gave me, I found Justin again. Without it, I might never have messaged him.

I pick up the box. "I'll take this inside and change, then we can go to Ann Arbor."

I leave Dave on the porch and head inside, where I put the present on the small white table in the entryway. I'll open it later. I want to get to U-M as soon as possible and deal with our daughter.

"Where's the extra key?"

I yelp, not realizing Dave followed me inside. "Where it always is. Under the middle cushion on the swing."

He shakes his head. "It's not there."

I roll my eyes. "Why were you even looking for it? I'll find it in a minute."

"I worry about you on your own here." He stoops a bit, like he always does when he's talking to me and he doesn't want his six-foot-three height to overpower my five-foot-four frame.

I huff a dark laugh. "Sure, Dave. You're so worried that you ended our marriage in a parking lot. You don't get to play the nice guy here."

He winces but as usual doesn't respond. He only pulls his sleeves down and looks at the floor.

I head toward the stairs to go up and change, when he starts walking to the kitchen. Leaning over the railing, I ask, "Now what are you doing?"

He turns around, flicks his eyes away from mine, and shoves his hands in the pockets of his beige chinos. "I need the credit card bill. I assume you have it. We still have a joint card, and I'm paying for it."

That annoys me. "Because you don't want to discuss what we're going to do about everything. Do you have a lawyer? Will I get surprise divorce papers on the doorstep?"

He shakes his head. "I wouldn't do that to you."

I gape at him. "Dave. Come on. I don't even know you anymore."

"I'm sorry," he whispers and looks at his feet.

It's clear he's suffering but equally as clear that he's not ready to talk to me. I can't fight someone who doesn't want to engage in battle, so I just say, "I'll get my own credit card. We can put Ava's stuff on the joint one." Then I snort. "Seriously, Dave, can you get your statements online already, like everyone else?"

He smiles at that. "You know I like to have things on paper so I can file them. They should be coming to my new place anyway. I rerouted everything, but the bill never arrived."

His condo, he means, that I've never seen. Now, when I'm reminded of how much he'd planned behind my back, I'm enraged. But I want this day to go smoothly—the quicker we leave, the quicker I can get back to Justin.

After changing into my usual simple black bra and underwear, a pair of black leggings, and an emerald green sweater, I find Dave shuffling by the front door. "Get the bill?" I ask.

He nods, and I glance at the pink gift box on the table. "I'll open that, then let's go."

I undo the ribbon and lift the top off the box. I gasp. And for a second, I wonder if it's from Dave, a peace offering, a surprise, a way to make amends.

"You love that book. Nice gift," Dave says.

Not from him then. And my chest skitters, because inside the box is a battered used copy of *The Unbearable Lightness of Being*. Quickly, I flip through the pages, which have pencil markings in the margins like the book that I was looking at in Pages today right before I went to my listing.

He points at the book. "Who's it from?"

"I'm not sure," I answer honestly, because I don't know what else to say. I had thought of my conversation with Justin about that book all those years ago but never mentioned it aloud to him.

"Someone left a box at the house, and you don't know who?" He sounds skeptical and narrows his eyes. "Is there a card?"

I shake my head. Maybe there's an inscription inside the book—but if it is from Justin, who knows what he might have written. I open it to the first page, angling my body away from Dave. Nothing.

"It was probably Jenna or Natalie. For my birthday." I look sharply at him.

He hangs his head. "I'm sorry," he mumbles. "I didn't forget your birthday. I didn't know if you'd want to hear from me."

I'm not sure if I did, either, because a meaningless greeting does nothing to salve the wound he opened.

"It doesn't matter. Why do you care who left me a present?"

He lifts his head. "I'm just concerned, okay? The extra key is gone, and now you're telling me someone anonymously left you one of your favorite books on the porch."

"You love this book, too, if I recall correctly."

He tugs his sleeves down again. "Eden, I only loved it because you recommended it to me."

Against my will, I soften. "That was a long time ago."

Turning so he won't see the sadness I know is evident on my face, I walk onto the porch. He follows, and I lock the front door. I also don't want Dave to know how rattled I am about the book. Could Justin have looked up my home address and dropped it on my porch? But how could he possibly know it's the same book I picked up off the shelf a few hours ago? Is it even the same book? Was he the person I felt watching me outside the store? No, that's ridiculous. Maybe he was thinking about that same conversation on the Diag I was.

I don't know whether to be alarmed or touched that Justin might have somehow discovered how much this book means to me, that it's always reminded me of him. Or is it just a weird coincidence? Jenna or Natalie could have just as easily gotten it for me.

While Dave heads down the steps, I shoot them a quick message in our group thread.

Eden: Hi, ladies. Thank you so much for the prosecco. I'm sorry I wasn't up to going out. Maybe another time next week? Also, did you leave a book for me on my porch today?

Jenna: Good timing! You caught me while I'm watching Ryder play soccer terribly. Lol. Sorry, hon. It wasn't me. And yes to going out sometime next week. I'll check my schedule. I hope your birthday was okay considering everything.

I don't want to tell Jenna and Natalie about Justin, at least not yet. We've only had a few conversations, and though they were racy and something I should discuss with my best girlfriends, I'm afraid they'll warn me to stop before I get in too deep. Justin has explained why he ghosted me all those years ago, but I know that Jenna, especially, never trusted him. I don't want to stop talking to someone who makes me feel so good when Dave can barely even look me in the eye.

Natalie: I didn't leave you a book either. Which book?

Eden: The Unbearable Lightness of Being.

Natalie: Dave?

Eden: No. I'm with him now. We're actually going to see Ava. She got caught drinking. I'll fill you in later.

Jenna: Uh oh. Ava's in trouble.

Natalie: Ugh. Is she okay, Eden?

Eden: Hope so. She's having trouble dealing with the split.

Jenna: Understandable. Keep us posted on Ava and the mysterious book fairy. Are you okay?

Eden: I'm okay. Talk soon.

I'm not okay. I'm not sure what I am. I put my phone in my bag and stick my hand under the middle cushion on the swing. Dave's right. The extra key we've kept hidden there since Ava was a baby is gone. I haven't looked for that key in a long time. Ava might have taken it and forgotten to tell us.

If the only odd occurrence today was the missing key, I'd let it go. But between that, the feeling that I was being watched outside Pages, and the same book mysteriously being left on my doorstep, I'm spooked.

I smooth my finger across my lips as though it will help me find the answers. Then something Justin said from our phone conversation comes back to me.

"Imagine I'm in the car with you."

I told him when to call me. I never told him where I'd be when he phoned.

CHAPTER FIVE

Unsettled, I follow Dave to the Range Rover that he's had for five years. The only change he's made is the **U-M Dad** sticker he's pressed onto the back window. While I'm having a torrid online relationship, his midlife crisis, or whatever he's suffering from that he won't talk to me about, seems as mundane as our marriage. I wish he'd have bought a flashier ride or gotten a tattoo—something that indicates he needed a change in his life and leaving wasn't all about me, like Ava believes. Like I believe too.

But Dave's problems aren't mine to solve, though I am worried about him. And myself. I don't recognize the person I'm becoming, but I don't want to go back to who I was before last night. I've never felt this exhilarated.

I can't tell if I'm looking for reasons not to trust what seem to be Justin's genuine feelings for me then and now, or if something is off. Should I message and ask him what his intentions are or extricate myself from whatever is happening between us before it gets even more out of control? Do I ask him if he left me the book? If he has our house key? No. I would sound insane.

"You okay?" Dave asks as he opens the passenger door for me. "I was right about the key, huh?" He smiles, but it's not condescending. It's a flash of my old Dave, who was enamored with my academic intellect and amused by my sometimes-wandering mind. And it calms me down.

Before I get in, I say, "Maybe Ava took it to college with her?"

"She definitely took her attitude."

I laugh, maybe to expel the bottled-up tension between us, and to my surprise, so does he, his body folding like an accordion, like it used to when we found joy in each other. I can't remember the last time Dave and I laughed like that.

As he straightens, though, pain flashes across his face. I can't stop myself from lightly touching his arm. "I'm sorry if I wasn't the wife you wanted."

He blinks, then takes off his glasses, which have filmed up a bit, and cleans them once again with his shirt. Without looking at me, he says, "It's not your fault, Eden. I think you're perfect."

I don't know how to take that. If *perfect* means *boring*, and I didn't excite him the way he needs. But he's turned his back to get into the driver's side of the car.

Dave always does the driving. Not because it's his car. He likes to think he's better at it than me. He's not. He's slow and overly cautious, so cars have to honk before he realizes the light is green. But I'm too keyed up to drive, too full of conflicting emotions that I won't be able to focus properly.

I reach to take the credit card bill in his hand so he can start the car. He snatches it from me and puts it into the glove box. "Sorry. You know I like to put things in spots myself so I remember where they are." He turns the key in the ignition and faces me again. "You look better without me."

It's such a powerful gut punch of a statement. And it's true. I feel like I'm glowing, but I'm also wrestling with how reckless I've been. "I think I like myself better too." I give him a pointed look.

His face blanches. I meant to hurt him, but it doesn't feel good.

Awkward silence fills the car, and I look out the window. There's a lot of traffic this gorgeous Saturday afternoon. It's cool but the sun is strong, and Dave squints to see the road. When he takes the ramp to get onto the I-94 West, I pull out my phone. There's no text from Justin. I'm both relieved and disappointed. I don't want to mention the gift until I'm certain he's the one who left it. Since it wasn't Jenna and Natalie, though, I can't think of anyone other than Justin who might have.

If Justin was in Grosse Pointe, why not ask to meet me for coffee or lunch? And he knew I was in my car when we talked. Is he hiding something?

I must be restless, because Dave glances over.

"Do you have to pee?" he asks.

I can't help smirking. "No, just getting comfortable."

"Maybe it's the lacy underwear making you uncomfortable."

So he did see my unzipped pants when I got out of my car. Was he always this judgmental?

"I'm surprised you noticed," I shoot back.

His neck muscles tense. "What's that supposed to mean?"

"Nothing, Dave." I put my hands in my lap. "What are we going to do about Ava? I'm really worried about her."

"I am too. But she's a firecracker, Eden. And we all make mistakes in college."

"Is that how it's going to be?" I shock both of us when I slam my palm against the door.

Dave jumps. "Calm down. I'm driving."

That makes me even angrier. I'm tired of suppressing everything I want to say. "No, Dave! This time I won't lay down the law and you brush off the fact that she's on *warning*. It's not fair."

His hands tighten on the wheel. "Okay. You're right. It's just that she's having a hard time—"

"Which isn't my fault, as you said."

He cringes and nods. "We were going to buy her the Les Paul guitar this week. What if we put that on hold until she can prove she'll follow the dorm rules and stay in line?"

"Now you're asserting your parental responsibility with her?"

Dave's hands curl tighter around the steering wheel. Being snarky isn't going to help, so I change tacks.

"Ava's wanted that guitar for so long. We promised we'd get it for her before the music faculty showcase next week. She's going to hate me for this."

"I'll lower the boom. I promise. If her record is clean, and her grades are decent, we'll get it in December for her birthday."

I'm glad he's offered to take the heat for this, but I know Ava will still blame me. He's right, though. Throwing money at the problem isn't a long-term solution.

We're both quiet the rest of the ride, but the tension in the car is heavy with all the things unspoken. As we pass Pierpont Commons, I'm hit with a stronger sense of nostalgia than I'd felt when we'd dropped Ava off. A mere six weeks ago, I reminisced about all the afternoons I strolled from the English literature department at Angell Hall to get some food at the student union. The day we brought Ava here, Justin wasn't on my mind at all. I was caught up with my discordant emotions: my daughter leaving home; freedom from being a full-time mother; my conflicting thoughts about my marriage, which became moot only a few hours later when Dave asked for a divorce.

It's shocking how quickly life splinters into before and after.

Dave keeps looking into the rearview mirror and pulling his right sleeve down. His fidgeting makes me tense. "Why are *you* so restless?"

"I could swear the same silver car has been behind us since we left the house. But it's gone now. I think I'm on edge about Ava and that key disappearing." He glances at me. "You don't have a stalker, do you?" He laughs, but it's nervous.

I flinch but belittle myself by snorting. "As if." I hear the slight tremor in my voice, though. "Do you?"

The twitch in his shoulders is lightning quick, but I notice it. Suddenly, I wonder if Dave's bizarre behavior over the last six months and now his weird focus on the credit card bill have anything to do with me at all. But he simply shakes his head.

Perhaps we're both hiding something.

But after Dave pulls into the circular driveway outside Bursley Hall and parks and we start walking a foot apart toward the dorm, I leave behind my pent-up grievances and mixed-up thoughts about Justin. I put my hand on his arm. "You'll tell her about the Les Paul?"

"I promise."

He promised to love me for better or worse, too, but for now, we're a team, here to support our child.

Dave reaches forward to open the door to the main entrance of the dorm, then stops. "I'll meet you up there. I forgot my phone in the car."

"I can wait here."

When he returns with his phone, we go together to Ava's floor, where outside her room, music bounces off the walls, but it's not unpleasant. It's my daughter's melodic, throaty voice accompanied by the scratchy plucking of her guitar strings. It warms my heart and pinches it at the same time. Ava is never happier than when she's creating and singing, and she'll have to stop to face her parents about the party in her room last night. Dave hesitates for too long, so I rap my knuckles on the door. We need to rip off the Band-Aid.

"Come in!"

I open the door, and there's my baby, sitting cross-legged on her single bed, strumming her guitar. It's such a familiar sight in an unfamiliar space. In a pair of pink sweats and a black Nirvana T-shirt, her slim build looks slighter. Deep circles are etched under her usually alert eyes.

She must see the concern on my face because she rolls her eyes to the ceiling. But there's also a tiny smile tugging her lips up that I can't make sense of.

"Seriously? It was one warning. I had two drinks. Ugh." She swings her long legs over the side of the bed. "I assume you're coming in to lecture me. Let's have it." She flicks her attention between me and Dave.

Quickly, I turn around and see Dave's eyes soften as he looks at Ava. I knew he'd have trouble giving her tough love. So, I harden as a reaction, like always. I nudge him with my elbow. Ever the gentleman, of course he lets me enter her room first, which is tidier than

I expected. At home, Ava's laundry was piled so high that one of her friends could have been living in between the sweaters and towels and I'd never have known. But in her single room, the bed is neatly made, and her clothes seem to be hung in the closet, since her floor is bare. Though I suspect she might have cleaned up after getting caught partying last night.

When Ava was in high school, I envisioned dorm shopping with her, laughing together while we chose funky art for her walls, a bold-colored duvet, perhaps red or with bright geometric patterns. I even started a list of records I wanted to surprise her with, along with a turntable. When I suggested a day out together, though, Ava informed me that she'd already bought everything she needed online. I never purchased the record player because I worried it would only prove how out of touch I was.

And as I look at the duvet that she must have recently bought herself—jet black with a skull and crossbones—I know she's right. I don't know my daughter or what she wants.

She follows my eyes, pointing at the duvet. "Too dark for you? Not a good look for me?"

I was thinking that the all-black background makes her room seem smaller. But I hold my tongue and say, "I like it. It suits you."

"Whatever." She flops back on her bed, covered in sheet music, and crosses her thin arms over her chest. I want to ask if she's eating enough, but I have to choose my battles. She'll be eighteen in December, officially an adult, but to me she looks like a lost little girl. I want to both hug and scold her at the same time. I want to ask her to forgive me for any wrongdoings but also show her that I'm only trying to protect her. What I also wish is to tell her that I'm as confused as she is by her father's decision to break both our hearts so she knows I understand her pain. But I can't, because driving a wedge between Ava and Dave isn't what I want for them.

"Honey," I start, but Dave cuts me off.

"What's going on, Ava Bug? We're worried about you."

I cringe inwardly—the best way to make Ava clam up is to tell her you're worried about her. And I thought our plan of attack was Dave's firm announcement that we're not buying her the Les Paul until she can show us that she's taking school seriously. Ava winces too. Then she glares at me when my phone buzzes in my bag.

"Work?" she asks snidely.

"Probably," I answer curtly, hating myself for engaging with her. But she always does this: makes me feel guilty for having a job and life of my own. For a staunch feminist, Ava has some very patriarchal ideas of how I should be.

Dave steps back toward the door. "I'm going to quickly tell Julia we're here in case she wants to speak to us."

Dave leaves, escaping the confrontation we need to have. I'm sure he's hoping I'll have solved it when he returns, which angers me. We were supposed to be a united front, with him taking the lead, and now he's gone. Typical.

Ava and I stare at each other. Well, I gaze, trying to figure out what to say as she glowers. I decide to wait for Dave to come back. I'm not doing this alone. I pull out my phone. It is indeed a text from a buying agent about my Lakeside Drive listing. There might be an offer with contingencies. I text back quickly that I'll call her in an hour.

My phone buzzes with another text. I look and wish I hadn't.

Justin: I want to hear you scream my name.

I can almost see the sparks fly from my skin. Immediately turning away from Ava, I put my phone in my bag and place it on Ava's desk. I can't look at her right now with cheeks I know are crimson, so I busy myself with straightening the papers next to her laptop.

"What are you doing?"

Ava's voice, that text, make me jumpy, and I bang my head on the shelf above the desk, knocking it askew. I try to right it, but it won't level. I point to it, relieved to have a distraction. "Dad can fix that. It's not safe. It can fall on your head." I hold my own head and turn around. "I want you to be safe. That's all Dad and I want for you, Ava. To be safe, healthy, and happy."

She scoffs bitterly. "No, you want to control me."

Before I can argue, Dave returns. He looks at me hopefully, like I knew he would. I give a quick shake of my head and sit on the bed, unsure whether to scoot closer to Ava or stay rooted to the end of the mattress. Dave leans his back against the desk.

"Look, I'm sorry that I had a few girls here." Ava pouts at Dave. "But it wasn't as bad as Julia made it sound. We were all fully clothed. Yes, we drank. Yes, it's against the rules and illegal. But I'm in college! Of course I'm going to drink. Isn't that how you and Mom met?"

Score one for Ava.

"Well, not exactly," I say.

Dave chuckles, but I look sharply at him because Ava needs to understand boundaries and consequences. I want her to love college, like I did, but I also want her not to get kicked out in her first semester.

"Ava, my love, I was twenty-two when your dad and I were at that party, so it wasn't illegal like what you did." She opens her mouth, but Dave jumps in.

"Your mom and I actually met at the Book Nook, which was an off-campus bookstore on South State Street. I went in once and saw her, and I kept going back. I only went to the party because I knew she'd be there." He smiles at me. "I might not have had the guts to ask you out without Tyler's encouragement."

I know Dave is trying to ease the strained conversation, but reminding Ava how much her father once loved me isn't helping. And after talking about Tyler and the party just last night, it hits me again how vulnerable Ava is away on her own with little adult supervision.

"Do you remember I told you about my friend, Tyler, honey?"

Ava bobs her head. "Yeah, Mom. Everyone here knows who Tyler Yates is. He has a whole memorial bench outside the athletic center. It's like an urban legend to scare us away from doing anything fun."

I swallow my frustration. "Except that it really happened, Ava. And he disappeared from the party where Dad took care of me and got me home safely." I debate how honest to be, whether to show my daughter my flaws. I have to. "I got so drunk that I blacked out. Anything could have happened to me. It was a wild party with a lot of very inebriated kids. And Tyler vanished without anyone even realizing."

"Or so they said," Ava retorts.

Dave jumps in. "The point is, Ava, alcohol reduces your ability to make good choices."

"You and Mom splitting up involved no alcohol. So, shitty things happen all the time."

I hear Dave suck in a breath.

Then she regards me with those brown eyes that have always made me feel like she can see straight into my soul.

"I have to rehearse for the music faculty showcase for homecoming. Just tell me how disappointed you are in me, once again, so we can get this over with."

I rear back. "When have I ever said I'm disappointed in you?"

"You don't have to say it. I feel it every time you look at me. You're always comparing me to you. How I'm not hardworking enough, motivated enough, goal oriented enough. My clothes aren't appropriate. My room is disorganized. I don't want to be anything like you, afraid of what everyone else thinks."

"That's not true, Ava," Dave says firmly. "Your mother wants the best for you."

I'm grateful that he's actually defending me, but Ava's assessment of me cuts to the bone.

My mind whirs through memories of her from birth to now, like one of those flip picture books she had as a kid. The faster you turn the pages, the faster the characters move to the end of their stories. Is that how she sees her childhood with me? A series of my parenting failures, not the kisses on bruises and scrapes, the cheering at her soccer games and music recitals, the laughter when I dyed the ends of her hair purple when she was fourteen, because she asked me to.

Have I viewed Ava as an extension of me, like my parents did? Still, no matter how angry and hurt Ava is, her cruelty toward me is unacceptable. "You're going too far," I say quietly, trying hard to keep calm. "I'm sorry if I've ever made you feel like you're not measuring up to my expectations, because I think you're amazing and strong and so much more self-aware than I was at your age. But this is not the conversation we came here to have."

Her eyes narrow; her sudden coldness worries me. I've seen Ava sever friends from her life faster than she changes socks. She's tough, and if you cross her, you don't get to come back. I want a closer relationship with her than I had with my mother, but I don't know how that's possible now.

My parents' absence in my life is more of a lost opportunity to have a real relationship with them than a gaping hole. I never felt like a priority to them, and I've never wanted Ava to feel that way. My love for Ava is unconditional and almost painfully deep. And I don't know how to care for her right now.

"Ava, your mom and I are going to talk outside for a minute, okay?"

Ava shrugs like she doesn't care, but I see the fear and also a flash of hope cross her face. As defiant as she's being, she almost seems happy that we're here.

I follow Dave into the hall, where we both wait for Ava's door to slowly thwack closed behind us.

He sighs heavily. "You're an excellent mother, Eden."

"I'm so much more than that. You and Ava just don't see it." A sob breaks free. Justin does see that, and I wish I could escape into my little world with him.

Dave shuffles, then scrapes his hand through his hair like he doesn't know what to do with himself. "For the record, you've never made me feel like I'm not good enough. It's that it can be hard for Ava to live in the shadow of your dreams for her when she's trying to find herself on her own terms."

I lean against the wall, for the support I can't ask for from him. "Are you talking about Ava or you?"

He flushes. "Ava."

"Right. Well, she can't get away with everything by turning us against each other, Dave. Or blaming everything on our separation." Something about this visit bothers me, though. "Did Ava look a bit . . . pleased to you?"

He squints. "What do you mean?"

"I think she might have wanted us to come here together."

"Oh," he says quietly. "To force us together, you mean?"

I nod. "Maybe. This *is* the first time we've seen each other since our last visit here."

"Look, why don't you take a walk and let me talk to Ava alone about last night."

I hesitate, because I don't want to run from our daughter. But the combustible energy between me and her isn't helpful either.

"Okay. And the Les Paul?"

"Yes." He looks at Ava's closed door. "I'll tell her we're not buying her the Les Paul until her behavior improves."

I move to open her door to say goodbye, and Dave says, "You left out some stuff about that fraternity party."

I turn around. "What do you mean?"

"That drummer douche you made out with in the front hall?"

I feel myself blush to the roots of my hair. "*Douche*? Really, Dave?" I remark on his word choice to delay talking about this. But I can't. "I never knew you saw that."

His cheeks go pink too. "Of course I did. I looked for you from the minute I got there."

I gawk at him. "So why didn't you ever say anything?"

He smiles sadly. "Because you went home with me."

I almost want to tell Dave that his leaving me has given me a second chance with Justin, but I can't hurt him like that. I don't have it in me.

Instead I say, "Hopefully if anything like that ever happens to Ava, someone will be looking out for her."

"And that she never meets someone who gets her wasted, then ignores her."

Now it's my turn to squint at him. "What are you talking about?"

"The drummer. Whatever his name was."

"Justin." I clear my throat. I really don't want to talk about him with Dave, but I feel a need to defend him. "He's not a douche. That's not fair. He didn't even know I was sick that night."

Now Dave looks surprised. "How would you know that?"

Quickly looking at the floor, I say, "Because I never told him why I left him, and I think he was with his band the rest of the night." I shrug like none of it matters.

Dave shakes his head. "You were completely out of it, so I don't know how you would remember anything, but he definitely wasn't with the band when we left." He laughs. "I clearly remember seeing them all in the living room, because the bass player gave me a thumbs-up, and I thought I was so cool. Anyway, the point is, I hope Ava has good people around her." He turns the knob on Ava's door.

My mind racing, I ask Dave, "Can I have the car keys? I might actually take a drive. It's been a while since I've hung out in Ann Arbor."

"Reminiscing?" Dave asks as he fishes his keys out of his pocket and hands them to me.

Nodding, I go back into Ava's room and look for my purse. It's not on the desk where I left it. I see it on the floor. I pick it up and kiss Ava on the top of her head. For a moment, I feel her relax.

"I'll be back soon," I say to the estranged members of my little family.

Ava stiffens. "You're leaving?"

"Do you want me to stay?" I ask hopefully.

"Will it change things with you and Dad?"

I press my lips together to stop the cry that wants to burst out of me. "I think that's a conversation for you and your father. I love you, Ava," I tell her and walk out her door, knowing exactly where I want to drive.

CHAPTER SIX

I stand on the circular driveway outside Bursley Hall, looking at the sprawling grounds of the north campus, memories washing over me. I can vividly recall so many moments from freshman year all the way to graduation. Only that one night at the Sigma Chi party is mostly lost to me. So much I never knew, so many things out of my control. I wish I could fill in the missing pieces.

Those aren't the only missing pieces in my life, though. And once I'm in Dave's car, his familiar citrusy scent enveloping me, I do wonder if Ava was hoping that her behavior last night would bring me and Dave together. The only times that he and I have really talked over the last six months were conversations about her. Even if they were arguments, they might have been better than our silence for Ava, who not only has embarked on a totally new stage in her life but has lost the stability she's always depended on.

It's up to Dave right now to be more honest with Ava than he's been with me. I can't keep trying to get through to him when all he seems to want is to push me away.

I need to take care of my own needs too. So, I google *Ward Contracting*—the company Justin owns, according to his Facebook profile—and click on the Current Projects page on the website. There are three renovations: a rental unit in Arbor Hills, a new build in North Burns Park, and a home being completely gutted in Kerrytown. The office is closed on Saturdays, and I don't know if Justin's crew works on the weekends or if he's on site. But the chance that I could see him today sends a tingle through my whole body, despite what Dave has told me.

I could simply text Justin and ask to meet, but it's more daring to show up unexpectedly, demonstrate that I'm thinking about him, that I want him. Then I'll ask if he dropped the book at my house.

I turn on the GPS, because I've never actually driven around Ann Arbor, and navigate to the furthest of the three sites, in Arbor Hills. Quivering with nerves when I stop at the curb outside a triplex, I see a bunch of men in hard hats hauling wooden planks into a dumpster in a driveway, but I don't spot Justin.

I get out of the car and as close to the rental unit as I can. I don't want to actually go inside, but I can see into each of the large double-hung windows on every floor. He doesn't seem to be here. I don't have that much time, because Dave and I need to drive back to Grosse Pointe and I'd like to speak to my daughter again before we do. I want to leave in a good place, with her knowing she can talk to me about anything.

Just in case, I ask one of the men if Justin is around or where he might be, but he doesn't know. I have no luck at the next location either. He's either at the last one or somewhere else entirely.

Somehow, not seeing him makes me more desperate, and I make the eight-minute drive to Kerrytown in five. When the GPS announces that my destination is on the left, I park in the only spot on the street, at the curb across from a house under demolition. In the steep, slanted two-car driveway, there's a big black truck with **WARD CONTRACTING** stamped on the side in white block lettering. I hear drills whirring and hammers banging, but I don't see anyone.

Sweat pools in my armpits, and my pulse quickens. He could be in that house, seconds away from me. Will he be happy I'm here? If he can give me an orgasm with only his voice, hunt down my address, drop a gift at my house—if it was him—surely I can stop by his worksite?

I pull down the rearview mirror to swipe on a bit of lip gloss and mascara. I definitely don't look twenty-two, but my eyes are shining, my skin is glowing, and I'm more animated than I've been since Chuck died and everything fell apart.

Blowing out a breath, I open my door and put one leg out as a man emerges from the front of the house.

It's Justin.

I lose all sense of space and time; my throat goes dry. My heartbeat thrums in my ears, and I can't move. He is the sexiest man I've ever seen in real life. From his confident, cool stride down the driveway, to the way his dusty black T-shirt hugs his taut biceps and broad chest and his faded jeans hang low on his hips—I'm an inferno. It's not just his looks or that he exudes sex; it's his allure.

I can't seem to get out of the car. Instead, I watch as Justin pushes his hair off his forehead—with the same casual flick of his long, slim fingers that I remember from college—walks to the black truck, opens the trunk, and rummages inside. His back view is as enticing as the front. I don't ogle every good-looking guy I see. I was married—technically I still am—and though of course I have found other men attractive, I haven't fantasized about them. Justin is the only person other than Dave I've wanted to touch me.

Now that I'm so close to him, I'm terrified. He slams the trunk, a box of tools in his hand. I need to get out of this car.

I do and call his name. Quietly, at first, and when he doesn't seem to hear me, I say it louder.

He swivels and faces me, shielding his eyes from the sun. I smile and wave.

He squints and doesn't wave back.

I drop my hand immediately as my insides plummet. Maybe the sun is blocking his view of me. On shaky legs, I step forward, crossing the street to clear the space between us. He's still squinting, but it's not because of the sun anymore. He looks confused.

He looks like he doesn't know who I am.

CHAPTER SEVEN

I'm shocked, then slammed with such a gale force of hurt and humiliation that I need to grab the tree trunk next to me for support. I don't understand. Why doesn't Justin recognize me? Do I look that different in person from my photos? Am I not as attractive, and he's trying to find a way out of the relationship he's started with me?

Up close, he looks older. His dark hair, once so black it was almost blue, is flecked with silver; fine lines spider at the edges of his eyes when he crinkles them in what seems to be bewilderment. It feels like half an hour has gone by while I stand dumbstruck at the end of the driveway, willing myself not to cry.

A crash from inside the house jolts us both. He doesn't give me a moment more of his attention. He hurries back up the driveway, toolbox banging against his hip, and disappears inside the house.

I'm alone.

The impact of his rejection makes my knees buckle, but I keep it together until I get back in the car, where I burst into tears. Guttural, raw, they pour out of me, not only because Justin must have been playing a cruel game with me, maybe back in college, too, but because no one wants me. What's so wrong with me that the people I care most about don't care about me at all? Why do I let them treat me like this?

Years of pent-up pain purge from my body in heaving sobs until I'm exhausted. I rarely cry for me, and this deluge of tears is even harder than when Dave drove away, leaving me alone in my car in the dorm parking lot. When I was little, I was told to be resilient when I was hurt; when Dave completely shut me out, I was told I was hovering and everything was fine; when Ava reduces me to a control freak who only cares about what other people think, I'm expected to be her human punching bag. Justin saw me as the woman I want to be—erotic, carefree, beautiful, exciting—at least that's what I thought. But now, as the sheen of this new relationship becomes tarnished, I realize it's the same thing he did in college: Catch and release. With me as prey.

I've been so caught up in the possibility of starting over with him, I forgot how much he could hurt me. The times he didn't bother showing up for sessions, leaving me sitting in the carrel by myself, feeling stood up. My obvious infatuation with him that he'd toy with while never asking me out on a date or letting me know that he was truly interested, until the Sigma Chi party. But then all the other sweet moments with him flood back: how he'd look at me with awe when I'd coach him to write a powerful opening line for his essays, helping him receive a B, his highest grade in English ever, and the way he brushed my hair from my face while kissing me. Was it all an act?

I look for tissues in the console, where Dave usually keeps them, but there are none. I open the glove box and don't find any there either. I also don't find the credit card bill that Dave *had* to get today, the one he practically shoved into the glove box before we left Grosse Pointe. When he said he forgot his phone in the car, was he actually getting the bill? But why hide it from me?

Confused, deeply wounded, and angry at everyone, I slam the glove box closed and wipe my face with my sweater, not caring if my mascara streaks all over it. Once again, I'm numb.

I turn the key in the ignition and leave Justin behind, not ready yet to see my daughter and her father. My coparent: that's what Dave is to me now. I'm truly on my own. I've had enough of letting people walk all over me.

I make a left and idle at the curb outside the white-columned Sigma Chi house, which still looks the same as the night of the party.

I swallow the nausea creeping up my throat because of how gullible I was then, actually believing I mattered to Justin as much as he mattered to me. How gullible I am now, trusting someone I barely know with my deepest, most intimate thoughts and my broken heart.

I check the time on my phone. I've been gone forty-five minutes and have received no texts from Dave or Ava, so I guess I have a few moments to go inside the frat house. Maybe it will jar my memories of the night, give me some perspective on how much importance I've placed on Justin coming back into my life. I need to shut the door on the past.

Right before I turn off the ignition, my phone rings. Justin's name, which I'd embarrassingly already saved in my contacts, flashes across my screen.

"Yes?" I say curtly, hoping to cover the catch in my voice, because I don't want him to know how much pain he's caused me.

"I'm so sorry, Eden. I was shocked to see you. And my wife was inside the house taking some photos for our company website. She can't know about you."

"Your *wife*?" I'm such a fool.

"Ex-wife. We're not divorced, and I don't know what to call her."

"You still work together."

"Yes. I told you, it's complicated. You can't show up like that. It can make things very bad for me."

My every instinct is screaming at me to hang up. But I don't. Since last night, I've been walking on air, elated and delirious with ravenous hunger for this man. Everything, even the sky outside my window is bluer; the sun, brighter, like I'm fully present in my life after so much avoidance and pretending. He reached out to *me*. I want to give him a chance.

Still, I have no interest in being the other woman. "Bad for you how?"

"I'll tell you everything, Eden, another time. I'm working now. But she and I still live together, on opposite sides of the house—"

"You *live* together? What kind of game are you playing with me, Justin? You lied to me. And not just about this."

"No. I didn't. Hear me out. Please." He exhales loudly. "Okay, my ex, Olivia . . . I don't love her. I'm not sure she knows what love is. But I can't move out just yet. And I don't want to lose you. I was afraid if I told you that, you wouldn't understand."

The corner of my lip curls in consternation. "You're right. I don't understand."

He exhales a long stream of air. "Look, my former wife is a bit unpredictable. I don't have the stability yet to start over on my own. And she can't leave the house either."

All of a sudden, it hits me that perhaps it's money Justin is after. Dave is a successful corporate lawyer; I'm a Realtor. If Justin knows where I live in Grosse Pointe, it wouldn't be hard to access any number of websites to find out the value of our house now.

"Did you come to my house today?"

"What?" He clears his throat. "No. You mean because of the book?"

"Yes."

"I found it in a used bookstore in Ann Arbor and remembered how much you loved it. A client of mine was driving to Grosse Pointe, and I asked him to drop it off. I meant it to be a birthday present."

I'm confused. Talking to him makes everything feel electric, but I don't know if I can believe what he says. It's possible that it's not the same copy of the book I saw. I didn't look closely enough in Pages to know if the pencil markings were the same as in the book his client left for me. I can't ask Justin if he was following me. But I can ask something else.

"How did you get my address?"

"The white pages online."

It makes sense. But he just dismissed me like I mean nothing.

"I appreciate the gift. But it's not okay, Justin, to make me feel like shit. Like you're using me for—"

"Sex?"

"Yes."

He sighs. I don't hear much in the background, and I wonder where he is.

"I care about you. And to be fair, you started the phone sex today. I'm not doing anything you don't want me to. But it's not about sex. It's connection. Don't you feel the energy between us?"

I rub my forehead, where a headache drills into my temples. "Yes, I feel it, but I don't trust you."

"I told you that you were the one who got away. I meant it, Eden. I thought about you so many times over the years. And out of nowhere, you friended me. It felt like fate."

I truly don't know if he's handing me a line or being sincere. "What do you really want from me?"

He lets out a grunt of exasperation. "I want you to feel as good as I do whenever I think about you, which is all the time now. I love talking to you. We've both been in unhappy marriages. We get each other. I just need some time to figure things out on my end. I'm risking a lot just to talk to you. I'm not sure how to handle it, to be honest." He pauses, then says, "And in terms of keeping this between us for now, would you want Dave to know what's going on with us? Have you told him? Or anyone?"

"Not yet," I admit. I watch as a young man saunters up the steps to the white-columned frat house. "Where are you?"

"In my truck outside the house I'm working on. Why, where are you?"

"The Sigma Chi house."

There's a crackling through the phone. "What are you doing there?"

"Trying to remember more about everything that happened."

"Why?"

"I don't really know." I look again at the house and those concrete steps I walked up so many years ago, full of excitement and hope, then only a few hours later, I had to be carried back down them. "I just hate that I lost a whole night of my life and my friend."

Justin sighs. "I know. I think about Tyler a lot."

I grip the phone tighter. "If you cared about me so much back then, why didn't you even look for me at all that night?"

"I told you. I thought you didn't want me. I wasn't about to go chase after someone who'd rejected me. I was a proud, cocky drummer who didn't often make girls run away from me."

"So you dealt by smoking a bong with your band?"

"I don't understand what you're asking."

"Where were you when I was throwing up in a bathroom?"

"I've told you all this already. I was with the band. Maybe *I* went to the bathroom first or got another drink after you ran off. Who even remembers? It was ages ago. I don't understand what's happening here. We're not the same people we were. And it's insensitive to throw that night in my face when you're the one who got wasted, took off, then I lost Tyler forever."

Shamed, I say, "You're right. We're not the same people. I'm not even the same as I was just a few days ago. We've . . . sexted and had phone sex. Maybe you've done this before, but I haven't."

The line is silent. I pull it away from my ear to see if the call has dropped, but we're still connected, so I wait.

"I never came to your house or place of work. I basically had the book delivered. Yes, as a romantic gesture, but I didn't knock on your door. You question my intentions when you shouldn't have any expectations here. I wanted this to make us feel free, but now it's like I'm not following some set of rules that I never agreed to. It's a turnoff. Even my wife wasn't this needy." His delivery is cold.

His sharp words pierce my heart. Am I too needy? I don't know what to make of his sudden mood switch, so I say nothing.

"Look, I care about you, but maybe we're not in the right place in our lives to start something together."

A crater opens in my chest. I don't want to lose this. I can't. He's the only person who's wanted to be with me. The only thing making me happy right now.

"I'm sorry," I say. "I've been unfair. I've had a hard day, and I haven't ever done anything like this either. I don't know how."

My stomach flips waiting for a response.

The line goes dead. He's gone.

CHAPTER EIGHT

I get back to Ava's room, despondent, hating myself for practically begging Justin not to leave me and confused about how things went so wrong with him so fast. Maybe I shouldn't have pushed about where he was at the frat house after I ran away from him. If it even matters. I'm clearly the problem in all my relationships. I don't know anything anymore.

Dave's sitting in Ava's desk chair while she's on her bed, playing a song on the Fender guitar Dave and I gave her when she was ten. It's her favorite of her three guitars, but for years she's coveted the Gibson Les Paul we said we'd put off buying her until she started college.

I look at Dave over her head, mouthing, "Did you tell her?"

He grimaces an assent, then says out loud, "Ava wrote an original for the student showcase next week. It's beautiful." Dave wipes his eyes from under his glasses.

"Can I hear it?" I ask nervously, not sure where I'm supposed to sit. I opt for the floor.

"No. And it would sound a lot better on the Les Paul." Ava levels me with a cold stare. "You promised you'd get it for me when I started college. You lied."

"We talked about this, Ava," Dave says firmly in a stern voice that I haven't heard in so long. "We'll still buy it for you once you prove that you're taking school seriously."

"You always protect her and take her side." Ava slaps the mattress with her hand.

"I want to protect both of you." Dave pushes himself up, and I hear his knees pop. "We should let you hang out with your friends. Mom and I will head home."

Ava is still watching me, though.

"What?" I'm troubled by the laser-sharp stare she's aiming at me, like she's figuring something out.

She looks away, shutting me out. I stand, unsure what else to do. "Ava, honey, I love you so much." My chest constricts, and I try not to weep. "It's going to be okay. Me, you, and Dad. Change is hard, but we always have each other."

Tears pool in her eyes, but she angrily swipes them away before they fall. "But we don't, though. Have each other. I'll do anything to help you get back together. Please."

Dave just wraps her in a hug and beckons for me to join him. I do, and Ava lets me into the huddle, or at least she doesn't shove me away. The three of us silently hold each other, and my heart breaks a little bit more.

Unable to make it all better, yet again, we leave our daughter behind and walk to Dave's car for the drive home. I'm quiet and lean my head against the window, watching the sky turn pink until we're on the I-94. Then I look at Dave.

"You need to make it clear with Ava that she's not responsible for getting us back together."

He nods, staring straight ahead at the road. "I tried. I told her it's not her fault or your fault. That it's about me."

"Did you ask her if she orchestrated that visit?"

He flexes his fingers, still not looking in my direction for even a second. "She sort of did."

I realize he's still wearing his wedding ring. I wonder if he's noticed I've taken mine off. I don't want to read into it, but it's hard not to. "If you keep your ring on, she's going to keep having hope."

I see him swallow.

I do, too, then decide to ask a question that he can't escape from in the confines of his car. "Why did you leave, Dave? It's not fair to me or Ava not to know why."

He breathes out so heavily that I feel it in my own body. "Do you like who you are, Eden?"

The question has been so much on my mind since reconnecting with Justin.

"You shuddered."

I shake my head. "Not a shudder. More of a startle. I've asked myself that a lot recently because of some conversations I've had."

"With who?"

I pull my bag closer, where my phone is silent, debating how much I want to share with the man I'm still legally married to and who'd called Justin a douche only a couple of hours ago. "Justin Ward."

His head swings toward me. "Wait. What? We just talked about him. You didn't say a word about being in touch with him again."

Rage bubbles inside me until it erupts. "Are you kidding me? You left me. Broke our daughter's heart, which she thinks is my fault. And you have the audacity to call me out for not telling you I'm speaking to Justin? No way, Dave."

He holds up a hand. "I'm sorry."

"People change. You don't even know him."

"You're right. I don't know Justin. I'm basing it off how he treated you at that party."

"Whatever. I don't want to talk about him with you." It's painful because I don't know if I've lost Justin for good. And that's not what this conversation is about. "Dave, I don't think the issue is whether I like myself or not. It's that I don't know who I want to be. Or who I really am."

"I get that." He pushes his hair off his forehead, causing the sleeve of his shirt to rise. I notice a black swirl that seems to be a stamp on the inside of his right wrist. He clocks me looking at it and quickly pulls down the sleeve.

"Do you really? Because for over twenty years, I was your wife, who believed with my whole heart that no matter how hard life became, it was always us." I lift my shoulders and drop them heavily. "You took one of the biggest parts of my identity away from me. You changed after your dad died. You refuse to talk to me about it. And it's me who seems to be the issue."

He puts his hand on mine. His touch used to soothe me. Now, it hurts, as does his total lack of response to my outpouring of emotion. I yank my hand away and gaze out the window until he turns onto Ivy Court.

Dave pulls into the driveway, shifts nervously, and pushes the button in the center console for the parking brake as though without it, we'll roll backward in the idling car.

He scrapes his fingers through his hair three times, then asks, "Are you free for dinner next week?"

I'm scared. Does he want to start divorce proceedings? Find a mediator? Talk about selling the house? "Can you just tell me everything now?"

"It's been a long day for both of us. I'd really like to talk when we haven't just battled it out with Ava."

It has been the longest day, and I don't have the energy to argue. "Fine."

He stares at me straight on, his face paler than it was a moment ago. "I'll text you, and we can coordinate a good time. Maybe Roberto's?"

"Fine. Though I question your choice of restaurant considering this doesn't feel like a family celebration. Should I come with a divorce lawyer?"

"Just you," he says quietly.

Again, my eyes are drawn to the stamp on his wrist. Did Dave go to a club? The image of him in his beige chinos dancing awkwardly in the middle of a group of young women is so laughable that I snort before exiting the car.

He waits, probably to make sure I get in safely because the sun has set and the house is dark, but I wave him off. I drag myself up the cockeyed steps, and the motion detector lights come on. I'm about to open the front door when I see something gold glint under the porch swing.

It's the extra key.

Bending, I pick it up, but instead of tucking it back into its hiding place under the cushion, I bring it inside. Dave might have inadvertently knocked it on the ground when he put his hand under the cushion to find it, but neither of us saw it under the swing. We were both distracted by Ava, but I'd rather not keep the key outside.

I immediately flick on the lights, but something feels different. The house is chillier than usual, though when I look at the thermostat, the heat is on. Still, I should check the furnace, something else I'll have to do on my own now, along with dealing with any plumbing and lighting issues. I can do them all—it's something I'm versed in as a Realtor, but I've never had to deal with those details in my own house. It's overwhelming to be responsible for everything here. Maybe I should look for a smaller place, like Dave has.

Heading down the steep steps to the finished basement off the kitchen, I'm sad all over again. As Dave started spending his evenings in our bedroom alone or at his office, I occupied myself by creating a "zen space" for Ava in the main room, with beanbag chairs, fluffy pillows, posters of her favorite bands, and a huge flat-screen television, hoping she'd invite friends over and find comfort at home, but she rarely did. At her friends' houses, they were apparently left alone to do whatever they wished, whereas I'd hover, bringing down snacks and chatting to blank-faced teenagers who didn't want me there. All I wanted was to be a part of her world. If I'm staying in the house, maybe I'll turn this room into a library just for me.

I'm buoyed by the image of walls of books, green library lamps, a cozy armchair, and soft blankets to curl under, but I shiver because it's even colder down here than upstairs. After heading to the furnace room next to the stairs and seeing the unit is working fine, I go back into the main room, trying to locate the source of the chill.

I push open the door of the small powder room at the far end, which looks out onto the backyard. The window is completely open. A trickle of fear slides down my back. I don't know if it's been open for a long time and none of us realized, or whatever the frightening alternative is. We don't have an alarm anymore, because one of us was always setting it off by accident. All the security we have is a sticker from the alarm company on the front window of the house.

I step around the toilet to access the window. The screen is unlocked too. It's a typical small basement window, but big enough that a person could stuff themselves through it. Quickly I close and latch the screen and window, sweeping my eyes around the space, which has a narrow shower with a glass door and a mirrored medicine cabinet. Nothing seems amiss, but I don't like the worry spreading in my chest. "You're being silly," I say, my voice reverberating off the walls. "You can take care of yourself."

I let the open window go as a simple oversight of my own making, but an ominous heaviness pervades the house—and me. Quickly, I run back upstairs and turn on every light. It's now close to 7:00 p.m. and it's dark outside. Drained from this entire day, I collapse onto the living room couch, where only last night I sent Justin a message and completely lost control of myself.

On a Saturday night at seven—before Chuck died, Dave retreated into himself, and Ava avoided being with us—I'd usually do the laundry. Then Dave would help me make meals to freeze for the week, and he and I would organize the weekly chores on our shared Trello board. If Ava was home, we'd microwave popcorn and sit together on the couch to watch a movie or play a board game. Now, the only laundry to do is these leggings and sweater I'm wearing, plus a few things in the hamper, and I don't have any food I need to prepare for anyone. I don't have anyone to hang out with.

I wish Jenna and Natalie were here with me, a huge bowl of mint-chocolate-chip ice cream between us, like we used to eat with three spoons in our cramped apartment. I want to pretend I'm not an adult dealing with adult problems. I need my friends.

I start a group FaceTime, add them, and luckily, they both join. I feel immediate calm when I see Jenna's big smile, her strawberry blonde hair in its usual messy weekend bun, and Natalie's warm brown eyes that fill with loving concern.

"I'm just making dinner," Jenna says, while her son, Ryder, still in his soccer uniform, waves in the background. "Did you figure out who gave you the book?"

These women know me better than anyone. And I've never directly lied to my best friends until now. Justin treated me poorly today, but I also made mistakes. I'm not sure Jenna and Natalie will see it the same way, though, because they remember the bad boy I, too, can't seem to separate from the man he is now. Am I lying to myself? Has Dave treated me any better than Justin? Maybe this is what love is like at middle age, with all its baggage and trauma.

"A client gave it to me," I tell them, feeling my cheeks warm with guilt. I look at the white living room curtains instead of the screen for a few moments, until I'm sure the lie isn't written all over my face.

"That's nice! It's because you're excellent at your job," Natalie comments, stirring something in a pot on her stove.

I smile, my stomach grumbling even though I'm not really that hungry. Natalie's a wonderful cook and used her grandmother's Indian recipes to make most of our meals when the three of us lived together in college. But I didn't eat lunch, and I'm not sure I even ate breakfast. I bring the phone with me to the kitchen, prop it on the marble counter, and open the freezer, which now only holds ice cube trays and freezer-burned lasagnas. I close it and grab a can of tomato soup, bread, butter, and cheese.

"Fancy meal you're making." Jenna laughs. "Seriously, though, Eden, what's up? Everything okay with Ava?"

I give them the rundown of the afternoon, ending with Dave possibly going to dance clubs now and he and I having dinner next week.

"Nat, do your boys ever say that you make them feel like they're not good enough?"

Natalie's heart-shaped face softens, and she tucks her long brown hair behind her ears. "Eden, honey, it's our kids' jobs to make us feel responsible for their insecurities. Sure, sometimes we mess up, but you love Ava so much, and deep down she knows it. She's just hurting."

"And we know you're hurting too. Will you please come over to my place next weekend? You can stay over?" Jenna offers.

Jenna lives in Dearborn, and Natalie in Lincoln Park, where I grew up. We're all within a half-hour drive of each other, so Jenna's invitation isn't because I'd need to sleep there. It's simply because she loves me. I agree, and we blow kisses at each other, our standard goodbye since college. After logging off, I take my soup and grilled-cheese sandwich to the living room, where I sit back on the couch. Soon, there'll be a permanent indent from my ass.

I shouldn't be so afraid to share my life with my friends. I don't like how insecure and self-conscious Justin made me feel. The emotional turbulence, obsessive thoughts, risky behavior, secret-keeping—none of it is me.

I should end this.

I pull out my phone. Justin has texted. I want to read it, and I also don't want to even look at it. Unable to withstand the temptation, I click on his message.

> Justin: I'm very sorry I was so reactive. I was on edge because Olivia was close by. I want to see you, but in a place where we can be alone.

I put my phone on the couch. Then I let out a scream of frustration. I do it again, because it's cathartic and no one is here to tell me to chill out.

Eden: You treated me like I don't matter. This isn't good for me. You're not good for me.

Justin: Wait. Let me explain. Please?

Eden: Tell me the truth and what it is you want from me, or I'm deleting your number.

Taking back control is empowering. He has one chance to redeem himself. Being alone is better than letting anyone lead me around on a leash.

Justin: Losing you would hurt very much. I've never had this kind of intoxicating relationship that revved up so fast. We haven't even talked to each other in person for over twenty years. My life hasn't been easy, and it sounds like yours hasn't been perfect either. We need each other.

Eden: This tells me nothing. Don't play me.

Justin: I'm not playing you. I'm protecting myself. I've been hurt. I'm afraid to get hurt again.

Tucking my legs under me, I read his message three times. I don't want to be a doormat, but everything he said rings true. Maybe I've been too harsh.

Eden: I care about you. You make me feel high. But you also make me feel really low. I'm not looking to feel worse than I did before we started this. I don't like the mood changes, how terrible you were at your construction site and on the phone after.

Justin: You're right. I take responsibility. I'm stuck living with someone unstable who I don't love, and who isn't a good person. I can't go through anything like that again. But I do trust you, Eden. I'm trying my best not to push you away and let you run from me like you did in college. Can I please take you on a date?

My body begs me to say yes; my brain insists I take some time to think. I listen to my brain.

Eden: I'll let you know.

I don't check to see if he responds. I click out of my messages, curious about the woman who Justin once vowed to love forever and whom he describes as *unstable*. What if she's dangerous to me?

I google her. But Olivia Ward seems to be an enigma online. While I find women with that name and with thumbnail images and social media accounts that could possibly be hers, none are in Ann Arbor, and Justin isn't friends on Facebook with anyone by that name. Perhaps she's not on social media; maybe Olivia didn't change her name when she married Justin.

I type in *Justin Ward wife* and get a single hit. It's their wedding photo in the Ann Arbor society pages. Justin, as good looking as always in a black tuxedo, stands next to an ethereal-looking blond. Her name is Olivia Walker. She's beautiful. They look so happy, like Dave and I did in our own wedding photos. Her father is Griffin Walker, it says in the short piece, the owner of Walker Developments, an apparently lucrative firm if Justin and Olivia's wedding landed in the news. It's all I can find about Olivia. I want to know more.

I can possibly track her down through the sales history of their home if they co-own it. Justin might be in the white pages online, like I am. If I agree to a date, I want to know if Olivia's instability is a worry for me.

All the agents at Greenwood Realty have access to the full MLS, the Multiple Listing Service database, through the brokerage. It's restricted from the public.

When I type in my credentials, it's restricted from me too. I'm sure I made an error. I was on MLS just this morning at my listing. But my next two tries into the database are denied.

Maybe something's wonky with my phone, or the site is having issues. I head to the seldom-used dining room next to the kitchen. My laptop rests on the farmhouse-style table we bought only a few months ago. It's almost 8:00 p.m., and through the window that faces the side of the house, the moon is barely visible tonight. I turn on the lights, sit on the pale-blue wing chair, shoving away dreams of the Thanksgiving dinner we might never have here, and open the laptop.

I try MLS three more times. Access denied.

I head back to the couch for my phone and am about to call Sylvie when I realize that I not only missed a text from her but also never called back the agent whose client was interested in the Lakeside house.

My stomach tightens with a dreadful cramp. Sylvie's text simply reads: Call me.

I do.

"Hi, Sylvie." I look at the time on the TV display. It's 8:15 p.m. "Sorry to call so late. I know you like to have an early night. I just got home from seeing Ava at U-M."

Silence. I know Sylvie is there because I can hear her breathing, but my anxiety goes into overdrive. Usually, she'd respond with a cheerful 'Hello' and ask about Ava. Tough but warm, Sylvie has been my mentor, guide, and—while not a close friend—someone I've trusted and looked up to since I joined the brokerage. I consistently sell the highest-commission homes, which is why she recently asked me to join her as a partner.

"Eden, I don't even know what to say." Her tone is steely and cold.

In response, I stutter, "I d-don't understand what you mean. I know I haven't called the agent from RE/MAX back yet, and I'll do that right after we get off the phone. Oh, and my access to MLS is blocked." That all came out in one garbled, frantic breath. I blow out a stream of air and more calmly say, "There was an incident with Ava, and it's been a bit of a trying day."

"Someone saw you. Parked outside the Lakeside house. Doing . . . what you were doing."

A crushing weight lands on my chest. *No, no, no.*

"I know you've been having a hard time, Eden. I, too, went through a . . . questionable phase after my divorce, but to engage in that kind of behavior at a listing, outside the house you are trying to sell . . . It's not only unprofessional, but it's also illegal."

Sylvie sounds so upset and disappointed in me; I fight not to cry. "Who saw me?" I regret the words the second after I say them.

"That's not what's important here. But a woman, one of the neighbors, she said, called me this afternoon to report you pleasuring yourself in your car. She also said a man pulled up and you talked with him." She clears her throat, obviously uncomfortable. "Are you using your listings to meet men?"

"No, I'm not meeting men!" I say too loudly and lower my voice, unable to stop the choke of tears from spilling out.

I remember the woman gardening. I thought I was hiding my hand down my pants, but clearly not. And Sylvie's right. The point isn't that I got caught. It's that I did it in the first place.

"I . . . I have no excuse for what I did in my car. I'm very embarrassed. I should never have done that. I didn't think anyone could see me." I bend my head in shame. "I'm so sorry. I'm not myself right now."

"I was shocked when I got the call, Eden. I know this isn't like you. But I can't have my reputation or the brokerage's called into question, much less a charge of public indecency if this woman actually reported it to the police. Who knows if she has photographic evidence? Those houses have excellent security cameras."

I didn't think about any of that. I put my entire career in jeopardy for a single phone call. What the hell is wrong with me?

I put my head in my hand. "Please, Sylvie. I don't know what came over me. I have no excuse."

"I don't want to do this, but I have to suspend your access to MLS, to our listings, and I'm giving the Lakeside house to Trina."

I needed that commission to keep my own financial stability. I don't know what to say to make this right. What I've done is inexcusable.

"I understand," I tell her.

She sighs heavily, and I now empathize with how Ava likely felt when Dave and I showed up today to discuss her infraction—ashamed, scared, regretful, and wishing she could turn back time and make better choices. Even if her ultimate goal was to unite me and Dave, she lost out on getting the Les Paul that she's wanted for so long. I've lost the house I worked very hard to sell.

"There's more, Eden. You committed a crime. You put me at risk, and yourself. I think you should take some time to work things out."

What I need less than anything is more time on my own, but Sylvie has made her decision. I'm powerless to change the outcome.

My throat hitches. "How much time?"

"As much as we both need for this to blow over. I assured the person who reported it that you wouldn't be back on the street or anywhere near the house."

Before I can say anything else, she hangs up.

I've lost everything.

CHAPTER NINE

I'm too devastated to cry, too tired to eat.

Dragging myself upstairs, I collapse on the king-size bed where Dave and I spent the last two decades with at least one part of our bodies always touching. Until, of course, he started sleeping as close to the edge of his side as he could get, lying with his arms crossed, on his back, like he was in a coffin. No matter how often I wash the sheets, it still smells like oranges and cinnamon, a scent that used to be home for me. Now it makes me lonelier than ever.

I crawl under the cool sheets and toss my phone onto what used to be Dave's space. I have no reason to wake up early tomorrow, no listing to show. Lying back on the pillows, duvet pulled to my chin, I start to run through the terrible decisions I've made. One of those is putting my financial stability in jeopardy.

I've always deposited my past commissions into our joint checking account and withdrawn from there, and I rarely view our finances. While Dave insists on having paper copies for his Luddite filing system, he set up automatic withdrawals for most of our bills, and he's always paid off the credit card. I did the cooking, cleaning, appointment making. Our household duties had been wordlessly delineated years ago, and it was an arrangement that worked while we lived together. But I'm on my own now.

I grab my phone, sit up in bed, and log on to our joint account. There's a healthy-enough amount of my own earnings for me to eat and buy necessities like toilet paper, but I'm going to have to be careful with my expenses so I don't withdraw too much from Dave's share. I want to be independent, but who knows when or if Sylvie will let me back into the brokerage?

I move the cursor up to log out, when the arrow skims past our credit card balance. I think about the bill Dave was so desperate to keep me from even touching. I click on "recent transactions." There are a lot of charges I don't recognize, which isn't unusual. We have separate lives. But two stand out as odd.

The first is a weekly charge of $300 to Celeste Rogers, dating back to March, totaling $6,600. That's a large sum of money to someone I've never heard about before.

I google her, and I'm surprised to see a website for a psychotherapist. Just like I'd never told Dave about my brief time with my therapist, Nancy, he obviously didn't tell me he was seeing someone either. I'm sad how much of ourselves Dave and I kept from each other when we should have been working together to fix our marriage. But I am glad he's been talking to someone, even if it's not me. Even though he refused to go to therapy with me.

On the landing page is a photo of a smiling Black woman, whose bio says she specializes in accelerated experiential dynamic psychotherapy. I have no idea what that is, and so many thoughts crash into me at once.

I research further and learn it's a form of talk therapy using someone's past traumas and experiences to unpack their current emotional state and heal them. Am I Dave's trauma? Was it Chuck? Or is it something darker?

The other charge is the most bizarre. There's a single five-dollar subscription fee to something called "Trisk Inc." I type that into Google but get nowhere, not a company or a website. I try just *trisk*. There are quite a few hits: a type of no-code software, a Hasidic dynasty, and interestingly, Urban Dictionary tells me it can mean when a girl gives a guy attention, but he ignores her, making her try all that much harder, as in playing a trisk with her.

I lean back against the headboard, alarm bells ringing in my head. Is that what Justin is doing to me? Running hot and cold to make me hang on to any loose thread he dangles in my direction? But how does that relate to Dave and this subscription? I'm missing something. I start typing *trisk* into the search bar again, and before I finish spelling it, *triskelion* pops up. I click. And I lurch at the symbol that appears in the images—three interlocked black spirals, each with a white dot in the middle making up the center, connected by a white curved line. It's the stamp I saw earlier today on the inside of Dave's wrist.

Suddenly warm, I push the covers off and sit up straighter. What the hell is going on? I find a link to what the triskelion symbolizes, and it has no connection at all to the Dave I know. Translated from Greek, it means "three legs" and is the oldest symbol of spirituality. Dave is neither religious nor particularly tuned in to anything intangible, but perhaps he's finding his deeper side. Between therapy and this, he's clearly trying to figure out who he is apart from me.

Besides the stamp on Dave's wrist, that symbol looks familiar. I know I've seen it somewhere. Closing my eyes, I try to conjure the image. My eyes fly open. It was in the local news. Adam Sumner, the state superintendent of education, a married father with two young daughters, was photographed coming out of a sketchy bar in Detroit, with that symbol on the sign. There was some scandal about it being a kink club and a lot of shame leveled at him until he resigned, and his wife moved away with their children because they were being harassed by the media and public. The trolls had a field day. I think Adam Sumner left town too.

I search Adam Sumner's name and find the articles. I open my mouth, but no sound comes out. They're from late March, a few weeks after Chuck died and when Dave's therapy sessions started appearing on our account. I don't know what the connection is between Dave, the symbol, and this club, or Adam Sumner, but there seems to be one. I type in *triskelion* and *kink*. A link immediately pops up. I click on it. A soft drone fizzes in my ear until it reaches a crescendo.

The triskelion is the international symbol of BDSM.

CHAPTER TEN

BDSM? Dave? I'd howl with laughter if the proof weren't right in front of me. Unless the stamp has another significance to him. My first instinct is to text Natalie and Jenna, even Justin, to try to make sense of what I'm seeing.

A sexual fetish of any kind is incongruous with the fairly repressed, sedate man I married. Sadomasochism seems shocking to me. Especially because the sex we had—from the first time in Dave's bachelor apartment a few months after the Sigma Chi party until March of this year, when it became nonexistent and he made up excuse after excuse not to be with me—was completely vanilla. We never talked about how we wanted it; we just did it, mostly with him on top. I once yelled out earlier in our marriage, but Dave looked pained and told me I didn't have to do that for him. I wanted to tell him it was for me, but I was embarrassed and barely made a sound with him inside me after that.

While he rejected my every sexual advance, was he out tying up other women in his secret condo? Am I not sexy enough, submissive enough for him? The moment Ava left the house, he left me. For how long was he biding his time?

I get out of bed and open the doors to our walk-in. It's so bare without Dave's color-coordinated suits, polo shirts, and chinos hanging precisely on their hangers. He's really gone. But it seems like he wasn't really here for a long time.

I don't find any magazines or DVDs, but of course he's likely looking at everything online, and maybe through that Trisk subscription. There are no whips or chains, which might not be what Dave's into, but it's all I know of the BDSM world. I do, however, see my blue-gingham keepsake box on the top shelf. I pull it down and bring it back to bed with me. I lift the lid.

"Oh," I say, taking out the concert and movie ticket stubs that I've saved, the funny birthday cards Dave wrote to me, and Polaroids of our years together before I used my phone for photos. I pick up a picture from Ava's first birthday, snapped by someone, maybe Dave's mom, because she's not in the photo.

But Dave and I are, standing behind Ava in her high chair, a huge grin stretching her chubby cheeks, her face covered in chocolate cake. Chuck is to the left of us, leaning against the wall, looking at his son with pride. Dave, beaming, has his arm around me, but his attention is on his father. We were so happy that day, and Dave strutted around like the king of his castle. I do recall, though, his relief when his parents left to go home and how he'd clung to me while we had sex after Ava was fast asleep. His eyes were closed the whole time.

What and whom was Dave imagining being with that night and ever since? Did he ever want me?

Deep down, though, I know why he's kept this from me. Even if I'd been secretly curious about his interest in BDSM, even a few days ago, I probably would have expressed my knee-jerk, deeply ingrained reaction of shock, anger, and distaste. When the articles about Adam Sumner came out, I did convey my dismay for his wife and children, declared the club "seedy" even though I hadn't seen the inside. I never once thought about how awful Adam's public humiliation must have felt. I would have made Dave feel ashamed, like my mother made me feel. How I've felt the last couple of days as I've been engaging in a sexual relationship with Justin, because I don't know how to let go without getting hurt in the process.

I've been so repressed that I'm stimulating myself in my car, but a deeper dive into the kink website Dave has a subscription to sparks my intrigue. I can't change how much he and I didn't admit to each other, and maybe ourselves, but we can admit what we feel now. Maybe we can salvage our marriage. If we want to. If I want to.

I text Dave. I have to gather my thoughts before confronting him, and a public place like Roberto's isn't the place to do it.

> Eden: How about coming to the house tomorrow night instead
> of going out? It might be easier to talk? I can cook something.

> Dave: It's Sunday. I can bring dinner.

Like he used to. I usually had open houses on Sundays, and Dave would grab pizza, Thai, Indian, Italian, because I didn't feel like cooking after working all weekend. But I don't have a job at the moment. I have secrets to confess too.

> Eden: Okay.

> Dave: I have a big case going to trial in a few weeks so I need to
> go into the office, but I can leave at five, get to you by five-thirty
> at the latest.

> Eden: See you then.

I curl up under the thick duvet, nobody beside me to press my cold toes against. A light drizzle streaks down the window. I grab Dave's pillow and slide it between my legs for solace. As I fall asleep, I wonder how I got to the age of forty-five and don't know who I really am.

The noise, a shrill, incessant beeping, jolts me awake. At first, I think I'm dreaming and ignore it. But when it doesn't stop, I realize it's the smoke alarm.

I push away my duvet, swoop up my phone from the bed, and race downstairs, where the screeching is piercing. Frantic, I don't know if I should leave, as I've always told Ava to do if there's a fire, or run to the kitchen where smoke billows. The acrid smell stings my eyes and tightens my lungs. I wish Dave, or someone, were here to help me.

There's a fire extinguisher under the kitchen sink, and I can escape to the backyard if I need to. I bolt to the kitchen, where the haze is thick, and coughing, I squint to see a smoking saucepan on the stovetop. The light for the element glares red. A tea towel is inches away from the element.

Panicking, I grab the charred saucepan and toss it into the sink. I turn off the element, throw open the sliding back door, then wave the tea towel over the alarm until the shrieking stops. All is silent, but the ringing in my ears persists. I sink to the floor. Did I leave the stove on after I made my soup last night? I've never done something so stupid before. My house could have caught fire; I could have died.

But why did it take so long for the smoke alarm to go off if the stove was on all night? It was around 7:00 p.m. when I talked to Jenna and Natalie and made dinner. I didn't smell smoke at all before I went to bed.

Shaking, I open the kitchen window to clear out more of the smoke, thankful Dave and I bought an electric instead of a gas stove. All alone in this house, I might not have heard a carbon monoxide alarm in time.

I can't tell anyone about this. I don't want people to worry about me; I'm the one who worries about everyone else. I'm safe, and nothing was damaged. But I'm sure I turned off the stove before taking my soup to the living room, before I called Sylvie.

Sighing deeply, I drag myself to the living room and sit on the couch, smoke clinging to the leggings and sweater I was wearing yesterday. Once again, I didn't change into pajamas, brush my teeth, or do the nightly moisturizing routine I've had since I turned forty. I'm a mess. My phone screen tells me it's 8:00 a.m.

I have nowhere to go.

I'm sick of this couch I'm permanently attached to, this house that feels like it's attacking me, and my thoughts. Digging my hand through my unruly hair, I decide a shower is the first step to making today a better, healthier, more productive day. I wash my hair twice and make some coffee.

The kitchen still smells awful, and it's now freezing because I left the door and window open. I close both, take a deep sip of my coffee, and contemplate what to do with my hours before dinner with Dave.

I have to laugh at myself; otherwise, I'll cry. My husband has had a secret fetish for who knows how many years. I've been having a sizzling online relationship with the guy I wanted for so long but could never have. I don't recognize my life. Is everyone hiding something they're afraid to be judged for?

I can't say I'm happy being suspended from work and with so much hanging in the balance, but I feel like I'm at a pinnacle and things will soon fall into place. They can't get any worse. And after riffling through my closet of boring baggy sweaters, button-downs, and loose dress pants, I realize I need some new outfits. Nothing too expensive, but slinkier, sexier clothes that make me feel beautiful and young.

For Dave, to show him that I've changed and I'm not as uptight, and he can tell me everything about himself without fear and shame. For Ava, to prove that her mother cares more about how she wants to express herself than what other people think of her. And most importantly, for me, to embrace my womanhood with all its scars and marks. As for Justin, I don't know what place, if any, he should have in my life.

At 2:00 p.m., after cleaning the entire house, washing down every surface with vinegar, and spraying peppermint oil to clear the air of the smell of smoke, I leave the house, pulling the knob three times after locking the door. As I make the quick drive to Kercheval Avenue, passing the houses I've sold over the last three years, I decide that today is my fresh start. I won't be stuck in limbo any longer, handcuffed to the past.

I park and stroll along the sidewalk, remembering the first time Dave brought me to the Village after we'd moved to Grosse Pointe Park, staying with his parents until we'd bought our house on Ivy Court. I loved this three-block area with its eclectic shops and restaurants, all of which we'd tried within the first four months of living here. It felt safe, clean—the perfect place to walk with Ava in her stroller and later hand in hand with Dave while she walked ahead of us.

I stop in front of a small boutique with wrap dresses, slinky tanks, and fitted trousers in the window display. I'm about to step inside, but first I take out my phone and text Ava, asking if I can visit her soon, just me and her. She doesn't respond immediately, but she never does. And she's probably still furious with me for delaying her gift of the Les Paul. No matter how Dave delivered the bad news, I'm sure Ava believes it was my idea. But I'm satisfied I've made the first move forward.

Looking around the elegantly designed store with neat piles of brightly colored cashmere sweaters and racks of chic dresses, I'm over-whelmed, not sure where to begin, because I don't know what my style is. A salesperson smiles at me, and I consider asking her for help, but instead, I grab anything that catches my eye.

In the changing room, there's no mirror, so after pulling on a pair of black pants that are tight but comfortable and a black sleeveless silk top that's so low cut, my cleavage is front and center, I exit the changing room.

Tears prick my eyes when I look in the full-length mirror. The pants make my legs look longer and shapelier, and though I cringe a bit at the crepey skin at the base of my throat, the top moves like liquid across my body.

"I love this look for you!" the young salesclerk says to me. "You know we have that top in pink too—it would look amazing. Can I grab it?"

I nod and grin, feeling confident and happy, feeling myself, in my own skin.

Just as I'm turning around to see the back of myself, I spot a woman who looks familiar at the jewelry stand close to the mirror.

Noticing me staring, she smiles tentatively and reaches for a necklace.

"I'm sorry. I'm trying to figure out where I know you from." When it dawns on me, I feel myself blush furiously and wish I'd never said anything. Now it's too late. "The open house on Lakeside. You came by."

"Oh, yes! Hi." She puts the necklace down and steps closer. "I'm sorry. I don't remember your name."

"Eden." I tick through my memory. "Lila, right?"

"You're good. I can barely remember my doctor's name."

I laugh, instantly more at ease. "Occupational hazard of realty, or whatever the opposite is." I bite the inside of my cheek. I'm not in realty at the moment.

She laughs, too, and glances at my outfit. "That looks really nice on you."

I beam. "Thanks. It's a postseparation identity crisis."

I'm surprised I blurted that out, but I'm not the selling agent on the Lakeside house anymore, so I don't need to be my usual professional self. And I'm tired of pretending everything is fine in my life, when it's not.

She chuckles. "Been there."

"You're divorced?" I put my hand over my mouth. "That's none of my business. Sorry."

She shrugs. "Not at all. I'm an open book. Yes, I'm divorced. Three years now. You?"

"A little over six weeks separated. Or on the way to divorce. I don't know."

"Wow, that's recent." She makes a face of sympathy. "It gets easier. I promise. Kids?"

"One. A seventeen-year-old daughter." I can't keep my mouth from turning down.

She must notice because she winces. "That's hard."

"Do you have kids?" I'm hoping she says yes so I can talk to someone, anyone, who's been through this. I don't have any close female friends who are separated or divorced. Neighbors and acquaintances, of course, but no one I've been able to share this with. Lila's eyes get misty, and I curse myself for being so intrusive—this is a lot to ask a near stranger to spill outside a boutique changing room.

She shakes her head. "No kids. Just never happened. I'm at peace with it."

The wistfulness on her face contradicts her words, but I'm not about to push.

Lila clearly picks up on my thoughts, because she says, "At times I wish things were different, but I've found my way forward on my own."

"And here's the pink!" The salesclerk is back, but she can see we're having a moment, because she steps away and points to my changing room. "I'll put this in here for whenever you're ready."

I smile at the girl and say thanks, but my thoughts are on Lila. I admire her honesty and strength. It makes me comfortable to share more. I lean against the wall next to the mirror. "That's amazing. I can't compare my situation to yours at all, but I'm trying to figure out how to move forward in the best way."

Lila nods. "*Best* is subjective. For me, it was understanding that the future was entirely different and new, so I had to navigate it like that. As though I was new." She smooths her hair. "Do you have support? Parents? Friends?"

"My parents have both passed away, and my friends are as great as they can be. But I don't know anyone else close to me who's going through what I am, and I feel like I should be over it."

"After six weeks?" Her eyebrows draw together. "You sound pretty harsh on yourself."

My phone buzzes from the changing room. It might be Ava, so I apologize to Lila and check it quickly.

Justin: I miss you. I want to show you how important you are to me. Please let me.

"Oh my God." I didn't mean to say that out loud.

"Everything okay?" Lila asks from outside the curtain.

"Yes. Sorry. Just answering a text. I'll be out in a minute."

"Take your time. I'm going to get some more stuff to try on."

What Lila said about navigating her life as if she were new after her divorce resonates with me. I, too, have been new these last couple of days, and I'm not sure I want to go back to the Eden I was before Justin and I started talking. I don't think I even want to go back to where Dave and I began, because there's evidently a lot we've kept from each other. I have so many questions I need answered from both the man I've spent so much of my life with and the man I once wanted to. I owe it to myself to get those answers.

Eden: I'd like to see you in person.

Maybe once I actually talk to Justin face to face, it will be the cold bucket of ice water over my head that I need to finally let him go. Or if there's something real between us that we can explore in a more natural, safer way without us misinterpreting each other on screen and over the phone. And I can figure out whether I should fight for my marriage and family, if Dave is at all willing. Or if I should completely start over on my own.

Justin: How's tonight? I can't wait to see you. ☺

Eden: I can't tonight. Monday?

Justin: If you find the place, I'll come to you. 7 pm?

Eden: Yes.

I slide my phone back into my bag. When I emerge, I can't hold back my smile.

Lila's at one of the racks. She comes back with a few sweaters draped over her arm and asks, "Good news?"

I chew my lip. Somehow telling a stranger about what I'm going through seems easier than telling Jenna or Natalie—there'll be no judgment, because she doesn't know me or Justin.

Twisting my fingers, I say quietly, "I started . . . talking to someone, I guess. He asked me out on a date."

Lila lays the sweaters on the white couch across from the mirrors. "Do you want to sit for a sec?"

"Sure."

We both sink onto the soft couch. Lila crosses her legs and leans back against the cushion. I mirror her body language.

"Talking is good. Having a little fling might be what you need."

I let my guard down more. "Dave and I met when we were really young, so this is my first experience with dating anyone else." I gaze in the mirror again, second-guessing myself and the sleek top I'm wearing. "Honestly, I have no idea what I'm doing."

Her blue eyes are full of empathy when she gently touches my arm. "The first date I went on after my ex and I split was a disaster. A friend set us up, and he started telling me about his son's championship basketball game, and I lost it there at the table. I don't even know why, but it was like, a whole mess of snot and blowing my nose on a linen napkin. Epic."

I can't help it. Giggles spill out of me until we're both dissolving on the couch in the shop. Lila's horrible first date shows me that none of us know how to do this in our forties; I'm guessing she's close to my age.

Another customer at the table of jeans glances over while the salesclerk eyes the two changing rooms, maybe wishing we'd hurry up and move on. Usually, I'd jump up so I'm not disturbing anyone, but I stay where I am, reveling in this moment of unexpected connection.

"Where are you going for your date?"

I reach to fiddle with my wedding ring, then remember I took it off. "Anywhere I think of that's nice I've already been to with Dave, and I don't want the memory of him hanging over me."

"I get that." She places a finger to her lips. Her nails are chewed to the quick.

I like that she has a bad habit, because it makes her even more approachable.

"Oh!" she says. "There's a super-cute place on East Jefferson that just opened up, which I can't remember the name of, that I love. Do you know it?"

"East Jefferson?" I shake my head. "I don't think so. If it opened in the last month or so, I've been distracted by life."

The salesclerk comes over. "Do you ladies need a different size or color in anything?"

I look down at the black silky top. "I think I'll take this."

Lila points to the sweaters she chose. "I wanted to try those on, but I have an appointment soon."

I stand. "Sorry for keeping you with my sob story."

Lila gets up too. "Not at all! I'd much rather stay and chat." She cocks her head. "I still have your card from the open house. Do you want me to text you the name of that restaurant when it comes back to me?"

"I can look it up." I hesitate before putting myself out there. Then I do it. "Do you want to give me your number? It's been really nice talking with you."

She grins. "Definitely. I feel the same."

I get my phone from my bag in the changing room, and Lila recites the digits. "Get in touch anytime."

I plug in her number.

"Did you sell the house?"

I should have realized she'd eventually ask that, and I feel my face fall. "No."

"Well, it only just went on the market. I'm sure you'll find a buyer soon. And I loved the little personal touches, like the candles you chose. Subtle and homey. Anyway, I'll let you finish shopping. I'll find the name of that restaurant. It's romantic but casual." She takes the thin silver necklace she was looking at from the stand, then hands it to me. "This would look great with that outfit." And with an elegant flutter of her fingers, Lila walks away.

I buy the black silk top and necklace, plus a pair of flattering black leggings and a form-fitting red sweater, and while going back to my car, I get a text from Ava. Her response to my question about visiting her soon is a simple thumbs-up emoji, but I'll take it. It's a tiny step forward. Humming to myself, I place the pretty pink bag in my trunk.

I might have made a new friend, and tonight, hopefully Dave will finally open up to me, and we can start to heal. Together or apart. But I can't contemplate my life with him until I truly know how I feel about Justin. It's not fair to anyone.

At home, I change into the leggings and sweater, nervous but eager for Dave to come. By 5:40 p.m., he hasn't arrived or texted to let me know he'll be late. He's always punctual, and a little niggle of worry creeps into my stomach. I peek out the front window and see that I parked in the center of the driveway, making it impossible for his Range Rover to fit. I must have been distracted. It's fine. Maybe he's driving around the block, looking for a parking spot. There are few ever available on our street. I call him to apologize. It goes to voice mail. At 5:45 p.m., I grab my keys to move my car.

From the driveway, I hear sirens, then red and blue flashing lights as a police car and an ambulance stop six houses down in front of my neighbor Parvina's house, which I'd sold her a year ago. Concerned because Parvina has a baby who recently had croup, I stand in the middle of the street to see better. Parvina is talking to a police officer. She points up the street. At me.

It's then that I see the gray Range Rover parked across from Parvina's house. My heart jolts. There's a **U-M Dad** sticker on the back of the car.

I run down the street. Parvina runs up to meet me, with her son, Roshan, in her arms.

"It's Dave!" she cries. "I was going to call you. I was inside feeding Roshan when I heard the screech of tires. I looked out the window and saw Dave on the ground. I called 911."

Speechless, unable to process, I race with Parvina to where Dave lies on his back on the road, eyes closed. Yellow tulips, my favorite flowers, are strewn around him. An open white box with our usual sausage-and-jalapeño pepper pizza from Roberto's is close to the sidewalk. Two EMTs are next to Dave.

"That's my husband!" I yell. "Is he okay?"

The female EMT turns. "We're transporting him now to Beaumont Hospital."

I drop to my knees beside Dave. "Is he alive?" I ask her, at a loss to check if he's breathing. I'm afraid to touch him. My heart smashes against my chest.

"Yes, ma'am, but we won't know the extent and severity of his injuries until we get him to the hospital. You'll have to step back, please, but you can meet us there. The police have some questions."

I can't stop myself from gently running my fingers over Dave's closed eyelids. No matter what's happened in our relationship, I love him.

A sob breaks free from my body as the two EMTs lift him onto the stretcher and place him in the back of the ambulance. A male police officer sets up a **ROAD CLOSED** orange barrier in the middle of the street to stop oncoming traffic, then approaches me. "Mrs. Miller, I'll meet you at the hospital after I've talked to Mrs. Nabi."

I grab Parvina's hand, which is shaking, and place my other hand on Roshan's tiny back. "Thank you. You saved his life." Tears cloud my vision as I begin to cry hard. "Did you see who hit him?"

Parvina shakes her head. "I'm not sure. It was all so fast. But when I looked up the street"—she points in the direction of where Ivy Court leads to the highway—"I think I saw a silver car."

PART TWO

OLIVIA

CHAPTER ELEVEN

It's the golden hour. The sky is fiery with red and orange streaks, creating long shadows on the cobblestone path as Olivia walks to the porch, overcome with relief that Justin's truck isn't parked in the driveway. But he could arrive at any moment, so she hurries past the garden, lush with pink hibiscus and orange butterfly weed, smiling in case any of the neighbors are watching her from their windows. Her mother planted the flowers; it's the only part of her left at the impressive Tudor, where Olivia's lived since she was six years old and her brother, Alistair, three.

Once Olivia enters through the arched oak front door and closes it behind her, her smile drops. After hanging her white puffer jacket on the brass coatrack by the door, she sweeps her eyes around the main floor, with its dark wood paneling on every wall and the L-shaped staircase in the center of the room, her gaze landing on the grandfather clock across the entryway, behind the stairs. The cuckoo stopped chiming years ago, but it still tells time. Seven o'clock. The energy in the air crackles with tension, a foreboding. Olivia knows Justin must be close to home. She can always feel his presence looming.

Rushing upstairs to the primary bedroom, she throws off her clothes and changes into black leggings and a pink wrap sweater. Pink is Justin's favorite color. Then she strides across the landing to press her face against the leaded glass in the upstairs diamond window. The streetlights have come on, and the houses lining their enchanted block in the Old West Side—an eclectic mix of Georgian Revival, Gothic cottages, and Colonials, all surrounded by old maples—offer a sense of serenity despite being so close to the hustle and bustle of downtown Ann Arbor.

Until she was ten, Olivia wanted to believe she lived in a fairy tale. She dreamed of marrying a man just like her daddy, who, when he was pleased with Olivia, called her his princess. She'd have done anything to please him. Her mother, father, and Alistair are all gone now. She's the only one remaining from the Walker family. Olivia and Justin inherited the house when Olivia's father, Griffin, died of an aneurysm two years after she and Justin had gotten married.

Picking at the peeling red damask wallpaper framing the window, she watches Justin's black truck roll down the street and turn into their driveway. A few moments later, he exits and waves amiably to someone. From his flirtatious smile, which Olivia can see under the amber motion detector above the garage, it's probably Bree, the gorgeous redhead who lives a few houses down. Yesterday, Justin helped Bree carry a long box containing her new flat-screen television into her house.

It's not just the pretty neighbors he helps, though. He's the go-to guy on their street, the one who brings in groceries for their elderly neighbors, shovels a car out of a snowbank, and sometimes even provides a warm hug, because Justin can make anyone feel like the center of his universe.

"You're so lucky," their Ward Contracting clients say when Olivia, the office manager, shows up at their company's ongoing renovations to take photos for the website and check out the progress on their builds, as do the women who gaze longingly at Justin when he jumps on the trampoline and plays soccer with their kids at block parties; even Mandy, the postal worker, a middle-aged U-M graduate and ardent fan of the Screaming Demons, swoons in the presence of Justin Ward.

Olivia understands. He's captivating. To outsiders, Justin not only hung the moon but also created it. It's a skill he learned from his mother, Yvonne, along with her cruelty and narcissism.

Olivia hears the front door close and the thud on the wide-plank wooden floor when Justin drops his toolbox with a bang. He brings the toolbox inside to upset Olivia. He knows she doesn't like to see clutter in the entryway. And the floors are already scratched from years of use.

She treads to the top of the stairs, trying to read his mood through his actions. His heavy steps head to the kitchen, and he gets a beer from the fridge, which he kicks shut. Once the neighbors can't see, he doesn't care what he damages.

She waits until she hears Justin move toward the living room.

Time to go downstairs, Olly, Alistair says.

Her younger brother was the only person who called her *Olly*; he was Ally. Deeply enamored with his big sister, Alistair was barely three when he burst into tears because he couldn't pronounce her whole name. Olivia, equally besotted with her sibling, made it easier for him, giving them each a nickname only for the two of them. It was always the two of them. "Like Velcro. Always sticking together," their mother, Diana, used to affectionately tease, placing the responsibility of caring for Alistair on Olivia's little shoulders.

Their mother suffered from frequent migraines, and while she rested in her bedroom, drowsy from the heavy medication she had to take, Olivia was more than happy to keep Alistair occupied with the make-believe games he loved. His favorite was king and queen of the castle, when they'd sit on the gold straight-backed chairs in the living room as if they were perched on thrones. Her favorite was hide-and-seek, because there were so many places in the Tudor that they could sneak into.

She didn't realize until she was much older that the punishments her mother received for not pleasing Griffin were far more severe than the spankings and slaps Olivia got. Diana sedated herself in her bedroom so her children wouldn't see how much pain her bruises caused her. Their castle was really a prison. For Olivia, it still is.

Sometimes her dead brother is the only person she talks to. Unlike Alistair, though, she knows the voice in her head isn't real. But it's a comfort all the same.

Gripping the railing, she goes slowly down the stairs, a cramp twinging inside her from her gynecologist appointment this morning, and sits on the last step before the landing platform. Then she puts her face against the oak railing bars, angling her head so Justin can't catch her observing him from behind the wall separating the front hall from the living room.

From the moment she first laid eyes on him twenty-three years ago at an open mic night at Benny's, the dive bar close to the U-M campus and the Alpha Phi sorority house, the sight of Justin Ward has made her weak.

Olivia hadn't even wanted to go to the loud, crowded bar, which had more neon, cheap beer, and fried food than she could handle in one place. But Amy, her best friend and sorority sister, had begged her because she had a craving for their curly fries. Olivia was certain her kitten heel slipped on blood on their way to a booth, but Amy laughed, saying it was most definitely ketchup. She hurried Amy through the plate of fries that rested between them on the sticky, wobbly table, her irritation spiking as a band clomped up the steps to the stage, dragging their equipment so it screeched along the floor. She rolled her eyes when the opening bars of a trendy, angsty Pearl Jam cover filled the cloying space.

"Can we go?" she asked Amy, pulling her miniskirt down after she caught a guy at the next table staring at her.

Her friend nodded, and Olivia gestured for the bill, when the drum solo started. She couldn't hear herself think. But when she looked at the stage, locked eyes with the shirtless, tattooed drummer, he winked. And something weird happened deep inside her: something she'd never felt before. It was like her bones had melted.

Olivia didn't want to leave so quickly anymore. But she pretended she did, walked Amy back to the sorority house, then said that she'd left her wallet at the bar. She hadn't.

And when she returned to the bar, the Screaming Demons were packing a beat-up van with their equipment.

"Need a hand with that?" Olivia wasn't really expecting the drummer, now clad in a black tank top, his inked biceps bulging as he carried an amp, to accept her offer.

He turned. Then he grinned, his whole impossibly gorgeous face lighting up at the sight of her, all pretty in pink, shiny blonde waves cascading over her delicate collarbones. He put down the amp, introduced himself in a deep, gravelly voice, and looked right into her.

"I was hoping you'd find me."

Justin didn't know anything about her. He didn't know the myth her father had spun for everyone that Olivia was required to repeat: her father mourned the loss of his beloved wife but bravely, lovingly took on raising his children on his own; Alistair was away studying at an elite boarding school; and Olivia was saving herself for the prince who was good enough for Griffin Walker's little princess. Olivia, lonely, was tired of pretending and wanted to be someone else for just one night.

So she agreed to wait for Justin in the parking lot while he dropped his bandmates off at the house they all shared. When he came back, he drove her to campus, led her by the hand through the Diag to the West Hall, lay down a blanket, and asked her why she looked so sad.

No one except Alistair—not her father, sorority sisters, professors—ever noticed the pain behind Olivia's practiced smile. And there under the glowing lamps that crisscrossed the Engineering Arch, she lost her virginity to Justin.

It was her first mistake but definitely not her last.

Now she only sees Amy and the rest of her sorority sisters twice a year, because that's all Justin will allow.

She watches as he bangs the beer bottle on the coffee table and pulls out his phone from the pocket of his jeans. Then after flicking his finger up, up, up, he places the phone on the table, angling it precisely. He unzips his jeans.

She hears the clang when his wedding ring hits his belt buckle, and she switches her stare from her husband to their wedding photo, hung to the right of the stairs. The gilt frame is slanted.

Olivia, with her white-blonde hair coiled into a ballerina bun, has her head on Justin's broad shoulder, and his fingers are on her arm. The photographer snapped the shot, while Olivia's father and Justin's mother, Yvonne, looked on with satisfaction. Olivia doesn't recall where Justin's father was at that moment—Henry always fades in Yvonne's presence, a wisp of a person, like Olivia has become.

But on that day in the backyard of the Tudor, despite Alistair's absence, when she and Justin exchanged their vows and he glided the stunning pavé diamond band onto her finger, Olivia was happier than she'd ever been. She'd found her prince. And as Yvonne pulled her into a warm embrace, Olivia nestled against her. She hadn't felt the loving arms of a mother since her own had died when she was ten.

Yvonne whispered, "You're too good for him" into her ear, and Olivia beamed at the compliment. It was only after all the guests had left and she was Mrs. Olivia Ward that she realized that it had been a warning.

Since Alistair died a month ago, Olivia's lost so much weight that she's had to wrap tape around her wedding band so it won't fall off. But the ring fit her perfectly twenty years ago when Justin dropped to one knee and asked her to marry him in the very living room where he's now jerking himself off to images and messages from another woman.

Olivia sees the notifications that flash on Justin's phone, which he leaves lying around whenever he showers—something he does at least twice a day. Filthy on the inside, Justin needs to feel clean on the outside. He plugs in his passcode—his own birthday—in front of her, as though taunting her to go into his phone when he's not around, just so he can trap her into invading his privacy, defying one of his rules. But he doesn't truly care if she sees the women's names that come up on his phone all the time. He does whatever he wants, because he can. Because she trusted him enough to confess her darkest secret to him the night they drove away from the Sigma Chi party.

Olivia's been lucky so far never to have gotten an STD from her husband. If he wears condoms with the Charlottes, Isabelles, and Sophias whom she's fairly certain he sleeps with, it's only to protect himself.

Olivia doesn't have definitive proof that he has sex with every woman he communicates with. She doesn't read every message. But she's seen enough messages to know that her husband uses the same tricks every time. He starts off warm and interested with an immediate compliment that makes a woman giddy with his attention. Then he makes himself sound vulnerable, so she wants to take care of him. Afterward he goes straight to the sex, reeling her in with the promise of his body and touch until she's helpless to resist him. Once she's hooked, he pulls back, gaslighting her into believing she's done something wrong to make her want him even more. He gets off on overpowering vulnerable women desperate to be desired.

It's exactly what he did to Olivia.

There's a clatter, and she jumps, looking at the living room, where Justin's knocked his beer off the coffee table. Sighing inwardly, she stands and gets a rag and garbage bag from the bucket of cleaning supplies under the kitchen sink, digging her nails into her palm when the door won't close properly. There's a loose hinge Justin won't fix, just like he won't replace the leaking faucet in the main floor powder room that she uses as her bathroom. Of course Olivia could handle these things herself. She grew up on construction sites, accompanying her father as he oversaw the progress on the many commercial properties that Walker Developments owned and sold. But Justin won't allow her to fix all the broken parts of the house, because he likes that it breaks Olivia bit by bit when things are out of order.

Like Olivia, the interior of the house has been falling apart for years. She often feels that the decaying Tudor is a metaphor for her whole life.

When she enters the living room, Justin's on the brown leather Chesterfield with his eyes closed, cruddy tissues strewn next to him. Almost everything in the house is the same as when Olivia grew up here, including the fear and isolation that eat her up inside.

"I'll clean that spill," she says softly so he knows she's there.

He opens his eyes but doesn't acknowledge her. He looks again at his screen. Olivia's heart beats a nervous rhythm. She can either walk away or wait until he's ready to speak. Both actions would be a mistake.

The spilled beer seeps into the pine floor, and Olivia drops to her knees to wipe it up before it stains.

"Those leggings aren't doing your ass any favors," Justin says, getting off the couch and stepping toward her.

Olivia lifts her head, cracking it into the sharp edge of the coffee table. Tears spring to her eyes; she presses the pads of her index fingers against her lids to stop the flow. Her tears either irritate Justin or arouse him. She's used to reading his moods, but he's nastier tonight than usual.

When she's sure no tears will fall, she removes her fingers from her face, then looks up into his green eyes, which change from hypnotizing to terrifying depending on to whom he's speaking. She watches as he takes in her hunched posture. After she finishes cleaning the spill, she stands.

"No," Justin says, gesturing at the soft pink wrap sweater she bought just yesterday. She was pleased with how it added shape to her slim build and made her pale skin glow.

She smiles to lighten the tense energy in the room and puts the rag in the garbage bag to take out to the trash later. "I thought you liked pink."

"I do, but not on you."

She looks down at the sweater. Maybe he's right. She should stick to muted tones that don't call attention to her. And she's too pale to pull off such bright colors.

Her husband lifts his arms above his head in a languid stretch, then winces as he drops his hands to his sides.

"Is your shoulder hurting, honey? Do you need the heating pad?"

He waves his hand in her direction, dismissing her. "I'm fine. Stop babying me. I'll tell you when I need something."

Olivia knows Justin pretends his shoulder aches worse than it does. The toolbox that ended his music career actually only nicked him as it fell—Olivia saw it happen. Justin claimed he couldn't drum anymore, but Olivia suspects he might have left the toolbox at the edge of the roof on purpose—to end a career that was going nowhere without having to admit that fact aloud.

Olivia ventures putting her hand on her husband's chest, softening the message she needs to give him. "Your mom called today. She said you're taking too long to respond about driving her to a wedding show in Detroit tomorrow."

Yvonne owns one of the preeminent wedding dress boutiques in Ann Arbor, where Olivia's father had paid an exorbitant amount for the frilly concoction Olivia wore on her wedding day—Yvonne didn't believe in a friends-and-family discount, and even now, the dress takes up half of Alistair's old closet. Fifteen thousand dollars that could have been better spent on the upkeep of their home.

At the mention of his mother, Justin stiffens. Whether by nature, nurture, or a horrible combination of both, Justin and Yvonne are very much alike. A stunning woman who possesses Justin's charm, magnetism, and effortless manipulation, Yvonne isn't used to hearing no, which is how Olivia ended up in a dress she never would have picked.

"Why can't one of my brothers do it?" he asks, pushing her hand off him.

"They all have work and stuff to do with their kids after school."

The youngest of four brothers, the only one without children, Justin is usually the son his mother calls to run her errands.

If Olivia had married any other man, if she'd never gone to the Sigma Chi party at the end of their senior year at U-M, she might have been a good mother.

Olivia could never bring children into their marriage—they would be as doomed as she is. Justin seems to believe that she has "unexplained infertility," that she's the damaged one.

She might not have had to use the IUD, still cramping inside her, that she replaced this morning. But bringing an innocent child into their house of horrors is a trauma she could never inflict. And if Justin ever suspects that she's lied to him in any way, he'll end her. He made that clear on their wedding night.

They were going to live at the Tudor with Olivia's father until they could afford to buy their own place. But for their wedding night, Griffin had gifted them a luxurious suite at a gorgeous hotel that he'd developed in downtown Ann Arbor. In the sumptuous king-size bed, exhausted but exhilarated, Olivia snuggled next to her husband, his body warming her the moment their skin touched. She kissed his shoulder, where she hoped he'd ink her name, and whispered, "I love being your wife."

Justin laughed. Olivia thought he was amused because she'd only been his wife for about five hours. And when he flipped her onto her back, she let out a gasp, excited to feel Justin's mouth and hands all over her. He could make her come like a rocket. He tugged a lock of her blonde hair. Hard.

Shocked by the sting in her scalp from where he'd yanked her hair by the root, she was more stunned by what he did next. His body went rigid, and when he brought his face close to hers, with disgust, he hissed, "You're a whore who barely knew my name before you sucked my dick but didn't want to be seen in public with me. Your dirty little secret, right, you bitch?"

Olivia's jaw dropped. Frozen, she was too terrified to cry, too disoriented to process who the man in front of her was. But he was far from done.

"You spread your legs so easily for me. You weren't even the girl I wanted to be with at the party. I didn't show up for you. But you just had to come and ruin everything." He pulled her hair once more before he smiled, but it was flat, cruel. "If you ever talk about what happened that night with anyone, you'll be the one to pay for it. You'll be locked away like Alistair—or dead."

Why was he talking about that party? She thought they'd left that night behind them.

Then Justin dealt the final blow, whispering, "Always remember that I know what you did. I have it all on tape. And I have copies." He took something out of the teak bedside table beside him. Then he pressed the button on the Dictaphone he used to record song ideas.

"Listen to me." He waved his finger in her face. "Whenever I want you, you will give yourself to me, because that is your obligation. You will never leave. You will never question me, tell me what to do, or get involved in my private business in any way. If you fuck with me, you will never see your brother again."

He made good on that threat.

Olivia looks at the black urn containing Alistair's ashes on the mantel above the peaked arch of the fireplace, which hasn't been used in decades. Grief rises swiftly to her throat, and Olivia swallows it down before it chokes her.

Justin walks past her, saying, "I'm going to shower, and I want dinner when I come back down."

"Of course. There's a nice beef bourguignon I just have to heat up." She follows him into the front hall, where he stops suddenly.

She bangs into his back.

Slowly he turns. "I own you." Then he pinches her waist in the sensitive spot right under her ribcage.

"I know," Olivia whispers, a chill settling deep in her bones. She's always cold no matter how high the thermostat is or how many layers she wears.

"Repeat it."

"You own me," she answers in the meek voice that turns him on, as she's expected to.

Justin happily bounds up the stairs, and Olivia heads to the kitchen to heat and plate her husband's dinner just like he wants it, as though they're a content couple.

She reaches into her pocket to rub her thumb over the smooth gold-and-brown stone that she'd given Alistair for his sixteenth birthday. The tiger eye had been her only way of protecting him. She had put it in his palm and closed his hand over it.

"This will help you ward off the evil spirits in your mind and anyone who wants to hurt you."

"Promise?" Alistair had asked, his hazel eyes wide with trust and love.

"Promise."

The tiger eye was the only possession Alistair had on him when his body was found four weeks ago in a stranger's backyard shed, three miles away.

Olivia had the stone made into a pendant with some of her brother's ashes inside, using part of the money she siphons from the weekly allowance Justin gives her, which she stashes in a tampon box under the powder room sink. She's very careful to hide the pendant from Justin—always deep in a pocket of whatever she's wearing—because if he knows how special it is to her, he'll take it, like he took her brother from her. One day, though, Olivia hopes to slide a chain through it, so the pendant lies close to her heart, without any questions from Justin.

If she'd been taking care of Alistair like she was supposed to the day their mother died, she's certain that her mother and brother would still be alive. This would not be her life.

You'll find a way out, Olly, her brother says now.

Her husband might own her money, her body, and her life. But he doesn't own her mind. Or what she does when he's not around.

CHAPTER TWELVE

Olivia wakes up groggy and unrested, as she always does. Justin is a deep sleeper, of course. He's unbothered by the worries that plague her. He's covered himself in most of their white duvet, and she carefully edges her way out of the bed. The floor is freezing when her bare feet land, and she immediately pushes her feet into the fluffy slippers she keeps beside the bed. A tiny delight he's given her.

She's about to leave the room when Justin's hand on her arm stops her cold.

She remains with her back to him, because she knows how he wants it. All of a sudden, he's behind her. Olivia shivers as he pulls down her pajama pants and bends her over the Eames chair that belonged to her father.

She knows exactly how long it takes him to be satisfied. During those six minutes, she thinks about how she and Alistair used to sit on this very floor watching their mother put on makeup for a night out with their father. Blissfully ignorant of what truly lurked beneath the tremble in her mother's hand as she applied silver eyeshadow, Olivia would engage Alistair in whatever scenario he'd come up with for her dolls. It wasn't until Alistair was a teenager that she understood he could actually hear the dolls talk, and it wasn't just in his imagination.

As Justin collapses with a shudder onto her back, Olivia wonders, as she often does, what other families are like. Whether the sorority sisters she still sees a couple of times a year ever suffer the assaults she does. If their husbands really love them.

Justin has never loved her. While her father was alive, Olivia was the project manager for Walker Developments, and Justin, the contracting manager. The three of them worked and lived side by side, but it was a boys' club of expensive cigars and scotch, backslaps and raunchy jokes—a club that Olivia clearly wasn't invited into. She didn't want to be, but she was desperate for her father to notice, even once, how viciously Justin treated her. He never did. Or he simply didn't care.

When her father died, it was Justin who became the successor of his trust, and she was a cobeneficiary. She relinquished all rights to the house and Walker Developments, which Justin turned into Ward Contracting, and gave him power of attorney over Alistair. She had no choice if she ever wanted to see her brother again.

She would have given her own life for Alistair's. She should have.

Her husband doesn't even look at her before he heads to his bathroom to shower.

As she's heading to the kitchen to prepare Justin's breakfast, the doorbell rings. Instantly, Olivia's adrenaline rushes into flight mode—this interruption will mean that his meal won't be ready when he comes downstairs.

She debates ignoring it. But the bell peals again, an old-fashioned, long, haunting chime that creeps her out every time she hears it. She asked Justin to replace it years ago, but he's seen how she reacts when it rings; he likes that it scares her.

Olivia goes to the heavy oak door and peers through the peephole above the small square stained glass window.

Yvonne.

Her mother-in-law shows up like this sometimes, no call or text. Olivia opens the door, glancing quickly at herself in the mirror next to the door. She doesn't need to look at herself, though. Her reflection is standing right in front of her.

"Hello, dear." Yvonne steps into the entryway, smoothing her blunt-cut dark bob, almost the exact shade as Olivia's, though Olivia's hair is cut to her shoulders, not her chin.

After Olivia had given up her rights to her property and her only family member, Justin took control of her appearance by handing her a box of black hair dye. "Blonde is for angels, not whores."

At the drugstore, she tossed out the box of jet-black dye Justin had given her, so he'd never find it, and plucked a mocha with copper tones from the shelf. Yvonne only smirked the first time she saw Olivia after she'd transformed herself into a version of her mother-in-law.

So, while Justin has never once mentioned the similarity between her and Yvonne's appearances, Olivia wonders if he gets off on screwing his wife because she so closely resembles the woman who makes him feel the weakest. Olivia certainly gains a tiny bit of pleasure from it.

Now Yvonne takes off her camel-colored cashmere peacoat, hangs it on the brass coatrack next to the door, and steps into the entryway, her heels clicking on the wood. Olivia can feel each tap on the floor in her chest. Justin probably never responded to his mother last night, and Olivia has to deal with the fallout.

"It's Monday. Why is Justin's truck still in the driveway? Isn't he at work? I imagine he's very busy if he can't even return a phone call," her mother-in-law says, scanning the room with judgmental eyes, then doing the same to Olivia, still in her pajamas. "You're not dressed yet?"

Olivia tugs down the bottom of her striped pajama shirt. "Justin's in the shower. I was making him breakfast, then I'll get ready for work."

"Humph. Is that another new truck outside?" Yvonne snaps the collar of her pristine white blouse. "He's like a greedy little boy who gets tired of one toy, so he begs for another one. Not that you two know what having a little boy feels like."

Olivia bristles on Justin's behalf. She can't help but feel some sympathy for him, considering how his mother treats him. It made him hate all women. "He leases the trucks."

Justin has a sixth sense when it comes to his mother. He calls out from upstairs, "Down in a sec!"

He handles Yvonne the same way he does everyone—with charm, though she's immune to it.

"Hurry up. I have an important meeting with my contractor for the second location today." She says it offhandedly, like it doesn't matter that she didn't hire Justin to renovate the new space for her wedding boutique.

He comes downstairs, his hair wet, his body sheathed in a tight gray Henley and jeans. He and his mother do their usual dance of Justin reaching for her and Yvonne pulling back. Her heel gets caught in the upturned edge of the Persian carpet covering the trapdoor that leads to the unfinished basement.

Yvonne falters; Olivia catches her so she won't hit the floor.

"That rug is so dirty and old. I don't know why you don't just get rid of it." She brushes Olivia's hands off her. "That whole basement is a disaster waiting to happen."

Yvonne has no idea how true that is. That unfinished basement is where Olivia's mother died.

Olivia will never unhear her father's raw, guttural scream. It was the last time she heard any emotion other than anger from him. That Sunday morning in May, Olivia was playing hide-and-seek with Alistair. But it was taking longer than the count of one hundred for him to find her.

Olivia heard a thud, then thundering footsteps. When the howl rang out, Olivia ran from her hiding place in the butler's pantry in the kitchen to the entryway, where the trapdoor, which was supposed to be closed at all times, was open. She and Alistair weren't allowed to go down there because the rickety ladder was old and playing in the basement was dangerous.

But Olivia knew something very bad had happened, so she had to scramble down the ladder. When her foot touched the cold concrete floor, she saw her father on his knees, next to her mother, who was face down, not moving. Her mother was in a sundress; welts and bruises Olivia had never seen before were visible on the backs of her arms and legs. Her neck was broken.

Where was Alistair?

There was a whimper. Her father whipped his head around and in three strides crossed the basement to the chest freezer, where her mother kept the ice cream sandwiches that she sometimes let her children have, when their father wasn't around. He dragged Alistair out from behind it.

"You little shit! You opened the trapdoor! You killed your mother! You killed her!"

Olivia watched her father slide his black leather belt from the loops of his pants. He struck Alistair's bare, skinny legs and arms.

"Stop it! Please, Daddy, stop hurting him!"

But he didn't stop.

Alistair locked eyes with Olivia. He didn't scream. He didn't cry. He silently took his punishment for causing their heavily medicated mother to stumble into the trapdoor, tumbling to her death.

Alistair was never the same after that.

Yvonne tightens her lips and steps back so she's not on the Persian carpet anymore. Olivia's staring at it, though, thinking about Alistair, when Yvonne says, "I need a ride to Detroit at noon and help setting up my exhibit. You'll need to stay all day so you can take me home tonight too. It's an important opportunity for me. That's why I came by. To make sure to tell you face to face so you don't forget."

Justin shakes his head. "I can't, Mom. I have plans tonight."

"What plans? Hammering a nail into a wall?" Yvonne rolls her eyes. "What about you, Olivia? You know I don't like driving in the dark. Can you do better than your husband and help out your mother-in-law?"

You took her son off her hands, Alistair says. Olivia stifles a laugh. She hadn't protected him, like a big sister should, yet he still protects her.

Clearing her throat, she tells Yvonne, "I have my Alpha Phi reunion dinner tonight. I'm sorry."

The only reason she goes to these sorority get-togethers twice a year is because Justin thinks they will be good for business—someone is bound to want to hire him to renovate their huge home.

Olivia hosted in the first few years after college, before the house fell apart from lack of maintenance and Justin's cruelty and emotional neglect disintegrated her into dust. It's hard enough sitting at a long, beautiful table with the women who once looked up to her as the girl who had it all. She never did, not with a mother who'd committed herself to an abuser, a brother committed to a psychiatric institution, and a father committed to the lie that Olivia Walker was the luckiest girl in the world.

But they're a good group, if only superficially her friends.

Yvonne stomps to the rack and snatches her coat from the hook. "No kids and all the time and freedom in the world, and you're useless. You've disappointed me once again, Justin. I don't know what Olivia sees in you." She opens the door and storms out.

Justin waits until Yvonne has driven off before he whirls on her. "Don't you ever talk to me like that in front of my mother." Then he, too, stomps away to the living room.

Alone in the entryway, Olivia replays the whole scene in her mind but can't think of a single thing she did wrong. It doesn't matter, though. Justin blames her for everything.

He occupies himself with his phone while Olivia walks to the kitchen to prepare breakfast. When she opens the shuttered door of the butler's pantry, she can't stop the cry that exits her mouth. Quickly, she slaps her hand over her lips so Justin won't hear. Her grief excites him.

Our time is coming, Olly. Hang on just a bit longer.

She's trying. She's tucked all her memories of her brother into her mind, where his voice lives, and transports herself there every moment she can. Each room in this house has special significance for her, but this pantry holds the remnants of their only refuge from their father's rage and her brother's final day in the house.

At least once a week after their mother died and Alistair's moodiness and social awkwardness slowly became hallucinations and suspicion of everyone but Olivia, she'd guide him into the pantry. There she'd take out the chocolate she'd hidden in a silver tin of flour—because, of course, they could no longer hide any treats in the basement freezer—and Alistair's beloved comic books and her sketches, plus her pastels and colored pencils, all of which she kept rolled in a yellow woolen blanket shoved under one of the two mahogany shelving units lining the walls. They'd sprawl out on the black-and-white tiled floor, lost in their own hobbies but always with each other.

And for one blissful year, from fourteen to fifteen, after Olivia had begged her father to seek help, Alistair was regularly seeing a psychiatrist and had been put on a cocktail of antipsychotics. He was able to keep the voices in his head at bay and see the world the way Olivia did. It all ended one night in her senior year of high school.

Her father was holding a soiree to celebrate a banner year for Walker Developments in the resplendent living room, while caterers bustled around the kitchen and serving staff rushed around with silver trays of canapés and champagne flutes. Olivia was supposed to be by her father's side in the peach chiffon dress he'd laid out on her bed for his trophy daughter. But toward the end of the evening, a man in a black suit kept looking at Alistair. It set her brother off into a tailspin of paranoia.

Olivia swooped in and, without her father seeing, brought Alistair to safety in the pantry. Her brother calmed down, and they were happily in the world she'd created just for the two of them, when the pantry door slid open. Her father had finally found their secret place.

"Get out of here!" he roared. "This area is for the housekeeper, not stupid teenagers who play weird games. What the hell is wrong with you, Olivia? I know Alistair is a lost cause, but you know better! How dare you embarrass me by disappearing all night!"

He dragged Olivia out by her wrist. She screamed in pain. Then her father slid his black leather belt, identical to the one he'd whipped

Alistair with the day their mother had died, from the loops in his pants. And Alistair snapped.

Six-foot-one at fifteen, three inches taller than Griffin and stronger, he was on top of their father so fast that Olivia couldn't do anything to stop it. He tackled their father to the ground, dug his elbow into his back, and told Olivia to run. The very next day, Alistair was shipped off to Ridgestone, a residential psychiatric care facility, where he was put on even stronger drugs, which, he told Olivia during her monthly visiting days, he hated taking. But he took them for her so he wouldn't cause any more trouble.

He'd never attacked anyone before the night their father caught them. He only did it to protect Olivia.

Her father never touched her again. He never once visited Alistair, as far as she knows. But he made sure Olivia could never hide from him again. He replaced the heavy wooden sliding door with white shutters, through which she can now hear Justin's heavy footsteps enter the kitchen.

Immediately, she takes the flour, sugar, and baking powder from the shelf to make him waffles, something sweet and solid to fortify him for his long day ahead visiting their construction sites.

With the silver tins stacked in the crook of her arm, she opens the shutter, knocking her elbow into the wall. The tins fall to the floor with a crash.

Justin simply stands there, arms crossed, regarding her with as much interest as he would a piece of trash while she bends down to pick them up. It was exactly what he did when she fell to her knees after the police left their house four weeks ago.

All the assaults and humiliations she's suffered are nothing compared to the agony she experienced when two uniformed officers knocked on their door and asked if they could come inside their home. Olivia had no choice but to agree. She had no idea why they were there.

Justin was in the living room, and he jumped up, all dimples and charm as he led the officers to the two gold straight-backed chairs that were once her and Alistair's pretend thrones.

"We're very sorry to inform you that your brother, Alistair Walker, was found deceased this morning."

The scream that tore from Olivia's throat was so piercing that she thought the windows would shatter. She wanted them to shatter. She wanted everything around her, especially her husband, to break into jagged little pieces like she just had. Because she knew he'd done this.

She never even got to say goodbye.

Since that day, Olivia waited for a tangible sign from Alistair that her life is worth living.

It came in the form of a Facebook message.

CHAPTER THIRTEEN

At 5:15 p.m. Olivia's in the powder room brushing silver eye shadow on her eyelids when the familiar dread mushrooms in her chest. A moment later, she hears the rumble of Justin's truck. She shoves the makeup under the sink and runs to the never-used dining room opposite the living room. The casement window provides a clear view of their driveway and the street, so Olivia crouches and, using the thick navy curtain as a shield, peeks over the ledge to watch Justin exit his truck, toolbox in hand. He doesn't come to the front door.

Olivia waits, and there's Bree, prancing down the street toward their house in a tight baby blue workout top and white leggings. As quietly as she can, Olivia opens the window a crack to listen.

"Hey, sorry," Bree says, once she's on the driveway. "Do you have a few minutes? I can't mount my flat-screen television by myself."

Justin grins. "Yeah, sure."

Together they walk to Bree's house. When she's sure they're gone, Olivia closes the window. As she's locking it, Alistair says, *He's probably mounting Bree too.*

Olivia laughs. She doesn't care if Justin is sleeping with their neighbor, but it's unlikely. With her large breasts spilling out of her tops and flowy waves of glossy red hair, Bree is too confident for Justin. He prefers blonds he can ruin.

It's time to go, her brother instructs.

She grabs her jacket from the coatrack and leaves the house. Before getting in the car, she looks up the street at Bree's pale-yellow bungalow. Even though it's only been a couple of minutes, Olivia has to make sure Justin won't come out yet.

When she merges onto the M-14, the anxious knots she's always coiled in unravel; she even turns on the radio, singing along to a Taylor Swift tune as the sun begins to set, dipping behind the trees, beyond which are many of the buildings her father developed. Olivia was by his side at the ribbon-cutting ceremonies, perfectly put together in whatever expensive outfit he liked the most. She'd plaster her fake smile on her face when reporters, looking for soft news, interviewed her. She feigned pride in her father's accomplishments and spouted the agreed-upon lie about Alistair excelling at boarding school overseas, on track to one day open a European branch of Walker Developments.

As the city recedes and a light mist makes the treetops glisten, Olivia can't define at first what it is she's feeling, then realizes it's hope.

She thought she'd lost every shred of it when the police sat stoically in her living room a month ago. All Olivia could do was lean into Justin, accept his support as the officers surmised that Alistair must have died trying to get to Olivia and Justin. Besides the tiger eye that she'd given him, all her brother had on his body was a card from Ridgestone in his pocket, with Justin and Olivia's address scrawled on the back. Olivia could barely speak through her tears when she asked why he was in a stranger's shed at all and not safely in his room at Ridgestone.

Justin's arms were around her, his hand stroking her back. The male officer said that after Alistair had been discharged from Ridgestone and told that he was moving to a halfway house, he left in the middle of the night without anyone realizing. How he'd made it all the way to Ann Arbor from Detroit, they didn't know, but he'd been killed when a metal shelving unit—in a shed that he'd likely found refuge in—had toppled and crushed him.

For a split second, Olivia considered catching the female officer's eye, giving her a look that said "Help me." Because with Alistair gone, all she had left to lose was her own life, which meant nothing to her anymore. Yet she couldn't, because she saw how the woman looked at her, seconds from collapsing, and at Justin, who held her up, as though he was the most loving husband. Olivia was certain the officer wouldn't believe her, because she had not a crumb of proof.

And the moment the officers drove away, Justin turned to her. "I warned you not to invade my privacy, but you didn't listen. You answered my phone."

She had answered Justin's phone a day earlier, because Ridgestone had flashed across his screen while he was showering. She was scared to pick up the call but was more frightened that something had happened to Alistair.

The director informed Olivia that their September payment was late. Embarrassed, both to be behind on the payment and, because she didn't control the finances, not to be able to say a check was forthcoming, she apologized and said she'd take care of it as soon as possible. After Justin got out of the shower and dressed that day, she had to ask him about it. That was one of many mistakes. He had no emotion when he told her he'd simply forgotten to make that month's payment and if she hadn't answered the call, he would have taken care of it, but that now, because she'd pried into his business, Alistair would no longer be able to call Ridgestone home.

Her next mistake was crying, begging him to keep paying, or allow Alistair to come home and live with them, sleep in his childhood bedroom again. Justin looked at her coldly and simply said, "I'm going out."

She hoped he would think about her request, but she should have known better. When Justin came home that night, he said he'd called Ridgestone and told the director they'd decided to move Alistair to a state-run halfway house and to please tell Alistair that Olivia no longer wished to shoulder the burden of him. She crumpled to the floor, devastated, crying harder than before, knowing that her brother had been lied to. Again.

For Alistair, she's about to do the scariest, riskiest thing she's done since college.

The trip is faster than she expects, and following the robotic voice of her GPS, Olivia makes a right onto a residential street lined with older houses that look snug and warm from the outside. It's amazing how much someone can hide behind the comforting glow of a lamp through a covered window. How deceiving looks can be.

Olivia checks her own appearance once she's parked, far down the street from the restaurant. Olivia had carefully selected the pale-lavender V-neck from her closet, a sweater from her sorority days, back when her pretty face, mane of blonde waves, and gray eyes were the envy of all her Alpha Phi sisters.

She knows how much she's changed. No longer slim and healthy like she was in college, but gaunt and hollow. Food is no longer a pleasure to her; not much is. No wonder Justin finds her so unattractive. Her collarbone juts out, and the feathery sweater that used to mold to her curves swims on her. She added a black belt around her waist, which helps her look shapelier than she is.

Olivia exits the car, shivering. The temperature has dropped considerably, and though she's wearing her puffer and the wind is buffeted by brown-brick low-rises, cold bites at her neck. From her bag, Olivia pulls out the turquoise cashmere scarf she bought yesterday, when she also purchased the pink wrap sweater that Justin didn't like on her. She rarely takes money out of her secret stash of cash, but looking good tonight is important.

The scarf is so soft, and Olivia brushes her face against it, soothing herself as she walks up the street and inside the busy restaurant, struck by how beautiful and happy the patrons look under the rose gold pendant lights hanging from the ceiling. She heads straight to the back of the bar, where she can see everyone who comes through the door in the long mirror above the shelf of liquor.

The door of the restaurant opens. Olivia glances up at the mirror. She smiles. The person she's waiting for has arrived. But she needs a moment to steel herself. Olivia reaches into her pocket and rubs the tiger eye, then ducks her head and weaves through the packed tables.

As she passes a small two-top by the window, she hears a gleeful "Hi!"

Olivia turns and makes an "O" of surprise with her mouth. "Oh, hey! Sorry, I almost walked right past you." She looks at the empty chair. "Waiting for someone?"

She watches as a shadow of a blush sweeps across the woman's cheeks, made more pronounced by the light outside the long window. Olivia wants to shake the anticipation out of her. Instead, she smiles at the angelic-looking blond who wants to fuck her husband.

Justin's words ring in her head: *You weren't even the girl I wanted to be with at the party. I didn't show up for you. But you just had to come and ruin everything.*

Eden Hoffman. The one who got away.

"I took your suggestion about the restaurant," Eden says. "I'm sorry I didn't text you to ask, but it was easy to find this place after you mentioned the name of the street."

Olivia pretends to be embarrassed. "Shoot, is tonight your date? I forgot to text you too."

Eden grins, tugging at the plunging neckline of the silky black sleeveless top she'd tried on in the boutique. She looks good. Different. She clearly spent a lot of time getting ready for tonight. Her shoulder-length hair has a bouncy curl to it, and her lips are slicked a glossy red that suits her rosy skin. But Justin wouldn't like the color. When they first started dating, Justin would lightly brush his finger across Olivia's painted lips, then kiss her like she was the most delicious treat.

Olivia stopped wearing bright lipstick a week after he'd played her the recording of her confession and laid out his rules. They were driving to see Amy, who'd invited them for dinner to celebrate being newly-weds. At a red light, he leaned over and dragged his thumb across her mouth, smearing her signature fuchsia lipstick. Before they went inside Amy's house, Olivia wiped it off her face as best she could. And she held back her tears when Amy gestured to her mouth, winked, and said, "A little make-out session in the car, huh? You two can't keep your hands off each other."

Olivia felt stained all night.

Tonight, though, she's finally cleaning up a mess that she made a long time ago.

"I swear I'm not crashing your first date after your separation." Olivia juts her chin at the take-out counter. "I was craving their Tuscan chicken and placed an order to bring home, but it's not ready yet. I was going to go outside and wait. It's almost too warm in here!"

Olivia is freezing, like she always is. But Eden has a line of sweat above her upper lip.

Eden nods, lifting her hair from her neck. "I turned forty-five on Friday, and I swear it's getting harder every year to keep my temperature stable!"

"Happy birthday!" Olivia exclaims, though she knows when Eden Hoffman's birthday is. She knows everything about her. She knows where she goes and what she does. The closer she can get to Eden, the closer she is to getting away from Justin.

Alistair told her so. The first time Olivia heard his voice was when she saw the Facebook push notification flash across Justin's phone while he was showering. She'd been wiping down the coffee table when Eden Hoffman's name appeared. She dropped the rag on the floor, every muscle in her body stiffening in fright as she was instantly brought back to the night that set off a future bleaker than Olivia ever could have imagined.

Olivia had arrived at the Sigma Chi party late because Amy had been prepartying too hard on tequila slammers and decided to give herself bangs while drunk. It hadn't gone well. Olivia and her sorority sisters had done their best to even out a pretty messy job, though it was clear Amy was going to be needing the proper scissors of a stylist. But Amy threw on a baseball cap and was still in good spirits while everyone laughed it off, all of them giddy from a round of tequila shots. Olivia was the only one who didn't take a shot; she was buzzed enough about seeing Justin.

But when Olivia showed up to the frat house and scanned the main floor for him, excited to see his reaction when he saw her—she watched him making out with a girl she'd never seen before. A blond in an ill-fitting jean skirt and a too-tight mesh shirt had her hands on Justin's chest and her tongue down his throat. Sloppy drunk, she swayed against Justin as he held her up against the wall.

Olivia knew then why Justin had repeatedly asked her if she was going to the party. She'd said no because she wanted to surprise him. She'd planned it out so perfectly in her mind—she would finally tell her sorority sisters who she'd been seeing those past few months. Yes, they could judge her, but school was basically over, and though she imagined staying friends with them for a long time, she also didn't care about whatever social ostracization dating him would mean. She knew his reputation as a bad boy and a flirt, but she'd seen a deeper side of him, and if her friends could know that, too, it would be amazing. She was even feeling bold enough to tell her father and knew he would grow to love Justin, even if he wasn't from a highly successful family, even if he wasn't studying law or medicine. She was in love with Justin Ward, and he was in love with her.

So many lies.

And so many secrets. Justin has been hiding something from her too. And Eden is the only person who might be able to tell Olivia what really happened that night. She's not worried that Eden will recognize her from the party or U-M at all. Olivia had never seen or heard of Eden before she watched her lay her hands all over Justin, and Eden was certainly too busy to notice anyone but him. Plus, Olivia looks entirely different than she used to.

Eden points to the empty chair. "Do you want to take off your coat and wait here until your order is ready?"

"What if your date . . ." Olivia trails off and asks lightly, "What's his name?"

"Justin." Eden's neck immediately flares red when she says his name.

"If Justin shows up, you don't want him to think you need a chaperone."

Eden giggles. "I might."

Olivia guffaws, as she's expected to. Eden wouldn't be giggling if she knew how much Justin could hurt her. "Let me see how much longer my order's going to be."

"Sure." Fanning herself with a hand, Eden says, "I'm going to order a glass of white wine to calm my nerves. Want one?"

"Definitely. Red for me, please." Olivia could use a warm infusion of alcohol. She's jeopardized so much to come here. After shrugging off her coat and scarf, Olivia hangs it on the back of the chair. "The necklace looks great, by the way." Smiling, Olivia points at the thin silver chain she handed to Eden at the boutique yesterday. She enjoys that Eden is wearing something she recommended, even if it's for a date with Justin.

Eden touches the chain. "Thank you. You have good taste."

If only that were true when it came to the man whom they both fell for in college.

While Eden searches out a server, Olivia moves her eyes to the door. She doesn't know how long she should be here or who might enter the restaurant at any minute. Quickly, she walks to the take-out counter. "If I order Tuscan chicken to go, how long will it be?"

The woman behind the cash register repeats the question into her headset, then answers, "About ten minutes."

"Great. I'm sitting at that table." She gestures to where Eden is ordering their drinks.

"Do you want to eat here?" The woman looks confused.

"No. Just waiting with a friend until her date shows up. Thanks." Olivia swallows. Tonight she actually does have a friend, even if Eden doesn't know who she really is.

"Your name?"

"Lila Cavanaugh."

"How will you be paying?"

"Cash."

Olivia hands over some bills, puts the change in the tip jar, then squares her shoulders and stands taller. About to saunter back to the table, she hears her phone buzz in her handbag. Olivia's heart pounds in her chest.

She catches Eden's attention, points to the sign for the restrooms, mouths, "Back soon," and heads straight for the women's restroom, the only quiet spot she can think of in the crowded restaurant. She's told Justin she'll be at Amy's elegant, hushed mansion for her Alpha Phi get-together. Justin doesn't know that the dinner is actually next month.

If he finds out there isn't a soiree tonight, that she hasn't been out securing job prospects, he'll be furious. But that's not what frightens her in this moment.

Inside the restroom, she answers the call, checking under each stall for feet.

"Where the hell is my truck, Olivia?" Justin's voice is low and dangerous.

She feels her insides quake and wills herself to stay calm. But as she looks at herself in the stark lighting of the mirror above the row of porcelain sinks, she sees her face has gone chalk white.

Taking Justin's truck tonight was a necessity and an act of defiance that makes her feel brave. But she knows how much it's going to cost her. Not only did she take Justin's truck without asking, but she also prevented him from going out tonight.

"My car wouldn't start," she lies.

He's quiet, which makes her pulse roar in her ears.

Nervous, Olivia starts to ramble. "I tried to start it three times, and you weren't home. I was going to be late for Amy's, and I didn't know what else to do."

His tone is low but brutish. "You stay home. That's what you do."

She thinks of Eden, steps away, waiting for this man who she believes is caring and thoughtful.

"It won't happen again. But I had to go to my sorority dinner. How would it look if I canceled last minute? Plus, your truck and our logo is now parked on Barton Shore Drive." Olivia quickly names Amy's street, one of the wealthiest in Michigan. "So all the rich neighbors can see it. Anyone looking to do renos now knows who we are."

"I don't care about goddamn renos. I told you I'm going out. I'm already late. I need my truck now."

He sounds like a pouty toddler. She straightens; she's in control for the first time ever. She's Lila Cavanaugh, a woman with a backbone and an untainted past.

"Take an Uber." Olivia's audacity startles her. She *never* tells Justin what to do.

"I'm not wasting any money on someone else driving me. Bring me my truck."

Yet he can waste money on beer, porn, video games, and whatever else he desires. And she knows exactly why he wants his truck so bad, what he plans to do tonight.

"I'm really sorry, but there's nothing I can do. Maybe your mom can drive you wherever you need to go."

And she hangs up, her courage evaporating as terror seizes her throat like his hands are around her neck.

Quickly, she exits the bathroom, leaving Olivia Ward behind. Shoulders back, head high, she strolls over to the take-out counter, where her food is waiting for her. Once at the table, she puts the bag on the floor and slides into the seat across from Eden, noticing that the glow on Eden's face has dulled and there's a slight sag to her shoulders.

"You okay?" she asks.

"He's late," Eden tells her.

"Maybe this guy isn't worth it." Olivia is telling the truth for the first time tonight.

Eden's eyes film with tears. "It's not just him. Dave's in the hospital. That's my husband, or whatever he is to me now. He was hit by a

143

car. The driver took off. It happened last night, but I just called him to check in and he seems so sad."

The clang of dishes and murmur of conversations around them seem to stop. "Oh my God. Was he badly hurt?" Olivia presses a hand to her chest to calm the roar of her heartbeat.

"He fractured his hip and the bone near his elbow." Eden indicates the lower part of her upper arm. "He had surgery and is in the hospital for at least a few more days, but it could have been so much worse."

Olivia nods. "I'm so glad he'll be all right."

And she is glad. She didn't want to hit Dave with her car. She'd followed Eden home from the boutique, only planning to watch her house for a little while, see the kind of life Eden lived. Olivia idled at the curb on Ivy Court—a simple, typical suburban street with basketball nets on driveways and bikes tossed on lawns, when suddenly there was Dave, getting out of his gray Range Rover, with a bouquet of yellow tulips and a large pizza box in his hands.

Hit him, Alistair said. *Just a tap.*

The thud when she banged into him has been thumping in her head since last night. She felt sick when she got home, checking every inch of her car for damage that might be from a body. She almost wanted there to be blood or hair, anything that could be evidence. But there was only a cracked headlight and a dent in the front fender. She didn't tell Justin about the damage. The car is still parked in their garage, and she's banking on him not caring enough to try to start it himself. She'll take the car to a mechanic to repair it before he notices anything wrong.

She doesn't think Dave saw her, and she wouldn't have known anything about him at all if his photos weren't posted all over Eden's social media. But she did follow his Range Rover when he and Eden drove to U-M to see Ava, whose own social media accounts contain far too much information.

And she might have made everything worse for herself.

"Can the police do anything?" Olivia asks.

Eden lifts her shoulders, then drops them with a slump. "They'll try to locate the driver, but all they have to go on right now is a vague description from my neighbor. She thinks she might have seen a silver car speeding off up the street."

Olivia needs to keep her hands busy, because she knows they're trembling. She takes her napkin from the table and bunches it once, twice, three times.

"I'm so sorry. What about cameras? Other witnesses?"

"The houses on that stretch of road don't have exterior cameras, and they've talked to everyone on the street to see if anyone was looking out their window at that time. It was already getting dark, though. And it happened so fast that Dave doesn't remember a thing." She twirls a strand of her hair. "I was going to cancel tonight, but he also wanted to be alone to sleep. Or so he said."

Olivia simply nods, and when Eden glances at the door again, Alistair speaks. *You're okay, Olly. No one saw you. Just the car.*

Right then the server approaches. "You two need refills on those wines?"

Eden smiles at Olivia. "Probably, don't you think? I mean, if you want to stay."

"For sure!" Olivia answers, reveling in having drinks with someone other than Justin, who only takes her out to dinner at a local restaurant for their anniversary every year so he can show their neighbors how romantic he is.

"You got it. I'll be right back, ladies!" The server is all spunk as she turns and walks toward the bar.

They're now close enough their elbows can touch.

Right then, Eden's phone buzzes, and her face lights up with hope, before she bends her head to read what's on the screen.

Olivia knows exactly who the text is from, but after Eden lifts her head, her eyes are wet. Olivia screws up her mouth in concern. "Bad news?"

"Justin's not coming." She puts a hand to her throat. "Maybe you're right, and I should let him go. But it hurts, because we started getting close, and I thought maybe there was something special between us. Something worth exploring that Dave isn't interested in anymore."

"I'm sorry." Olivia mews in sympathy. "Did he say why he isn't coming?"

"Just that something happened with his truck."

"That's a shame." Olivia makes a sad face, but she can't believe what she's done. How dangerous all this is. She's definitely afraid to go home tonight, but right here, right now, she wants to stay in this little cocoon as long as she can. She's realized that Eden makes her feel safe. If she can get the other woman on her side, make her see the things about Justin no one else sees, Olivia might finally have a life of her own.

She reaches for the plastic bag she picked up at the take-out counter a few minutes ago, puts the container of Tuscan chicken in the center of the table, and picks up her fork, motioning for Eden to do the same. "We can share?"

Eden laughs sadly and spoons a healthy amount onto her plate. "Thank you. It looks amazing."

The aroma of the tomatoes and spices waft temptingly into Olivia's nose. Usually, she'd only eat a few bites and barely taste them. But tonight, she's ravenous and puts a large forkful into her mouth, swallowing with rare pleasure.

Eden smiles, but she looks pained as she takes a bite, then puts down her fork.

"I think his weird behavior might have something to do with his wife."

Indeed, Olivia thinks, as her stomach fills and her mind sharpens. "He has a wife?" She alters her tone. "No judgment."

"It's complicated. They're separated but still live together on opposite sides of the house, until he can afford to move out."

Olivia can't stifle her laugh. Surely Eden can't be that naive. She takes a sip of wine and says, "You believe that?"

"I know how it sounds. I want to believe it. I like to think people are telling the truth." Eden lifts her wineglass but puts it down without drinking from it. "Have you ever been with a man who makes you feel so good and so bad at the same time?"

Olivia's pulse quickens. "Haven't we all?" she answers, then takes a deep sip of her own wine so Eden can't see the nervous twitch of her mouth.

"Justin is the only guy other than Dave I've ever had strong feelings for. I don't know where things stand between me and Dave. And I don't know why I'm letting Justin treat me like this again."

"Again?" Olivia squeaks, then clears her throat.

Eden sighs. "He hurt me when we were younger too."

Olivia stays as calm as possible, desperate to rub the tiger eye in her pocket, but knows it might elicit more questions than she can answer. She recalls the message Eden sent Justin that set her whole plan in motion.

I wish I'd never gotten so drunk. I'd never lost control of myself like I did with you that night. Everything that happened, honestly, was so unlike me. I blacked out.

The next day, I thought I remembered hearing Tyler say my name while I was sick in the bathroom, but the police said I was too drunk to make a reliable account. I felt awful about that.

Tyler did say her name. To Justin.

Maybe something about tonight *has* jolted Eden's memory.

Olivia asks quietly, "What do you mean he hurt you when you were younger?"

But Eden falls back into her chair and says, "Forget it. Enough of my pity party." And the moment is over. "Thank you, Lila. You're the only person I've told about Justin. I don't normally reveal so much personal information. But you make it easy for me to talk."

Olivia puts her hand on her heart, shattered so many times. Laughter from another table drifts over. Olivia looks to her left, where two women are giggling. She can see the sparkle around them, like a rosy aura.

Without thinking, she reaches for Eden's hand. Eden holds Olivia's fingers before letting go. Olivia wants to feel the soft touch again, savor it. She wants to tell Eden who she really is right now. She doesn't want to lie a minute longer.

Careful, Olly. You'll scare her away if you tell her too soon. She has to trust you more.

So all she says is "Lust is a heady drug. And finding someone you can talk to when you're all alone is hard to let go of."

Eden nods.

Then Eden's phone, which is on the table right next to her wine-glass, lights up with a call.

When Eden answers, her entire body goes rigid; her eyes fill with alarm. "Oh my God," she says, making Olivia want to climb over the table to try to hear the person on the other end of the line, her own adrenaline spiking in response to Eden's obvious distress. "Are you sure?"

Eden ends the call, tosses some cash on the table, and stands up so fast her chair falls over. Her skin is now white and clammy looking with fear. She leaves the chair where it lies and says, "I'm sorry. I have to go."

Before Olivia can ask what's happened, Eden runs out into the night.

Follow her, Alistair says.

So Olivia does.

CHAPTER FOURTEEN

Olivia has only a breath to catch up to Eden. Leaping from her chair, she races out of the restaurant, hurrying as fast as she can to Justin's truck, parked way down the street. Justin has the only fob, but she has a key in case she ever needs to move it for him. She jams the key in the lock, opens the door, jumps inside, and starts the car, her knuckles white as she grips the wheel.

She turned off her phone soon after Justin called. She didn't want to know if he sent threatening texts or called again. She didn't want to be Olivia Ward at all. But now she has to be careful not to let Eden see the Ram, the white lettering of **Ward Contracting** bright under the streetlamps. She lets Eden's blue Camry move ahead enough that Eden hopefully can't spot Olivia or the truck in her rearview mirror. But Eden is driving like it's life or death, and Olivia has to keep up.

When Eden merges onto the ramp for the I-94, Olivia's confused. Eden doesn't need to take the highway to get to her house on Ivy Court.

And then abject terror almost paralyzes her as she wonders, for the first time, if Justin could be tracking her or his truck. She's almost always at home, unless she has a doctor's appointment or is needed on site to take photos for their website. He couldn't have caught her doing anything wrong before recently. But now that Olivia's been living instead of merely existing, he has every reason to try to trap her in a lie. She has to outmaneuver him.

Eden turns off at exit 175, and Olivia gets her bearings. Perhaps Eden's going to see Ava at her dorm. She breathes properly for the first time in an hour. Maybe Ava's the one who phoned, needing her mother, and Eden ran. Ava's social media accounts don't have a single shot of Eden, but Eden's show how much she loves her daughter.

Still, Olivia has to be sure exactly where Eden is driving. She tails her to Kipke Drive, full of buildings and dark, empty parking lots. This late at night, it seems an odd place for a mother-daughter meetup.

A wave of vertigo makes the sky glow above her spin when Eden pulls into the lot of the Division of Public Safety and Security for the University of Michigan.

A police station.

Olivia immediately turns off her headlights, parks at the lot across the street, and watches Eden walk through the doors of the building. Olivia swallows the acid burning her throat, thinking of every possible reason Eden could have gotten a call that made her take off for the police division at U-M.

Could it be about Dave's accident? Fear zips up her spine. Even if the Mazda is in Justin's name, she's the one who drives it most of the time. What if someone saw her? After twenty minutes, the doors open. It's not Eden. A woman shields herself from the wind to light a cigarette. Even with the windows closed, the imagined acrid, burning odor of the tobacco and nicotine finds its way into Olivia's memories.

A cigarette was Olivia's downfall.

Smoking was her secret habit. She only smoked when she was really stressed or upset—after a dinner with her dad, before a big test, on her way to and from visiting Alistair at Ridgestone, which her father allowed her to do once a month. She'd make the hour drive by herself in the red Jetta her father had given her for her sixteenth birthday, purchased from one of his client's dealerships, of course. She relished the trip there because she was so excited to see her brother, but the medication he was on dulled his energy, and she always cried and chain-smoked all the way home.

Smoking was also how she dealt with the betrayal of seeing Justin and Eden making out at the Sigma Chi party. It was Tyler, sweet Tyler, her friend, whom she'd met in freshman year when they were both pledges, who spotted Olivia sobbing in the upstairs hallway. Tyler brought her into his bedroom at the far end of the hall next to the bathroom and onto the balcony for a smoke and chat.

The balcony extended across the entire second floor, above a patch of grass and overlooking a gravel lot, where only a few cars, including the Screaming Demons' white van, were parked. It was a cool May night, and the fresh air calmed Olivia slightly.

She sat down on the cold concrete, her back against the white railing, staring into Tyler's bedroom through the sliding glass door and out to the hallway, where the party raged on.

Tyler sat beside her, put his red Solo cup down, and draped his arm around her, until her tears finally subsided. She lit a cigarette, and Tyler plucked it from her fingers for a drag before handing it back to her.

"You smoke?" Olivia was shocked. Tyler, with his shaggy hair always smelling like chlorine from swim team practice, seemed like the epitome of health.

"We all have our vices. Like you and skeezy drummers. That why you were crying?" He raised his eyebrows and took a sip from his cup.

Olivia sucked on the cigarette, then exhaled a sob. "He's not skeezy. And how did you know this was about Justin?"

Tyler rested his elbows on his knees. "When I see a girl crying, he's often involved."

Olivia wrinkled her nose. "What does that mean?"

He shrugged. "Nothing. Forget it. He just doesn't seem like your type."

She nodded and took another drag from her cigarette, blowing out the smoke hard. "I know. But honestly, I don't even have a type. And he's actually really sweet."

Tyler snorted. "I went to high school with that guy. *Sweet* is not how I would describe him. A user, yes. A poser, for sure. He was on the track team, then it was school council and on to band. Whatever gets him the most attention. I think he only came here tonight for the free weed." He gently knocked his knee into hers. "What did he do that's made you so upset?"

"Kissed another girl."

Olivia offered her cigarette, and he took another drag. "Was she blonde?"

Olivia jerked her knee away. "You saw them too?"

"Nope." He laughed. "*He* has a type."

She shook her head. "I know we have something special. He told me yesterday he loved me." She rubbed her eyes with the heel of her hand. "I've never felt like this about anybody."

Tyler shrugged and gave Olivia the cigarette back. "I'm just telling you how I see it. I don't want you to get hurt. But even in high school, he was a player." He pointed at her. "And the girls were a mess after he was done with them. Trust me, it's better you found out now what he's really like and stay far away."

A door slammed. A light went on in the bathroom next to Tyler's bedroom.

"Keep this between us, though, okay? I mean, I think the guy is a dick, but everyone else thinks Justin Ward is the shit. I don't need the headache of dealing with him."

The sound of loud retching came from the bathroom.

"Hang on a sec," Tyler said. "I'm going to see if that party animal needs any help." He stood up, and a moment later Olivia could hear a murmur of voices. Then the bathroom window slid open.

When Tyler came back, he said, "It's Eden Hoffman. She's super drunk and out of it. I've never seen her like that. I didn't even think she drank." His eyebrows knit with worry. "She told me to leave her alone, but I cracked a window so she can get some air."

"Who's Eden Hoffman?" Olivia asked, taking one last drag of her cigarette before tossing it through the railing slats behind her.

"We work together at the Book Nook." He rubbed his jaw, glancing at the open bathroom window. "I don't like leaving her on her own in there."

"What is happening to me?" a female voice moaned.

Olivia stood, too, biting her lip. "Yeah, she doesn't sound good."

Tyler shifted from foot to foot. "I should go in and take care of her. Something's not right."

"I'll go. She might be more comfortable with a girl helping her." Olivia went back inside and over to the bathroom, where the door was closed. She knocked, but there was no answer.

She didn't want to violate anyone's privacy, but she had to make sure that the sick girl was okay, so Olivia turned the knob. There hunched over the toilet was the blond in a mesh top and jean skirt, puking her guts out.

Quickly, Olivia left, leaving the door open so someone else could help the girl who'd just had her tongue down Justin's throat. It wasn't her problem, and Eden was probably some drunk groupie.

She went back onto the balcony, where Tyler leaned against the railing.

"So? Is she okay?" he asked, putting his drink on the ground.

"You mean the chick who was fooling around with Justin?" Olivia picked up Tyler's red cup and took a large sip. "She'll be fine. She's just wasted."

Tyler scoffed loudly. "Eden and Justin? No way."

"Yes way," Olivia argued.

Tyler looked at the bathroom window, then back at Olivia. "That makes no sense. I invited her to the party so she could talk to a different guy. Something's off here."

Then Justin came onto the balcony.

Distracted by her thoughts, Olivia doesn't see Eden leave the police station. It's only when she hears a car door slam that she focuses. Olivia slides down in the driver's seat, throwing her head back so hard she feels a pop in her neck, and jams herself as far under the wheel as she can until she hears who she hopes is Eden driving away.

After counting to two hundred, Olivia slowly, carefully sits up, darting her eyes around the police station parking lot and into the starry night to make sure Eden is long gone. Olivia starts the truck and pulls out onto the road. She's been away from home for over three hours. No sorority dinner lasts that long. She can't possibly follow Eden anywhere else tonight. She does send her a quick text, though, using Burner, an app she installed to get an untraceable number on her phone.

Lila: I hope everything is okay! Let me know when you get a chance or if you need anything.

She reads it five times before sending it to make sure it has the right friendly tone. Hopefully Eden will respond.

On the short drive home to the Old West Side, sweat dampening the armpits of her pretty lavender sweater, the pungent scent of her fear filling the car, she stops quickly at the twenty-four-hour 7-Eleven to get Justin's favorite fudge ice cream in an attempt to make up for taking his truck.

Their house is dark when Olivia arrives, and she's counting on Justin being asleep. She tiptoes to the door, suddenly realizing that Justin might notice how many miles she's put on his truck tonight; it's the kind of thing he tracks. As she inserts her key into the lock, she thinks of all the places she could have driven—the dinner at Amy's, the store; maybe she gave a lift home to one of her sorority sisters—to explain the difference on the odometer should Justin ask. Thinking about these possibilities, she steps into the entryway.

"Where the hell have you been?"

Olivia screams, dropping the bag of ice cream to the floor.

Justin moves from behind the door, where he's clearly been waiting for her. He closes the door, then turns around to face her.

She's in trouble now, and her mind goes blank. Even Alistair's voice is silent.

Justin comes toward her with a single measured step. Olivia can hear her heart thundering and stays rooted to her spot. But when Justin presses his hard chest against hers and gently strokes his fingers through her hair, she relaxes.

Of course he's only toying with her. His hand guides her head down. And for the next four minutes, Olivia thinks of the dinner with Eden. How nice it was to have someone to talk to and pay attention to her. And she enjoys a small sense of accomplishment because she's doing what Eden would have to if she'd seen Justin tonight. In a way, Olivia is protecting her. After he's done with her, Justin sniffs the air. "I'm taking a shower. You should too. Whatever you ate tonight is seeping from your pores." He pulls up his track pants and smiles at her.

Once he's upstairs, and after putting the melting ice cream away, Olivia heads to the powder room, feeling sick no matter how many times she brushes her teeth. The brief respite from her reality is over. How much longer can she pretend to be Lila Cavanaugh before Justin finds out what she's been doing? It was useless to think she could hurt him in any way.

As her foot lands on the first step of the stairs so she can go up and shower in the guest bedroom, she hears his phone buzz from the living room. Olivia hesitates.

Go, Alistair says. *You need to know what he's doing. Your life depends on it.*

Olivia steps back onto the main floor and walks into the living room. Justin's phone is on the coffee table. On her own phone, she sets a timer for five minutes. Then she picks up his phone and types in his password.

There's a text from Yvonne that makes her smile.

Mother: Thanks for nothing, Justin. Shawn took me to Detroit even though he should have been with his kids.

There's also a message from someone named Madison Lassiter, a name Olivia's never heard before. Olivia scrolls down to the first message, sent at 1:00 p.m. today.

Justin: Good to talk to you today, Madison. You seem bright and talented. If I can find something, you'd be a positive asset for the Ward Contracting team. You have a special spark, and I like your energy on the phone. I felt electric the rest of the day.

Madison: Thanks for taking the time. I'd love to work for you, even as an intern. Like I said, I'm super good with my hands. I can get down and dirty on a construction site. I felt a spark, too. I'll do anything.

"I'll bet you will," Olivia says to the screen.

A spasm twists in her chest. Olivia already knows how this text exchange is going to go, and she wouldn't care, except now he's involving their company. She doesn't know if it's the first time.

Justin: You're sweet to say that. I'm sure I'm a bit older than most of the guys who get your attention. I might have something, actually. Part-time. Could be some late nights. Are you able to do that?

Olivia snorts. They can barely pay the staff they have. Olivia does the hiring, and she only hires men. Her husband is such an asshole.

Madison: I like men with experience. I can do anything you want.

Justin: I think we should meet in person for an interview. A private space, perhaps, so we can really build on this connection? I'd like to hear all about you.

Madison: I'd like to show you. I can meet tonight.

Justin: I can't tonight. I'll get back to you with a time and place. I'll think about you until then.

Madison: I haven't stopped thinking about you.

Justin: What kinds of thoughts?

Madison: Naughty ones.

Justin: You can get into trouble with me, so be careful when you tease me.

Madison: I'm not just teasing.

Olivia wants to throw the phone across the room, scream at her husband for being so stupid. Sending inappropriate texts to a woman looking for a job opens himself—and Ward Contracting—to a sexual harassment lawsuit. That would completely wipe them out financially and ruin his entire good-guy reputation that he's worked so hard to maintain. Does he think he's untouchable because Olivia will solve all his problems for him?

She has three minutes left before Justin gets out of the shower. At 7:20 p.m., after he'd berated Olivia for taking his truck, he texted Madison again.

Justin: Plans changed. Let's meet at Rocco's in the Old West Side at 8.

A seedy bar that's a ten-minute walk from their house, Rocco's is the last place Olivia would interview a potential hire, but that's clearly not what's happening here. Of course he wouldn't let his missing truck stop him from getting what and whom he wants.

Madison: Can't wait.

At 8:45 p.m., right before Olivia got home, Justin sent another text.

Justin: You don't get the job. You stood me up.

Madison: I was just about to text you. I'm sorry. I couldn't get into the bar.

Justin: I don't like to be kept waiting.

Madison: If you give me another chance, I'll show you how sorry I am.

Justin: I know a place I can take you. Tomorrow night. I'll text you the location. Be ready.

Madison: I'm so ready for you.

"Jesus, Justin," Olivia whispers. "You're such an idiot." This Madison girl is clearly underage. Olivia hopes she's at least eighteen or this could blow up into a bigger disaster.

The timer dings. She can't read any more of his messages tonight.

The shower turns off. The bathroom door opens, and she hears Justin pad down the hall to their bedroom. Olivia gets up to shower, as Justin instructed.

Dizzy with too many secrets in her exhausted mind, she sits on the shower floor. Under the spray, which feels like needles on her skin, she wants to drown herself. Let the police find her, her car, and everything she's so carefully buried. She's so tired of the lies, the subterfuge, and this life.

Please don't give up, Olly.

She hauls herself up and turns off the shower, then wraps herself in a towel. Looking in the mirror, she doesn't know who the bedraggled, hollow shell of a woman staring back at her is.

"I can't go on like this, Ally," she whispers.

She has to end it.

CHAPTER FIFTEEN

The next morning, after barely sleeping, Olivia's in the pantry about to take the tin of steel-cut oats from the shelf for Justin's breakfast when she hears the front door close. Justin, of course, slept like a log beside her all night, but he wasn't in bed when she opened her eyes. She didn't know where he was, but she had to get up and prepare his meal. Olivia maintains their shared calendar, so she knows that Justin has a 9:00 a.m. meeting with Larry, the owner of the Kerrytown house, who wants to speed up the renovations.

Taking her phone from her black sweatpants, she looks at the screen. It's 8:30 a.m. Perhaps Justin left early to grab breakfast on the way. He never tells her anything he doesn't want to.

She needs to be sure that Justin has actually left the property, though, so she runs to the dining room and peeks through the curtains. The driveway is empty. Justin's truck is gone. She exhales and smiles.

After putting the tin back on the shelf, she flops onto the couch in the living room, looking straight ahead at the black ceramic urn. Alistair's ashes and her pendant are all she has left of him, except for the secret album folder on her phone, where she hides the photos that she's taken of him. She opens the folder to the very last picture of her brother.

It's from Labor Day weekend, about two weeks before he died, and the usual monthly visit Justin allowed her, like her father once did. If Olivia had known it was the final time she could talk to Alistair, touch him, she would have told him everything, no matter how violently

Justin would have punished her. No matter how disappointed Alistair would have been in her.

Olivia snapped this shot of him standing under the white oak in the center of Ridgestone's expansive grounds. The leaves were still dark green, and the sun shone on Alistair's honey-brown hair, the same shade as their mother's. He was a bit thinner than Olivia liked him to be, but his hazel eyes were alert, and his smile was genuine. He had friends and a stocking job at a grocery store. He looked happy.

Justin had been right beside her, of course. She hadn't visited Alistair alone since she'd graduated from U-M.

At his door, they hugged one last time. Alistair waved with his whole body like he always did for her, never caring how silly he looked as long as he made her smile.

If Olivia had defied Justin before now, Alistair would still be alive.

You're a survivor, Olly.

"I am a survivor." This time it's her own voice she hears, loud and clear.

The front door bangs open.

Olivia bolts up from the couch and walks to the entryway, where Justin stands. With Bree. And all Olivia's bravado vanishes.

"Hey, sleepyhead." Justin smiles as he bends to put down his toolbox, then comes over to kiss her on the cheek.

"Morning, Olivia," Bree chirps, coming straight into the entryway and shutting their door behind her. Today she's in a hot-pink athleisure outfit that hugs her generous curves.

"What are you doing home?" The words fall out of Olivia's mouth before she can stop them.

Justin laughs. "I told you this morning that I had to drop off the truck at the car wash around the corner. I'm getting it detailed. It smells funny." He grins. "Maybe a skunk sprayed it after you brought it home last night." He casually drapes an arm around Olivia's shoulder.

His touch makes her ill. But she says, "Oh, that's too bad, honey," like she's supposed to.

"Anyway, I walked home, and Bree was running past, so she stopped and asked if I could quickly fix a loose tap. Busy morning for some of us." Then he winks at Bree. "Olivia had a late night."

"Nice!" Bree grins. "Where did you go?"

Olivia's throat closes; she isn't used to sharing anything about herself, as no one usually asks. Justin speaks for her.

"Olivia has these fancy dinners a couple of times a year with her sorority sisters." He shrugs sheepishly and drops his hand from her body. "I sometimes can't believe she fell for a rough-and-tumble guy like me."

Bree laughs. "Which sorority? I was in Kappa Alpha Theta."

"Alpha Phi," Olivia croaks.

"Where did you go to college?" Bree puts a manicured hand to her chest. "I went to Stanford."

Of course you did, Olivia thinks, managing to say, "University of Michigan." She moves an inch away from Justin, quickly looking at the grandfather clock behind her. It's 8:45 a.m.

"Just down the road! I didn't realize you went there! I have a few Kappa friends who also went there—let's get drinks sometime and see if we have anyone in common!"

Bree is way too peppy, and Olivia knows that a drinks date will never happen, but she responds, "Sure!" trying to muster the same energy as her neighbor while desperately hoping she'll leave.

Olivia breaks out in a prickly cold sweat before telling Justin, "Honey, you've got that meeting with Larry at nine."

He shakes his head at Bree. "I don't know what I'd do without my wife." Then he smiles at Olivia, but she feels his hand land tensely on her shoulder. "I actually called Larry and changed the meeting for this afternoon."

Thunder rumbles in the distance, and Olivia flinches.

Bree notices and says, "I'm afraid of thunder too. I'd better let you guys start your day and get home before it starts to pour." She smiles prettily. "Thanks again, Justin. Let's make that date for drinks soon, Olivia."

After Bree is gone and a few moments have passed, Justin grabs her by the waist. Olivia shrieks in fright. He ignores her cry and digs his finger into her clavicle. "Something's going on with you."

Olivia hears herself swallow. She waits for Alistair to tell her what to say. But he's quiet. So she is too. She doesn't know exactly what Justin means. It's better to say nothing.

He tightens his grip, then squeezes her nipple hard. "I know you think with Alistair gone that you don't need to be afraid of me anymore. But I know everything, and if you screw with me, Olivia, no one will believe you. You'll go down for everything. Not me."

Justin ascends the stairs for his shower. Olivia is immobile until she hears the water turn on. It's 9:00 a.m.

She checks her phone for any texts from Eden about what happened last night. Nothing. Olivia checks another app she's downloaded and hidden on her phone. Her heart stops.

We're in trouble now, Alistair says.

She drops the phone on the wood floor. It clatters loudly as her entire world collapses, again. This time, Olivia might not survive it.

Justin doesn't know everything. But he's about to find out.

PART THREE

CHAPTER SIXTEEN

EDEN

I park my car at the curb in front of an elegant brown Tudor, the largest property on this fairy tale–looking street. Shaky from lack of food and sleep after driving around all night long, I almost fell to my knees in relief when Justin told me to come to his house so he could help me look for Ava.

She's been missing for twelve hours.

I've never moved as quickly as I did when Julia called me while I was at the restaurant with Lila last night. Ava was supposed to check in with Julia at the end of every day to make sure she was staying on track, following the rules. By close to 8:00 p.m., Ava hadn't come back to the dorm. She also hadn't shown up to any of her classes yesterday or the rehearsal for the upcoming showcase next week.

She's not answering any calls or texts from me, Dave, Julia, even the police. After the call from Julia, I drove to the U-M police station, and they printed off my most recent photo of Ava, took all her information, and said they'd do a sweep of the campus and surrounding areas. I'm grateful for Suzanne's Law, which the police explained means they have to open an investigation immediately when a minor under twenty-one is reported missing. Maybe if the law had existed when Tyler disappeared, they might have found him.

But I can't think about Tyler now, especially in any way connected to Ava, or I'll completely lose it.

Through my windshield, I see the sky darken, and a crack of thunder makes me jump. I quickly make sure I haven't missed any calls or texts from the police. They assured me that they'll do everything they can, including notifying the National Crime Information Center. They said they've seen cases like this before with college kids, and it's likely Ava's taking a breather from the stress of school. Either her phone is turned off or she's blocking everyone, because all our calls go straight to voice mail.

I'm not sure Ava knows that Dave was hit by a car. I called and left her voice mails several times Sunday night, and when she didn't call back, I texted her, hoping that would prompt a response. Nothing. The last communication between us was the thumbs-up emoji she sent on Sunday afternoon. I've looked at it again and again, holding on to that like a hug from my daughter. The police are going to track her phone this morning, but they can only do that if her phone is actually on.

A mother always knows. Something is very wrong. I have to do anything I can to find her myself.

But I'm helpless and very alone. Dave is stuck in the hospital with a broken hip and elbow. Jenna and Natalie both offered to come to Ann Arbor and help me look, but I need to be proactive now. Before the sun even rose, I texted Justin that Ava is missing. He responded immediately, gave me his address, and told me to come at 9:30 a.m. I'm not exactly sure why I'm here—whether it's for me, so I can confront Justin about his lies and find out if he's been manipulating me, or because he really is the only person in Ann Arbor who can help me locate Ava.

I'm more than half an hour early, so here I sit in my car outside his home, canopied with maple trees. A gorgeous garden of vibrant perennials lines the front lawn. It's a beautiful property, yet I'm surprised by the hairs that instantly stand up on my arms when I look at his windows. Each one is covered in thick navy curtains. Though a lovely cobblestone walkway leads to an expansive front porch, there's something off about the house. It sags in sadness.

I feel the same. So, I decide to use my extra time to talk to the people in my life who matter the most. If Dave hadn't been hit by that car, I think we might have sat down to dinner together and finally told each other everything we've been holding back. I wanted to, and I think he did too.

When I saw him unconscious on the ground, it made me realize that I've always taken for granted that he'll be there. Maybe not with me but around for me to rely on if I need him. I could have lost him forever. There's no guarantee of tomorrow. We never know when our last conversation with someone might be.

After Dave's accident, I stayed awake all night in a chair beside his hospital bed, watching him sleep. I didn't even want to leave Monday morning, but Jenna and Natalie each came to take a shift with him so I could rest. None of them knew I also had to get ready for my dinner with Justin that never happened. That I was torn between my past with Dave and a possible future with another man.

When Dave finally opened his eyes after surgery, though they were clouded with morphine, his words were clear when he said, "Don't be afraid to live your best life."

I'm not sure if he meant with or without him, because he hasn't wanted to talk about anything but Ava since.

He's doing the only thing he can from his hospital bed: monitoring our debit and credit card transactions, but there's been no recent activity. Wherever Ava is, she could be using cash, but there are also no new posts on her TikTok and Instagram accounts, where she constantly updates her life.

I start by texting Jenna and Natalie, because though they won't be happy at all that I've reconnected with Justin, they are my best friends who love me unconditionally. I think I forgot that recently.

Eden: No news yet. But I wanted to let you both know where I am. Please don't ask questions now. I promise I'll explain everything after Ava is found.

Natalie: You're scaring me.

Jenna: Go ahead. I'm listening.

Shaking as I type, I do it.

Eden: I've been talking to Justin Ward online. Romantically. I'm at his house. I'll drop you a pin. I'm hoping he can help me find Ava. I'll be okay as long as I have her in my arms. The rest doesn't matter.

Natalie: What??? I'm trying not to react, but honey, Justin Ward? But yes, Ava is the most important. Please keep us posted.

Jenna: WTF, Eden. Justin Ward? I can be there in an hour. Please let me come.

Eden: It's okay but thank you. I promise to let you know if I need you. I have to go. Love you both.

One hurdle jumped, I drop them a pin. I'm sure the two of them are now talking about me. But I need to call Dave next. No matter what, Dave is Ava's father, and I've got to let him know where I am too. I also have questions for him.

"Anything?" Dave asks immediately when he picks up.

"No, but I found someone to help me look for her."

"Who?"

I feel too wretched to do anything but be straightforward, too cowardly to admit my own actions first.

"Before I tell you, I need to say a few things. Things I wanted to say when we were going to have dinner, and I couldn't do it at the hospital because you weren't up for it."

"Okay." Dave's tone is low and scared.

"This isn't the time to get into it, but we need to be a team and honest with each other. We have terrible communication." I open my mouth and just say it. "I know about the BDSM."

Dave sucks in a breath so sharp I feel it scrape my own throat. "I made a huge mistake. I got our marriage all wrong."

He starts to sob. I've only seen Dave cry once, when he held Ava for the first time. But those were happy tears. The ragged sound through the phone is torment.

"What did you do?" I whisper, my hand on the car door handle as though I can make a quick escape from a confession that I'm not sure I want to hear.

"It's what I didn't do," he says so softly and tenderly that I start to cry too. "I thought that I was supposed to be like my father. A provider and a protector. And I saw you as a version of my mother, a nurturing caregiver. Unconsciously, I wanted to re-create my parents' relationship, but I didn't understand what their relationship really was at all."

"Are you high on morphine?"

He huffs a laugh. "Yes, but I've never been more aware. I know that I've been such a shitty person to you since my dad died. I'm so sorry. I unraveled. I lost the most influential person in my life, the person I wanted to make the proudest. With him gone, I felt like I couldn't pretend anymore to be the righteous man everyone thought I was." He sighs. "For years, Eden, I've pushed down all these sexual thoughts and desires. Not just for BDSM. But freedom and excitement and exploration of a whole world I've never experienced."

I take my hand off the handle and press it to my throat, where another sob rises. "Because I wasn't enough for you?"

"No, it's the opposite. It's always been you. Only you. You're the star of my every fantasy, Eden. But you're also the mother of my child. I felt perverted and ashamed thinking of you as a sex object. So, I pushed you away."

"But I'm your wife, Dave. We've never even talked about sex. There's something wrong with that." And in this car where I risked everything to talk to Justin, there's something wrong with me too. But I have to let Dave get everything out because he might lose his nerve.

"I realize that now. Maybe too late." He blows out a breath. "Something happened when I went to visit my mom at the home recently. She thought I was my dad. And she asked me if I remembered the letter that I, meaning my father, left under her pillow the night I graduated high school."

"Oh, Dave. That must have been so hard."

"It was, but then it changed everything for me. I told her I remembered the letter, because I didn't know what else to say. The look on her face . . ." He makes a murmur of joy I'm not expecting at all. "It was like she was all lit up from the inside. She let out this girlish giggle I'd never heard from my mother. So, after I left the home, I went to my parents' house, because I'm still packing up their stuff. And in the box with all their photo albums, I found a stack of letters tied with a ribbon. Romantic letters from my parents to each other."

I try to picture opinionated Chuck, with his booming, stern voice, and docile Marsha, with her twinsets, penning love letters to one another. "I can't imagine that."

"Neither could I, and they're the kind of letters between parents a son shouldn't read. But I'm so glad I did, because I'd misunderstood what their marriage had really been like. Everything I knew about relationships, I learned from watching my parents. Everything I knew about being a man, I learned from my father. But I was watching as their son, and I confused how they parented me with how they loved each other. Just because they weren't that physically affectionate or playful in front of me didn't mean they weren't living a whole separate life together behind closed doors. The things my father wrote to my mother were so open and emotional and . . . sexy." He stops.

"Keep talking, please."

"I'm trying to find the right words." He clears his throat. "When I read the letters, all the shame that I've carried fell away. I saw my father in a new light. He had desires, too, and never stopped himself from telling my mother about them. My parents actually had the marriage I've wanted with you but was so afraid to tell you I wanted. I didn't even try. I should have tried."

"Why didn't you, though? How could you leave me? I don't understand what you were looking for if I'm the one you wanted." I ask this all in a rush to get out everything I've longed to know for months.

"Because I never wanted to see your disappointment and shame in me. Or God, Ava. I was actually at Trisk, that club, the same night Adam Sumner was. It was supposed to be a totally confidential, private event. I wasn't there to be with anyone. I just wanted to see what it was all about. I was grasping for any understanding or a way to stop myself from wanting a different sex life than we had. I was still inside when the photographers got there and had to sneak out the back so I wouldn't be caught on camera. I was terrified." He chokes up again. "I imagined you seeing me online, or Ava's friends posting it on her social media. My employees and clients seeing me in the news. I could have blown up your lives and mine. I needed to let you go. I waited to ask you for a divorce until Ava was in college so I wouldn't ruin that experience for her." His voice cracks with so much pain. "But I ruined us."

It's too much to take in. I look again at Justin's house, where everything seems dark and shut tightly. "Thank you for being so honest with me. I know how hard that was for you. I need time to process this, but our issues aren't all on you, Dave." My heart is racing. I exhale, wishing I could expel my past mistakes as easily as my breath. "I've been having a sexual and emotional online relationship with Justin Ward. He lives in Ann Arbor, and I texted him to help me find Ava. I'm in front of his house right now."

There's complete silence.

"Dave?" I ask gently.

"That guy? Why?" His voice is gruff.

"I've been so lonely," I say honestly. "He's been there for me recently in ways you haven't for months. I've learned a lot about myself through talking to him, and it's time *I* figure out exactly what I want."

While I'm not sure how to do that, after talking to Dave, I realize that it's possible I've been so consumed by Justin's words because it's what I've yearned to hear from Dave.

He makes a sound of discomfort. "This is a painful conversation."

"It's real, and it's about time that we had that."

"But that guy, Eden"—he pauses—"didn't care about you."

"I didn't think you did either until just now."

Dave lets out a long, deep sigh. "It should be me there with you. I'm so sorry I can't be."

I shake my head even though he can't see it. "That's not your fault, and we'll talk more about us once I find Ava, because I am going to find her." I'm grasping, too, when I continue. "Justin might also be able to help me with that. He knows Ann Arbor better than I do. I'm not thinking straight. I'm exhausted. Maybe he can drive me around to all the places a musician would stay out all night. And I don't want to be alone right now."

"Do you think Ava played somewhere or went to hear music and . . . what?"

My shoulders tense in frustration. "Met a girl and went back to her place? Got drunk and passed out in an alley? I don't know. But Justin used to play at bars and cafés all the time. I don't even know where live music is around here anymore. He might."

"Google can do the same thing. Do you love him, Eden?"

The anguish in his question hurts me, but hiding how I really feel will cause more damage. "I don't know right now, Dave. I was infatuated with him in college. But I fell in love with and married you. I have a lot to work out."

He's quiet, then says, "Okay. Whatever you have to do to find Ava and for yourself." But he sounds skeptical. "Just be careful, and keep your phone close, please."

"I'll keep you posted."

I hang up and drop him a pin too. I'm still fifteen minutes early, but I can't wait any longer. I exit my car right as the sky suddenly splits open and lightning flashes. Rain pelts me as I hurry up the porch steps and cross to the thick oak front door. I don't really know what I'm hoping to accomplish by coming here, but I've been in the dark about my own life for too long. I tap my knuckles on the wood.

I hear the click of the lock turning. The door creaks open.

I step backward, stupefied.

The woman in front of me, in a black long-sleeved shirt and black sweatpants, places her body in the center of the frame.

I take in her slim build, blanched face, brown hair sticking out wildly from her scalp as though she's been pulling at it. Instead of the bright-blue eyes I saw just last night, they're gray. As understanding reaches my scrambled brain, I'm slammed with a shock so powerful it steals my voice. She's been wearing colored contacts every time I've seen her.

Pushing my wet hair from my face, all I can murmur is "Lila?" as I raise a trembling hand to my throat. "What—I don't understand. Why are you here?"

Her hand flies to her neck. She's wearing a diamond band I've never seen on her ring finger before. I glance above her head at the wall, where to the left a picture hangs. A wedding photo of a gorgeous couple; the blonde bride is resting her head on her husband's shoulder. I falter, reaching for the doorframe for support.

It's Justin and my new friend, Lila Cavanaugh.

"You shouldn't be here," Justin's wife says.

Then she pulls me inside the house and shuts the door behind me.

CHAPTER SEVENTEEN

OLIVIA

Olivia's chest squeezes so painfully it's hard to breathe. Eden is inside the house. Justin is still in the shower. She waits for Alistair to tell her what to do, but all she hears are her own jumbled, frightened thoughts.

She couldn't leave Eden on the doorstep. She looked like she was about to pass out. Now in the entryway, Eden still seems off balance, her eyes ping-ponging between Olivia and the wedding photo on the wall. All the color has leached from her face. Her hair drips rainwater onto the wood. Olivia has so much more to worry about than the puddle seeping into the floorboards, but she can't look away from it.

She's also scared to face Eden as herself with Justin right upstairs. Olivia knew it was only a matter of time before Eden came to the house. The GPS app that she installed on her phone after she'd dropped the tracker into Eden's purse, trustingly left on the kitchen island at her Lakeside listing, clocked Eden parked at the curb for over fifteen minutes. She should have met Eden outside, come up with some plausible explanation why Lila Cavanaugh is really Olivia Ward, Justin's wife, and not a childless divorced woman with good advice and all the freedom to do as she pleases.

Olivia cocks an ear toward the stairs behind her to make sure the shower is still running. She has maybe two minutes to get Eden out of here before Justin sees her. He wasn't supposed to be home.

She wanted it to be just her and Eden, two women joining forces against an abusive narcissist. Now they're both in danger if Justin finds them together—if he finds out how much Olivia has been plotting behind his back.

She gets close enough to Eden that she can see her pulse jump in her neck. "I can explain later. But you need to leave right now."

Eden's eyes are ringed with circles so black it's like she hasn't slept in days. Eden trusts Lila, and if Olivia can get into character, they'll be safe. But with Justin steps away, Olivia is not equipped to slip on the facade, and she doesn't have enough time to get Eden on her side before Justin comes out of the bathroom. Alistair hasn't said a word to her since Eden walked into the house. All she can do is beg.

"Please. There's so much you don't know about him. Go."

"I don't understand. Who are you really?" Tears pool in the corners of Eden's wide brown eyes. Her body is shaking. She leans against the wall by the door, as though she needs it to hold her up. "Why did you lie to me?"

"So you would help me leave him."

"Leave him? *He* wants to leave. He told me that."

Olivia shakes her head. "He's a liar and a con. You got away once, Eden. Go before we both get hurt. I promise I'll tell you everything later."

Eden opens her mouth, squeaks something unintelligible, then closes it. She looks at the door and back to Olivia. "Olivia? That's your real name?" She speaks carefully, tensing, as though she's afraid of what Olivia might do to her, the way everyone used to speak with Alistair, even though he'd never have hurt anyone unless he had to. He could always sense when Olivia was in danger.

When she and Justin walked down the hallway at Ridgestone, the last time Olivia saw her brother, she looked once over her shoulder.

Alistair mouthed, "It will be okay."

He knew she was suffering. He couldn't help her escape, but he could still comfort her. Now, though, he won't even talk to her.

When Olivia doesn't respond, Eden says, "I don't know what game you're playing or what's going on between you and Justin. But he asked me to come here. He offered to help me find my daughter, who's been missing for twelve hours now. Is he home?"

"I told you to come here," Olivia whispers.

Eden shakes her head. "No, he did." Her face softens. "Look, you know I've had trouble dealing with my separation. I understand how hard it is. I'm not trying to come between you and Justin. All I want right now is to talk to him and find my daughter." Eden reaches into her purse.

Olivia waits a second for Alistair to guide her next move, but when he doesn't, she yanks the purse from Eden's shoulder, tossing it across the room. It lands at the bottom of the stairs. She doesn't want Eden to access her phone and alert anyone about Olivia's strange behavior. That would definitely be the end for her.

"Hey! I just wanted to see if anyone has texted or called about Ava. There are a lot of people looking for her, including the police."

At the mention of the police, tiny needles of panic spread through Olivia's body. When Eden makes a move, Olivia—bigger and stronger—impedes her, no matter which way Eden turns.

The steady flow of the rain outside quiets for a moment, and the running shower sounds louder than any other noise in the old house.

Eden stands still. "Is Justin here?" she asks firmly.

Olivia nods. "He can't see you here. I'm trying to protect you."

"He's my friend. This is between me and him." She holds up her hands. "I don't know what he's told you about me, but I've known him for a long time. We were close in college."

At this, a strangled laugh bursts from Olivia's mouth. "I know exactly who you are, Eden. I was at that party too."

Eden's eyebrows knit together, as though she's trying to make the pieces fit. "I don't understand. Is all of this about a party twenty years ago?"

"There's so much you don't understand." Olivia grabs her arm. "Justin did something to you that night. I've been trying to tell you since your open house."

Eden gapes at Olivia's hand on her arm; fire flashes in her eyes. "Oh my God, you've been stalking me. The shop in Grosse Pointe, the restaurant you recommended . . . not coincidences." She pulls her arm from Olivia. "Justin was telling me the truth. There's something wrong with you."

The shower turns off.

"Justin!" Eden yells out.

The bathroom door opens. Justin comes out in only a white towel wrapped around his waist and takes one step down the stairs to lean over the dark wood railing above them. He grins. "We have company?"

Olivia is sure only she can hear the undertone of menace, because Eden walks straight to the bottom of the stairs. Olivia doesn't know what to do other than follow and stand beside her, like a shield, for both of their protection, even though the other woman has no clue whom she's really facing. She puts a foot on one of the straps of Eden's purse to prevent her from picking it up.

But Eden no longer seems worried about her purse. She calls up, "Justin, it's me. Eden," in a voice that to Olivia sounds hopeful, hungry, and relieved all at once.

And with those words, Olivia knows that no matter how horrific any of her previous days have been, this will be rock bottom. There is nothing she can say or do, no way to hide all the secrets she and Justin have been keeping and all the ones she's carefully hidden from him.

Justin casually brushes his hair with his fingers. "Hi, Eden. Let me just throw on some clothes." He laughs as though embarrassed to be in nothing but a towel, when he knows full well that his muscular chest and broad shoulders make most women light headed. "And I'll come down."

And he's back so fast, in gray sweatpants, pulling a black T-shirt over his head, his left bicep bulging with his tattoo of a mythical griffin. Oh, how Olivia's father hated tattoos, but he loved that his son-in-law inked one on his body in honor of him. He even proudly showed it off to anyone he'd introduce Justin to. But Olivia knew that Justin had only gotten that specific creature because it symbolized possession and he wanted her to see it every time his hands came near her body.

Her husband begins his descent, his steps solid. But to Olivia, everything is moving in slow motion. She wishes she could sprint right out the front door. But she can't leave Eden all alone with Justin. As Justin hits the floor, inches now from her and Eden, a roar in her head starts up—it's not Alistair's voice; it's like sand is filling her skull—and she claps her hands over her ears to muffle it.

Still, she clearly hears Eden say to Justin, "I didn't know your ex-wife would be here. I don't want to cause any issues. And I'm sorry I questioned you so much, because you were right that she's unstable. She's been stalking me, Justin. Following me everywhere I go."

He squints and slowly moves his eyes to Olivia, drilling them into her. His shoulder twitches. Olivia knows what that means: he's working hard to keep his cool. She doesn't want to look at Eden. She's too scared.

Then like the flick of a switch, Justin smiles and separates the women by taking Olivia's hand and drawing her close to him so they're in front of Eden. Olivia has to remove her foot from the strap of Eden's purse. Eden furrows her brow and looks down at the purse, then up at their clasped hands, which might seem affectionate, but Olivia knows Justin is keeping her in place.

"I'm sorry, Eden. I don't know what's going on here." He rubs his stubbled jaw and presses his thumb hard into Olivia's palm. But she doesn't say a word.

"Did you text me to come here?" Eden asks. "To help me find Ava?"

Olivia wishes the trapdoor would suck her down to the basement, away from this mess she's created.

In a flash, Justin nods. Olivia knows he's not looking out for her. He's buying time to figure out what she's done and how to keep himself out of it.

"Please, can we talk privately for a minute?" Eden sways.

Immediately, Justin releases Olivia and is at Eden's side, holding on to her. "Absolutely. Why don't we sit down on the couch, okay?"

"I need my purse." She points to it on the floor.

"Of course." Justin picks up the black bag and hands it to her. "My wife clearly isn't well, and I don't want this to get out of hand."

Olivia bristles, but he's right: she's not well right now. She has to follow Justin's lead.

Eden rummages in her purse. "Where's my phone?"

Olivia says, "I don't know." And it's the truth.

Eden closes her eyes for a second, a cry of lament releasing. "I just had it outside! Did I leave it in my car?" She's looking at Justin, but she's really asking herself. Again, she plunges her hand inside her bag, frantically searching. Then she takes something out and opens her palm to look at it.

There's a tiny square black tile in Eden's hand. "What the hell is this?"

Oh no.

Justin looks at it. "I'm not sure. May I?" he asks, his fingers brushing Eden's palm to take the tile, letting them linger on her skin for a moment.

He's leaning into the narrative, using seduction, the best weapon in his arsenal, but doing it right in front of Olivia makes her feel so small and insignificant.

He pockets the black square and gestures to the living room. "Why don't you rest for a moment, and I'll bring you a glass of water." He switches his attention to Olivia. "Come with me?"

Before Eden can reply, Justin leads Olivia to the kitchen and into the pantry. He closes the door behind them. With both of them in here, Justin's imposing size taking up so much space in her safe place, Olivia shrinks into herself.

"What. Have. You. Done?" he says quietly through gritted teeth, laying his hands on her shoulders and pressing her against the back wall between the shelves.

The tremor starts in Olivia's legs, quickly moving up her body until she's shaking so hard that her teeth chatter. Justin closes in on her, his chest now hard and unyielding against hers, and she reaches for the tiger eye pendant in her pocket. He clamps his hand on her wrist.

"Touch that stone, and I'll kill you." His nails dig into her delicate bones so hard she's afraid he's going to break them.

But she doesn't cry out, because she knows that's what he wants. All she wants is for Alistair to talk to her. But he's completely silent. And she understands that the fantasy she's created of his voice in her head—having a friend, someone to help her—has vanished, because she's made too many mistakes and lied too many times. Her brother is dead. She'll never get away from Justin.

"Why does that woman think I texted her to come over?"

Olivia can't help the gasp that releases from her mouth. "Don't you know who she is?"

"Should I?"

"That's Eden Hoffman."

"Eden. My *tutor* from college?" Justin's jaw drops, and he wraps his fingers around her arm. "How dumb are you?"

Olivia has no fight left in her. "I know you sleep with other women." She looks up at him to see if his expression registers regret, remorse, anything, but she only gets a cold, blank stare. "I also know that Eden's the one you wanted to be with at the party instead of me."

"The party? What are you even talking about? What did you do, Olivia?" he whispers, but she's so frightened that it sounds like a yell.

There's no more hiding. "My phone. It's all on there."

Justin lets go of her and holds out his hand. She takes her phone from her pocket, gives it to him, and sinks to the black-and-white tiles, huddling in a ball with her head between her knees. She wishes for the yellow wool blanket that used to be tucked under the shelf so she can wrap it around her freezing body. She can still smell the mustiness of it and taste the bittersweet chocolate she and Alistair would share in here. But it's only her and Justin. She has to face the consequences of her actions all alone.

She can't bear to look at Justin's face. Nothing she says will make him empathize or sympathize. He's not made for that level of humanity.

"I should have been keeping a closer eye on you. You changed your password from our anniversary."

I did so much more than that, Olivia thinks. Then she recites her new password—*eighteen nine forty-two*—the day, month, and age Alistair was when he died.

She hears Justin's breathing speed up.

"Tell me right now what I need to look at."

"Go to the hidden apps."

She stares at the floor while he scrolls through her messages and calls and all the texts that she scheduled to send whenever she was with Eden.

"You're lucky that woman is here." Justin crouches in front of Olivia and flips the screen so she can read what's written there.

I want to hear you scream my name.

Effortlessly, he grabs her by the armpits, hauls her up, then jams his fingers into the hollow at the base of her throat. "You hacked my Facebook page?" Justin slides his other hand up the back of her neck and tugs at the baby hairs.

Olivia coughs, struggling to breathe. Justin lifts his fingers a tiny bit so she can speak.

"You never use it. But you never turned off the push notifications, so when Eden sent you a friend request Friday night, I saw it on your phone. You left it on the coffee table like you always do."

His hand pulls at her hair again.

Olivia winces at every yank, but she keeps talking, because at least for now it will stop him from hurting her even worse. "You use the same password for everything, so I changed it. Then I answered her as you." The tears flow freely.

His face has an expression of surprise, maybe even amusement. He looks down at her phone again. "And you took a screenshot of this selfie of me from my phone, obviously. And the voice-changing app? So, you didn't just message, but you talked to her on the fucking phone?"

"Yes," Olivia says. "I practiced with the voice changer until I had your tone and cadence, and I played with the different male voices until I found one that sounds the most like yours."

Justin gapes at her. "Why?"

She can't do anything but tell him the truth. There's no escape. "Because I wanted to find out if she remembered what you did to her at the party. What Tyler knew."

When Justin came out onto the balcony that night and saw Olivia and Tyler both leaning against the railing, he ran his eyes over Olivia's face. Then he came closer as though to hug her.

She held him back and jutted her chin at the bathroom window. "Your other girlfriend is puking her guts out in there."

Justin laughed. "Oh, that's where she ended up? Nah, Eden's not my other girlfriend. Maybe she's interested, but I very clearly told her I'm not. I love *you*."

Tyler scoffed. "You say that to all the girls you mess with, I'm sure."

Justin clapped a hand on Tyler's shoulder. "What's your problem, man? You've never liked me since freshman year in high school. What have I ever done to you? Our moms are friends. We're like brothers."

Olivia saw the hesitation in Tyler's eyes. But then he flung off Justin's arm. "And since high school, I've watched you play with girl after girl. You put on a good act. But I see right through you."

"Okay, whatever. I think you're drunk. Let's hash this out tomorrow, all right?" Justin held out his hand. "Olivia, let's go."

She should have taken Justin's hand and walked away with him. Instead, she stayed next to Tyler.

"Eden's not a big drinker. I've never seen her get this wasted," Tyler said.

Now in the pantry, it's just Olivia and Justin, and he cocks his head. "Wait. You don't know what I did to Eden?" He starts laughing and doesn't stop until water springs to his eyes, the only time Olivia has ever seen tears from him. He wipes his eyes. "I only married you because I thought you knew. You idiot, I roofied her. There's no way she'll ever remember anything after she had that drink." Then his hand circles her neck. "What were you planning on doing with that information?"

Olivia shakes her head. She can't say the words.

His face goes stony. "You will never get away from me, if that's what you want. If you think what happened to Alistair was bad, it's nothing compared to what I'll do to you. I was just tired of spending my money on him for no reason. But you've really made me angry."

More attuned to the sound of footsteps than Justin, because she's spent her life listening to learn how close in proximity both her father and husband are to her, Olivia hears the click of heels before he does. She waits until they tap the kitchen tiles, getting louder and nearer, until a shadow passes the pantry. Justin's back is turned away from the door, so he couldn't have seen it.

Alistair's name in Justin's mouth and the fact that she's been chained to this monster for no reason at all make every blood cell in her body boil with rage. She can't physically attack Justin, but she has one chance to make him pay.

"I promise you. Eden doesn't know that Tyler is in the house."

Justin definitely hears the squall of shock outside the pantry, because his head whips around.

Run and help me, Olivia begs Eden in her mind.

There's a loud thud.

Justin pushes away from Olivia and peers through the white slats. She moves from the wall and looks too.

Eden is on the floor. She's unconscious.

Olivia's husband says, "Well, now she knows. You have to get rid of her."

CHAPTER EIGHTEEN

EDEN

Every bone in my body screams with excruciating pain. My eyes are heavy and gritty, but when I reach to rub them, I can't move my hands. Searing heat burns into my wrists. I pull with all my strength, but a rough material abrades my skin until I'm sure I'm bleeding. Blinking over and over, I finally adjust to the darkness. And panic shoots up to my throat, cutting off my air supply.

I'm lying on my side on a cold concrete floor. My wrists are bound with rope, tied to a metal pipe that juts out of the floor and connects to the ceiling maybe seven feet above me. Frantically, I move my head around the room. Brick walls, a rickety wooden ladder reaching from the bottom to a trapdoor in the ceiling. A small window to the right of me is covered in a navy curtain, and I hear rain pound the glass.

"Help!" I scream until my throat is raw, violently shivering, trying not to hyperventilate or pass out again.

Black dots obscure my vision. I'm underground in this old Tudor, which could have been built in the nineteenth century. No neighbors will hear me scream.

Breathing in and out as slowly as I can to control my paralyzing fear, I sweep my eyes across every corner of this dank cave as if I were showing it to potential buyers. It's the best way for me to try to find an escape route.

It's a large space, musty, possibly filled with mold, and the walls appear to be a dilapidated brown brick. There are some cardboard boxes shoved to the end farthest from me. I have to wonder why it's such a horror show down here, why Justin and Olivia's whole house appears to be untouched by even the minimum of updates. As gorgeous as it looks on the outside, the inside is dark, unwelcoming, and claustrophobic.

I have to get out of here. My teeth clack together as I tug and tug at the rope, but I'm only rattling the pipe. Where is Justin? Has Olivia hurt him? Why didn't he tell me that talking to me would jeopardize my life? His wife isn't merely unpredictable. She's a psychopath who's kidnapped me. I have no way of knowing if anyone has found Ava. I can't look for her. Self-pity and shame flood me. I did this to myself. I'm an insecure, lonely woman who might never see my family again.

My clothes and hair are still damp from the rain, and weak with hunger and exhaustion, I can't stop shaking. But for the brief moments that I manage to stay still, I hear a hum, like something is plugged in and running. It could be from the furnace room to the far left, but it sounds closer.

I hold my breath to find the source of the noise, and my gaze slowly travels around again. I stop on a large white chest freezer, elevated on bricks, pushed against the wall next to the furnace area. Nothing that will help me get away from Olivia.

I don't know why she wants to hurt me so much, though my mind keeps wandering to the Sigma Chi party. Was she dating Justin when he kissed me? I have no idea, but if that's the case, she should be angry with him, not me. Yet thinking about seeing the two of them together, I realize she didn't seem like a furious wife; she looked terrified. Of what? Her husband?

I'm afraid of her. Terror grips me in a stranglehold as it occurs to me that Olivia might have stalked Ava too. I listen again, in case there's any chance she's down here with me. That Olivia has gotten to her, kept my daughter here since last night while she was having dinner with me in Grosse Pointe. Nothing makes sense.

"Ava!" I cry, but it comes out a strangled snivel.

No moan, scream—nothing at all comes back to me but my own voice echoing off the walls and the faint buzz of the freezer.

"Ava!" I try again until the force of my roar feels like it's peeling off layers of my throat. "Someone, help me!"

I hope that my mind is playing tricks on me. That Ava's out there somewhere safer than here. I don't know if Olivia plans to just keep me down here or kill me.

Something living crawls up my leg, and I jerk to get it off me. I left my jacket in the car. In only my silky sleeveless top and my dress pants from last night, I have nothing to insulate my joints from knocking painfully against the concrete floor.

"Justin!" I yell again as loudly as I can, hoping he's safe.

I hear two sets of footsteps, one heavy, one light, walk above me. Then a sound of something scraping, wood against wood. Light beams down onto me from a flashlight. My head is pounding, but I can't close my eyes against the glare. I need to see who's coming for me.

A boot lands on the first rung of the rickety wooden ladder. Horror almost paralyzes me, but it's Justin. My relief is so immense that it comes out in heaving sobs that rack my body.

"Help me. Please. I'm over here," I whisper roughly, desperate for water. My throat's on fire.

As Justin gets closer to me, though, my pulse speeds up, and I can't pinpoint why. And the moment he sits down in front of me, instead of looking shocked that I'm tied to the metal pipe, a prisoner in his basement, he shakes his head ruefully and pats my leg.

"Eden Hoffman. I never thought I'd see you again."

Woozy, I don't understand. He clicks his tongue and places the flashlight on the floor so the light beams around us. The shadows it creates on his face are monstrous. I look into his eyes, expecting warmth or alarm at what his wife has done. But they're empty.

He turns off the flashlight. The room plunges back into darkness, so when his fingers squeeze my shoulder, I'm not expecting it. I shriek, jerking away from him. "You're very jumpy, Eden. Stay calm, okay?"

I use my legs to scoot closer to the pipe, farther from him. "You have to call the police."

He ignores that and says, "So, you still want me after all these years, huh?"

I don't understand his playful tone. "Can you please untie me?"

"No can do. I've just seen our messages to each other."

It takes a moment for what he's said to reach my brain. *I've just seen our messages to each other.*

Icy dread makes me rigid. I can't speak. I can't move. And at the same time, I have total clarity. It was Olivia I was talking to the whole time.

It was all a lie.

More than anything, I don't want to cry in front of this man who doesn't know me, doesn't love me, but I'm helpless as I curl in a ball on the concrete floor and cry into my arms, which are hanging uselessly from the pipe. I've risked my job, safety, a potential reconciliation with Dave, and most importantly, my daughter, for nothing.

The Justin in our messages, the person I bared my soul and opened my heart to, doesn't exist. Of course he doesn't. How could I be so blind? The emotional, romantic, attentive man I thought I was talking to is a woman. I should have known, because the real Justin toyed with me in college, didn't give a damn about me when I was sick, like Dave said, and ghosted me without a second thought. I ignored every red flag because I wanted to be desired so much.

I'm too crushed to feel the full weight of my fear. I could have, should have stopped it the moment my gut told me something was off with Justin. I should have told Natalie and Jenna about him before today, because they might have been able to wake me up from my fever dream. I'm ashamed at my stupidity.

"None of it was real." The sexting, the phone sex, the intimate exchanges—the ruthlessness and humiliation scald my insides and burn a path up my throat.

I lean over and vomit all over the floor. I've had nothing to eat or drink in so long that it's almost all water. Justin flicks the flashlight back on and looks at me with disgust.

"You definitely puke a lot. I remember that about you. I'll have Olivia clean it up."

"Why would Olivia do this to me? What does she want from me?"

Justin reaches out and fingers a strand of my hair. Then he turns the flashlight on and off repeatedly, disorienting me so I can't see where his hand will go next. It lands on my thigh. "My wife lives in a fantasy world, like her brother did. You can't take anything she says seriously."

I don't believe that Olivia hasn't been trying to tell me something, because she said it herself when I showed up today. She lured me here, engaged me in an intimate relationship, pretended to be my friend. There's something specific she wants from me. All I want is to get out of here.

"My husband knows I'm at your house. He'll call the police if he doesn't hear from me." This isn't quite true, because Dave thinks I'm out with Justin looking for Ava. He won't worry about me for at least a few hours.

And when Justin turns on the flashlight again, I know I've made a mistake. He's sneering at me.

"Husband? You're a whore like my wife. But you were always smarter." He takes my phone out of the pocket of his sweatpants. "Password, please."

I tell him, because I have no choice. My password is Ava's birthday, and I think about my perfectly imperfect daughter, maybe hungry, cold, afraid. I will not think anything worse than that or I will give up right here.

He taps on my phone, my only link to the beautiful life I'd do anything to return to.

I can't see what he's typing, but a moment later he flashes me a satisfied smile. "Dave says he's glad I wasn't home and agrees that you should definitely find a hotel and sleep for a bit. He's sorry for doubting me, but something about me always made him uncomfortable." He snorts. "That's not very nice." Then he reads from the screen in a monotone. "Oh, he also says: 'I'm so relieved we finally talked. I can't wait to see you.'" He sucks his teeth. "Don't think that's going to happen."

I want Dave with an ache that's stronger than my physical agony. I hold on to that. "Let me see the texts."

Justin's hand clamps my leg tightly. "You don't trust me? We were friends, Eden."

I try to reconcile the boy I loved so long ago with this person I don't know in front of me. I'm clearly not going anywhere for a while, if ever. I don't think asking questions will save me, but they might answer why I'm down in this basement at all. "You never gave a shit about me, so why did you invite me to the party and kiss me?"

He turns off the flashlight again, plunging me back into darkness. "You were such a prude. I liked it, though." I hear him chuckle. "I knew you wanted to fuck me but were too scared. It was fun. Virgins always are. And you never forget your first. But we never got there, did we?" Then he splays his hand between my legs. "I'm a bit turned on from those messages. My wife is a filthy bitch. Are you?"

I gag. I've been consumed by fantasies of his hands on my skin; now every part of me tenses against him being anywhere near me. Mustering all the strength I have left in me, thinking about Ava and Dave, I wrap my hands around the pipe so I can sit up. I will not give Justin the satisfaction of seeing me on the ground like an animal. It clears my head enough to quickly run through the conversations I thought I was having with him.

Maybe I did something to hurt you.

My ex, Olivia . . . I don't love her. I'm not sure she knows what love is.

My former wife is a bit unpredictable. I don't have the stability yet to start over on my own. And she can't leave the house either.

I think Olivia was talking about Justin, not herself. She's afraid of him, and she can't leave. And she told me that she's been trying to tell me something about Justin since we met at my open house. Justin did something to me at that party.

Without another word, he ascends the ladder, scraping the trapdoor closed behind him.

With Justin gone, the hum of the freezer becomes louder, a steady buzz that makes every hair rise on my body. I don't think I'm the only one who Justin hurt at the party, because suddenly the words I heard behind the pantry door, right before I passed out on the kitchen floor, come rushing back to me horrifyingly clearly: *Eden doesn't know that Tyler is in the house.*

Slowly, I turn and look at the freezer. I don't think I'm alone down here.

I open my mouth. And I scream and scream and scream.

CHAPTER NINETEEN

OLIVIA

Eden's screams split Olivia's head open. Then the banging starts. It's Eden, hammering on the pipe with what sound like her fists and feet.

On the living room floor, Olivia rocks back and forth. She never wanted anyone else to die. But what other choice does she have? If she runs out the front door right now and goes to the police, while Justin is getting dressed for his meeting with Larry—which he told her he's still attending—they'll both be arrested.

She'd rot in jail, but Justin would probably go free. Even if Olivia tells the police everything about the night of the Sigma Chi party, Justin has a stronger alibi. She's the one who cried in the upstairs hallway, went with Tyler onto his balcony for a smoke, and left the cigarette behind. Justin's band will back him up. She has no one.

Now that she's faced with imprisonment and death, not only the threat of them, every reason she had for impersonating Justin and having an online relationship with Eden seems as worthless as she is. Being Justin's slave was far better than having a woman tied up in their basement, another body in the house. Another innocent victim. Olivia didn't want her relationship with Eden to end like this. She didn't want it to end at all. She can't protect the only friend she has.

Alistair must hate her. That's why he won't speak to her anymore. Olivia's thumb is chafed and raw from rubbing the tiger eye pendant. She's so cold and ashamed.

Justin walks into the room. He doesn't even look in her direction before he plucks the black urn with Alistair's ashes from the mantel and hurls it to the floor.

Olivia can only watch in shock as the ceramic shatters and a gray cloud of her brother's remains clogs the air, some of the ashes landing on her clothes. She can taste the dust in her mouth.

"Clean that up. Clean all of this up!" he yells.

Olivia doesn't move. Every assault, insult, and act of terror against her doesn't hurt as much as this cruelty. But a small sense of relief flows through her. She still has the last of Alistair in her pocket.

Justin walks closer to her, mashing his steel-toed boot into the ashes, an inch from her fingers. Right now, he can smash her bones, rip out her throat, slam his foot into her face. She wants the pain. She deserves it. He crouches so he's in her face. He leans in and drags his thumb along her lips. "You're as dead as your brother if you don't take care of this. Stand up," he commands.

Following her husband's orders, she rises unsteadily, leaning into him. He holds her only to stop her from crumpling to the floor. Still, his arm supporting her—the sheer size and strength of him against her body—undoes her, and she presses her face to Justin's chest.

"I only wanted you to love me," she whispers into his soft T-shirt.

"Well, all I want right now is for that woman to shut up. We should have duct-taped her mouth, at least. The neighbors might hear. Do that when you go down." Justin checks his phone, types something, then makes an odd face Olivia can't define. "Her car is right outside our house. We can't keep her here. Not another missing person. You'll either have to drive it into the lake with her in it and make it look like an accident, or we burn the house down."

Imagining the house that she's been shackled to since she was a little girl exploding with flames and the bones in the basement turning to cinders sounds like heaven.

"I'll take care of it," Olivia vows. "I'll take care of you. Please forgive me."

Justin ignores her. "Find out if she told anyone about her sexting." He laughs. "I still can't believe you have such a dirty mouth. You really are disgusting."

Olivia hears a phone buzz in his sweatpants pocket. "Is that Eden's phone?"

He shrugs. "Maybe. I snagged hers when I picked up the purse, so I have all the phones now. You've gotten us into a mess. When this is over, we're going to have a good, long talk about privacy and following the rules." He gives her an appraising look. "This is why you have no friends. You can't be trusted."

Nodding slowly, Olivia holds back the tears threatening to spill. For a very short time, she had a friend.

His voice is eerily calm when he says, "I'll postpone my meeting until tomorrow. I can't meet Larry when I'm upset. Fix this."

He stomps upstairs, and moments later, the aggressive, rage-fueled drum beat of "Helter Skelter" by Mötley Crüe fills the house. That propels Olivia to move. That song is what he played in his van on the way to her father's house after the frat party, with Tyler in the back.

CHAPTER TWENTY

EDEN

The voices upstairs have stopped, but the walls shake with a heavy metal song. I stare at the freezer, hoping with everything in me that I'm wrong. That Tyler's not inside, frozen and dead. That I won't end up next to him, and my family and friends will never know what happened to me, why and how I disappeared. Because of an entire relationship that never existed.

My screaming and banging on the pipe have stripped me of any energy I had left. Blood drips down my wrists. I'm broken.

The trapdoor scrapes open again.

Olivia steps down, her brown hair, once blonde like mine, skims her shoulders, and she grips the ladder with one hand, pulling the door closed with the other.

At the bottom, in her bare feet, she moves her eyes around the room. I hear a tinny sound. The room floods with a dim orange light. She's pulled the silver chain hanging from a bulb in the center of the room.

Before I can get a closer look at what may become my grave, Olivia's by my side.

She drops to her knees, reaches out a hand as if to touch me, then pulls it back. "I never wanted it to be like this," she says, furiously wiping her eyes with her fists like a small child.

"Then why? Why pretend to be my friend? Why pretend to be Justin and involve me in your sick games?" I moan when a spasm of pain from fear and nausea rocks my stomach.

She sighs deeply, like she's held in the breath for a long time. "You don't know what it's like to be married to someone, to live with someone who hates you." She moves so she can sit cross-legged. "Your spouse, I mean. I know you and Ava have your issues."

At this, I recoil. "Did you stalk my daughter too? Where is she?"

"She puts too much information on social media. But I'd never have hurt her. Truly Eden, I don't know where she is."

A dark laugh escapes my chapped lips. "I don't believe anything you say. What do you want from me, Olivia? Or do I call you Lila?"

She hangs her head, like she doesn't have the strength to support its weight any longer. "I wish I were really Lila." Sitting back, she pulls her knees to her chest and takes something from her pocket.

I lurch, scared she has a weapon. But it's a gold-and-brown pendant that she rubs her thumb across.

"My brother died four weeks ago. He was my best friend. My only friend, really, until you came along."

"We are *not* friends." I say it curtly, but even after how much she's done to hurt me, I sense a very lost, damaged woman in front of me. I lower my voice. "Why catfish me? What is it you're looking for from me?"

"When I saw your friend request, I thought it was a sign from my brother that I deserved to live. While you and I were talking, he started talking to me. In here." She taps her head, then hands me the pendant. "It contains some of his ashes. All I have left of him now."

I take it from her, because it might bond us even more, which could be my way out of here. The stone is cool in my hand, oddly soothing. "Why did you think you didn't deserve to live?"

She glances up at the beams on the ceiling. "I've done awful things to save myself. I thought if we could save each other then maybe I'd be worth something."

I snort, because that's ludicrous. "You saved me by catfishing and stalking me, engaging me in a sexual relationship? You humiliated me."

"That wasn't what I wanted."

I stare at her. "Were you planning on telling me you catfished me?"

"No," she says in a very quiet voice. "I wanted you to understand how awful Justin can be. I pretended to be him so you'd see the kind of horrible, dangerous man he is. And how hard it is to get away from him. I don't want to be a bad person, Eden." Olivia chews on a fingernail.

"What exactly did you do so I'd see that, Olivia?" I ask carefully, my mind skimming through all the frightening incidents in my life these past few days, the worst of which was Dave getting hit by a car.

Now she does touch my leg. "I never meant to hurt Dave that bad. I just wanted to prove to you that Justin could hurt you. Did hurt you. So you'd believe me."

"You actually tried to run over my husband?" I shake my leg to get her hand off me.

She stops touching me. "Ex-husband." She sighs. "I'm so sorry."

"You abused me the way Justin abuses you. You used sex to manipulate me."

Her palm slaps the concrete. "No! *You* wanted the phone sex. I was just talking and acting like Justin does with women. I did whatever you'd want him to do. I never forced you."

And more of the pieces click into place. "Does he force you?"

Her face freezes. "He would have done the same thing to you if you hadn't gotten so sick at the party." She looks me straight in the eyes, hers clouding with pain. "Justin drugged your drink."

Every muscle in my body tenses, and suddenly everything I didn't understand about that night makes sense, far too late. Those personal conversations in the library carrel, Justin's flirtatious touches to make me question whether or not he was interested, the compliments I drank in, my joy when he invited me to the frat party—all a ploy to sexually assault me.

I feel sympathy for Olivia, because no woman should ever have to experience rape, but I'm also so angry that I bark, "You *knew* Justin drugged me? And didn't care?"

She snatches the pendant from my hand. "I only found out today. But Tyler knew—or suspected."

I fall back against the pipe. A wave of dizziness makes the basement spin. I struggle to focus on her. "Is Tyler dead in that freezer, Olivia?"

She opens her mouth, and a deep, keening wail of grief, misery, and loss breaks free, as though she hasn't sobbed in years. It echoes in the basement and lasts so long that I can't stand it. I extend my leg to touch her foot.

"This wasn't the life I was supposed to have," she says, when she's finally out of tears.

"Me neither."

I cough, and she lays her hand on my back, like I did with Ava when she was young. I hate Olivia for holding me hostage, but deep down, I don't think this is what she truly wants. "I'll help you. That's what you wanted. This doesn't have to be your life. Tell me, how did Tyler die?"

The wood beams above our heads vibrate with the loud, pounding music.

She comes closer to me and says in my ear, "If I tell you, we can never let you go. You know that, right?"

Now I huff a raspy laugh. "Were you ever going to let me go?"

I might never get out of here alive, but maybe if Olivia tells me, she'll eventually be able to tell Tyler's family what happened to him. And tell mine what happened to me. Gently, I say, "Let go of the burden. I know you want to."

Suddenly the music stops. Heavy footsteps tread above our heads. There's a long, loud creak, like a heavy door is opening.

Hope rises inside me. "It sounds like Justin is leaving. You can let me go," I beg. "Please, Olivia. I think he coerced you into hiding Tyler's body because you're terrified of him. I think Justin killed Tyler, and you're covering for him. I'll go with you to the police. It's not too late."

Olivia opens her mouth.

A female voice rings out, loud and clear, through the ceiling.

"Hey, Justin. I hope it's okay I just showed up."

Justin's response is harsh. "It's not okay. You can't be here, Madison."

A bold laugh. "Oh, you're going to want to hear what I have to say. I'm a minor. I have screenshots of everything. The police, media, your neighbors would be very interested if they saw them. I think you should let me inside."

My blood runs cold. I know that husky, melodic voice and cocky laugh. And now I'll do anything for her to hear me. "Oh my God."

Olivia holds her fingers over her lips, then murmurs, "That's a girl Justin's been chatting with. He'll find a way to get her to leave. Just be quiet."

I shake my head furiously. "No. That's not some girl," I hiss through my teeth. "That's my daughter. It's Ava."

CHAPTER TWENTY-ONE

OLIVIA

Olivia stares at Eden, who wrenches hard enough on the ropes binding her wrists to make something crack.

"Let me go!" she shrieks so loudly that Olivia's ears ring.

Olivia slaps her hand over Eden's mouth. "Shut up!"

Eden bites down on her palm, and Olivia howls, pulling her hand from Eden's sharp teeth.

"Ava! It's me! Mom!" she screams.

"Stop it! You're delirious! It's not Ava," Olivia hisses. "Do you want Justin to come down here?"

"I know my daughter's voice." A moment ago, Eden was so weak she could barely sit up. Now her voice is steel, and she's rattling the pipe with all her might.

"Please. Stop!" Olivia darts her eyes to the ceiling. "I'm telling you that's Madison. A girl Justin's been texting with. I saw the messages."

"A girl Justin or *you've* been texting with? Oh my God, did you catfish my daughter too?" She kicks out again and again, landing a hard blow to Olivia's ankle. Then she howls, "Ava! I'm in the basement! Run and call the police!"

Eden's writhing like a woman possessed, and Olivia doesn't know what to do. If Madison hears her, she'll call the police—if she can get out the door fast enough. If she can't, there's no limit to what Justin is capable of. Like a snake, he strikes when cornered.

"I am her mother. That's Ava. I don't care what you do to me, but get her out of here safely." Eden gets on her knees, spittle hanging out of her mouth. "Please. I'm begging you. I don't know how she knew I was here, but I think she came to find me."

Olivia needs Eden to stop talking so she can think. Before Justin answered the door to that girl, she was about to reveal everything, because there's no way Justin is letting Eden out of here alive. If it's true that Ava is upstairs, the rules have all changed.

Everything is too loud—her breathing, Eden's voice, the argument upstairs, and all the dead men in her life. Could it be Ava is Madison, who asked for a job with Justin, then flirted, made plans to meet him at a bar she couldn't get into? From what Olivia's seen on Ava's TikTok and Instagram accounts, the teenager is focused on music and other girls.

Eden slams her elbow into the pipe over and over. "Do you ever take any responsibility? You hid a dead body, lied to the police, let Tyler's family suffer, ruined my life, and now my daughter is upstairs with your abusive husband. Let me go! Do you want to be like Justin?"

Eden's skin is clammy, and sweat covers her forehead despite how cold it is down here. Olivia pulls her shirt over her hand and gently wipes Eden's face. No, she doesn't want to be anything like Justin. Ill and harmless, Eden is the woman who genuinely made Olivia feel like someone special. She gave her hope. Now all she's left with is terrible regret.

"Please, Olivia. If you can't save me, save my daughter." Eden looks at the pendant still in Olivia's hand. "If not for me, or yourself, do it in your brother's memory."

There's a horrific crack that rocks the foundation, then the ceiling shakes with a crash that can only be a body hitting the floor.

"Ava!" Eden screeches, bending her head, curving into herself.

The trapdoor lifts open, creating a diabolical shadow on the concrete as Justin's head appears.

"We have a problem."

"What did you do to my daughter?" Eden screams. "You won't get away with this again. Everyone is looking for her!"

Justin waves Eden's phone. "No, they're not. Your hubby texted that Ava called him half an hour ago. She was so upset about your breakup that she stayed at a friend's off campus overnight. She turned off her phone and fell asleep. Dave thinks you're very relieved and will be in touch after you speak to Ava and get some more rest." He snarls, "Your daughter's a piece of work."

"You're going to get caught, Justin."

"I see things differently, Eden. And you know what? I tend to come out on top. Hey," he says, his eyes on Olivia now, "I thought I told you to duct-tape her mouth. I need silence."

Eden struggles against the ropes, her wrists etched with deep abrasions. Olivia puts her hand under her shirt, feeling her own deep scratches from being bent over the arm of the Eames chair. The scratches scar.

Justin turns his attention to Olivia. "I'll get into Ava's phone to erase everything. You deal with the rest."

And he's gone. But her secrets are still in the house. She didn't tell Eden the whole truth.

Eden bucks uselessly against the ropes.

"I'm so sorry," Olivia whispers in her ear.

Then she says one more thing, and following Justin's orders, she duct tapes Eden's mouth closed before heading up the ladder.

"Please no," Olivia says when she gets to the main floor and sees the horrific scene in front of her.

Justin sits on the bottom step of the staircase in the entryway, where Ava Miller lies face down, crumpled on the hardwood floor, blood pouring out of the back of her beautiful brown hair and turning the purple streaks as crimson as the Persian carpet rolled up near her. More blood stains her light-gray U-M hoodie. Olivia gasps and turns away. The sight of blood has always made her light headed. There was no blood when Tyler died.

If he'd kept his mouth shut the night of the party, never accused or touched Justin on that balcony, he'd still be alive.

When a terrible whimper came through the open bathroom window, Tyler growled, "I know you did something to Eden. I'm going to find out what."

Then Tyler put his hands on Justin's shoulders to push him out of the way so he could get inside the frat house.

Olivia watched Justin shove Tyler's hands off him, too hard. When Tyler toppled backward over the railing, she wanted to step forward and grab Tyler's shirt, his hand, anything to prevent her friend's body from falling through the air to the ground below. She could have stopped it. But she didn't move quickly enough. Tyler hit the gravel parking lot with a thunderous crack.

The music blaring from inside the house and the sounds of everyone partying were muffled, like she was in a tunnel. Olivia opened her mouth to scream for help. Justin clapped his hand over her lips.

Drawing her close, he whispered, "Quiet. No one is out here. Everyone inside is trashed. Not a single person heard."

"But Tyler—"

She looked down at the golden boy with the sunny smile, her friend, his eyes closed like he was sleeping.

Torn between right and wrong, Olivia jumped when a door slammed inside the house. She and Justin whipped their heads to the sliding glass door and looked into the hallway through Tyler's bedroom. Justin put a finger to his lips, tiptoed into Tyler's room, peered into the hallway, and closed the door. Then he came back out to the balcony.

Justin brought her body close to his, because she was shaking so hard. "It was just Eden. Some guy is carrying her downstairs. It's fine.

No one saw me. She's still completely wasted. She won't remember a thing." He stroked Olivia's hair. "But someone else could see us. We have to get out of here."

They took Tyler's red Solo cup and went through the sliding door into his bedroom and out to the hall, where a fire escape was at the far end. Quickly, making sure no one was around, they ran down the steep steps to the back of the house, where Tyler's body had landed close to the grass under the balcony.

Justin checked Tyler's pulse and nudged him with his sneaker. "He's dead. There's nothing we can do for him."

Olivia started to cry, but Justin shook his head. "Listen to me. We were never here. Say it."

"What? No. We can't just leave him here, Justin. It was an accident. We have to tell the police."

He cupped her chin. "We can't go to the police. He fell backward. It could be hard to prove it was an accident, especially when your mother also died in a fall. And with Alistair's issues . . . I worry you'll be held responsible for this."

"But it *was* an accident. And I wasn't even facing him. I was next to him."

"But no one knows I was even upstairs. Tons of people might have seen you crying or talking to him. Before Eden basically attacked me in the hallway on my way to the bathroom, I was jamming with my band in the living room. The rest of the guys were smoking a bong. I'm sure they're too high to even notice how long I've been gone." His face suddenly went white. "No one knows you and I are together, because you wanted it that way. Tons of people probably saw Eden all over me."

Olivia's chest skittered with fear. "What are you saying? You'll make me look responsible?"

"Of course not. I'd never do that to you. I love you. I need to protect *you*. Can you imagine how furious your father will be if he knows you were with Tyler when he fell? That you were drinking and smoking?"

Olivia panicked. Justin was right. If Olivia was in any way connected to a scandal or simply behaving in an uncouth manner, he'd punish her by taking access to Alistair away.

"We were never here," she said, because she wanted to believe it so much. She didn't want to even think about what Tyler thought Justin did to Eden. It was so obvious to her that Eden was just another girl infatuated with Justin Ward. He didn't need to do anything for Eden to throw herself at him. Most girls did, just like Olivia had.

She started to walk away, but then she remembered the cigarette. "Justin," she whispered frantically. "Tyler and I shared a smoke."

His eyes widened. "Shit. We have to find it."

They ducked and ran under the balcony, where dirt, leaves, and other garbage were piled in mounds on the grass.

Olivia dropped to her knees and pulled a lighter out of her pocket to see better in the dark, but it kept burning her fingers.

"I don't have a flashlight, and we can't turn on the headlights on the van." He pointed to the Screaming Demons' white van parked across from the balcony with the other cars.

Olivia couldn't hold back her tears. They leaked out of her eyes and down her cheeks. Even if she found a cigarette, how would she know it was hers? She'd chewed her lipstick off hours ago, and so many people smoked Marlboro Reds.

"This is really bad. The police could find your cigarette." He pulled her toward him, his broad chest comforting against hers, slowing her racing heartbeat. "I'm so in love with you. We're more than soulmates. Plato says that humans can be split in two. Halves of the same whole. It's called twin flames. That's what we are. It's you and me. Always. I'm going to marry you one day, Olivia Walker. And I'll bring Alistair home to you."

She'd waited her whole life for a love like this. Someone who wouldn't leave her; someone who would take care of her and her brother.

So, she stayed quiet and helped Justin move Tyler's body into the back of the band's van and cover him with blankets. They came up with their alibis. Justin went back to the living room to take a hit from the bong with the band, and Olivia started walking. In thirty minutes, he met her in a woodsy area about twenty minutes from the Tudor.

Once at the Tudor, knowing her father wasn't going to be home for a few days, they turned on the freezer in the basement, which no one had been allowed to enter since her mother's death. Then they placed Tyler's body inside, shut the top, and padlocked it.

Tyler's fatal injuries must have been internal—a broken neck or spine, maybe a traumatic brain injury. There was no evidence to clean up, except the cigarette she and Justin could never find—and the only witness now in their basement while her daughter lies in a pool of blood on their floor.

"Is she dead?" Olivia finally asks, wanting desperately to run to the teenage girl.

Justin doesn't answer.

Olivia ventures a few steps toward Ava and forces herself to look to see if she's still breathing. She's too afraid to touch her. She's always so afraid.

"What did you do to her?" she asks Justin, who is eerily nonchalant.

"Me? Are you kidding me? You're the one who involved us with this family. She thought I was seeing her mother and threatened that if I didn't stop, she'd post screenshots of our texts. And she blathered on about some guitar she wants. She tried to blackmail me."

Olivia bends down and touches Ava's delicate neck to feel for a pulse. When the beat moves faintly under her fingers, Olivia strokes the unconscious girl's cheek. She turns to Justin, still sitting on the stairs. "We have to help her. This isn't right. None of this is right."

He laughs coldly. "She targeted me, seduced me, tried to entrap me." He stands and approaches Olivia. "And you, my sweetheart, are in big trouble for getting me into this."

Olivia doesn't step back. What's the point? He's going to kill her eventually. She's gone too far.

From beneath her, it's silent. Eden isn't rattling the pipe. Olivia looks again at Ava, not knowing how she even knew about Justin.

"You did this, Justin. Your mother is right. You're worthless."

He seizes Olivia by the throat, lifting her off her feet. She hears a gurgling moan. It's not coming from her.

Ava is waking up. Justin has heard it too.

He drops Olivia, who falls to the floor, and he moves toward Ava. The girl is prone, and with her fingernails digging into the plank floorboards, she drags herself forward, collapses, then rises to her hands and knees, crawling ever so slowly toward the front door.

"Mom," she says in a desperate whisper.

Justin steps over Olivia and presses his steel-toed boot to Ava's back, pushing her down to the floor.

Olivia can't bear to watch. She closes her eyes, but they open when Justin yanks her head back by her hair. "Help me, goddamn it. We have to cover her mouth and stop her from moving. Give me the duct tape."

"I . . . I left it in the basement."

"Moron. The rope then."

On autopilot, no fight left in her, Olivia rises. She brings him the toolbox, clicks it open, and takes out the rope, avoiding the terror in Ava's eyes, trying to block out her own from making her collapse to the floor again, herself.

Justin flips Ava over onto her back, and his boot now holds her down by her stomach. He spits in her face. "All you women are out to ruin my life. You're trash."

Ava spits right back at him. It's clear that Ava is petrified, but she has an inner will only possible because she was raised by an excellent mother. Maybe if Olivia and Alistair's mother had been able to take them away from this house, she and Alistair would be together now. None of this would be happening. She disappears into that reverie, into her mind, so she doesn't have to watch when Justin places himself in front of Ava, swinging his boot back and smashing her in the face. But no amount of daydreaming can block out the sickening crunch of bone breaking.

"Get the fuck away from my daughter!" Eden screams, pulling herself out of the trapdoor, the yellow ropes dangling from her bleeding wrists as she rushes toward Justin.

CHAPTER TWENTY-TWO

EDEN

I lunge at Justin, leaping onto his back to force him away from Ava. He shakes me off easily, and I hit the floor on my tailbone, feeling like my spine has snapped. I'm close enough to Ava that I see her beautiful face covered in so much blood that I can't make out her features.

I don't have time to look at what Olivia is doing or think about any of my own pain because Justin grabs for me as Ava rolls onto her stomach, trying to crawl military-style toward me, the way she did when she was a baby. Her hand weakly bats at the back of Justin's leg.

He spins around, kicking out again with his boot right into Ava's throat. Using every ounce of power I have, I stand and clutch the back of his T-shirt, trying to pull him toward me, away from my daughter. It's not enough to stop him. Nothing is. He elbows me hard in the chest, winding me enough that I have to let go. I slam into the brass coatrack by the front door. It topples into Justin and Olivia's wedding photo on the wall, shattering the glass frame, then crashing to the floor.

Justin reaches for something in the toolbox beside him.

He turns. In his hand is a hammer. He swings his arm back. There's an almighty scream.

"Stop, Justin! Enough!"

Olivia leaps in front of me, shielding me with her body, taking the slam of the hammer on her shoulder. But she doesn't even flinch. With almost superhuman power, Olivia places her hands on Justin's chest.

The hammer drops onto the rolled-up Persian carpet with a bang that rattles the floorboards.

One shove is all it takes.

Down Justin falls, backward through the open trapdoor. The thud when he hits the bottom isn't deafening. But it is final.

Olivia rushes to the trapdoor. I bolt to Ava, who's crumpled in a heap in the entryway, covered in blood. I lie down beside her, gently cradling her against me, my chest to her back, the way I did when she was a little girl and she'd call for me in the middle of the night when she had a bad dream.

There's a hole in the plaster by the front door. I look at the gash at the back of Ava's head, now bleeding a light trickle, and realize he must have cracked her skull against the wall. With the lightest touch, I stroke Ava's shoulder, my tears falling onto the floor.

She squeezes my hand and nestles in closer to me. My brave, reckless daughter, who—for so many reasons I don't understand—played Justin like Olivia played me.

"Olivia, call 911!" I yell.

She doesn't seem to hear me, because she moves from the trapdoor to the living room where broken pieces of black ceramic surround what looks like gray piles of dust. On her knees, she grabs a fistful of the dust, then lets it sift through her fingers back to the floor. She returns to the trapdoor and peers down into the basement. "I killed him." She's not crying.

I don't know if her lack of intonation is from shock, grief, guilt, remorse, or relief. Olivia saved my life and Ava's. For that, I'm thankful, even if none of this would have happened had she not deceived me.

I shift slightly from Ava, and after crawling to the trapdoor, I look down at Justin. His neck is bent at a horrifying angle, his body splayed out on the floor. Blood seeps out from under him, scarlet against the light-gray concrete. His gorgeous face is unmarred; his eyes open in a blank stare. Impaled through his left forearm is a shard of black ceramic.

If not for Ava, I wouldn't have had the strength to move. Now that she's safe, I press my forehead to the floor in thanks and also contrition. I didn't want anyone to die, not even the sociopath who tried to destroy his wife, my daughter, and me.

Revenge isn't in my blood. Justice is.

I reach for Ava's phone, which must have skittered across the floor in her struggle with Justin, and press Emergency Call. I reel off Justin and Olivia's address. After the dispatcher assures me that the police and rescue squad will be here momentarily and that she'll keep me on the line talking to her, I can barely speak.

She tells me to open the front door.

Depleted, I crawl over and unlock it. Then I end the call with the dispatcher, because I want to talk to Dave more than heed her request to stay connected. I move back to hold Ava again. "I need to phone Dad, honey. What's your password?"

"Your anniversary," she whispers.

And that unravels me. With the deepest cry, I dial Dave's number and fill him in as much as I can.

"I love you, Eden. I'm so sorry I'm not there. This is my fault for hurting both of you. I told Ava where you were." His voice is hoarse with emotion. "I love my girls so much."

He tells me that Jenna and Natalie have been texting and calling him all morning. Both my best friends knew something was wrong, because I'd never have gone to a hotel to rest while Ava was still missing and I hadn't answered a single one of their messages.

"I should have known. I should know you better," Dave says, guilt and regret evident in the sobs I hear through the line. "I should have called the police. I didn't think you were in actual danger."

"This isn't your fault, Dave. You're a good man."

"I want to hold you," my husband tells me.

"Me too." It's the truth. "There's time for that later, Dave. There's time for everything."

Olivia tears her eyes away from the basement and looks at me. "You still want to be with him."

I don't answer, because sirens ring out in the distance, getting louder and closer until flashing red lights bounce off the small stained glass square window on the front door.

A woman in an elegant charcoal pantsuit enters with a man in a wrinkled sports jacket and jeans. She flashes a badge and quickly surveys the hole in the wall by the front door, the blood on the floor. "I'm Detective Lieutenant Linda Phan, and this is Detective Keith Lonergan. We're with the sheriff's office of Washtenaw County." She sweeps her eyes around every corner of the dark room before they land on me. "You're Eden Miller?"

"Yes," I say with relief.

"Is there an active threat in the home?"

I glance at Olivia. "No."

The detectives step to the side, and two EMTs, a male and female, carrying a stretcher enter the house. The female, whose name tag reads **Raquel**, heads straight for Ava, while the male, Frank, points to the open trapdoor and asks, "Is that ladder safe to climb down?"

I nod. He heads down the ladder, and Raquel flashes a penlight in Ava's eyes and checks her vitals. And all the while, my baby girl is clutching my hand. Or I'm clutching hers. I never want to let go.

Three firefighters come through next, and while two also head down to the basement, one stays to help Raquel attach a collar around Ava's neck and transfer her to a stretcher, which they elevate so she's semisitting. Then Raquel inserts an IV into the back of Ava's small hand.

Olivia has not moved from beside the trapdoor. She only rocks back and forth. Helplessly, I stroke Ava's free hand, wanting to beg Raquel to tell me she's okay but knowing I have to let everyone do their jobs.

Raquel looks at me. "Ms. Miller is stable. She has a possible concussion, maybe fractures, and internal injuries."

I need to release Ava's hand so Raquel can check my vitals, place me on a stretcher right next to Ava's, and secure an IV. "You're dehydrated. Definitely some bruising on your lower back, adhesive trauma around your mouth, and possibly other injuries."

Then Raquel stands to walk over to Olivia and does the same check on her. She doesn't need an IV, and she refuses a stretcher.

Raquel's radio crackles. "Need an officer down here."

Detective Lieutenant Phan nods at Detective Lonergan, who descends the ladder. A moment later, the firefighters run back up the ladder and out the door, returning with a basket and ropes.

The noise seems to shake Olivia from her stupor. She reaches into her pocket.

Phan is immediately at Olivia's side and seizes her arm. "Mrs. Ward, slowly remove your hand from your pocket, please."

Olivia complies, pulling out her hand and splaying her fingers. The brown-and-gold pendant that means so much to her is in her palm. Gently, the detective takes it from her and pats her down. Olivia has nothing else on her but the tiger eye.

"It was her brother's," I tell Phan.

Olivia's gray eyes lock on mine. She offers me a small, harrowing smile and a nod. I nod back. Her eyes move to her wedding photo, spindly cracks obscuring her and Justin's faces, on the wall near the front door, where only a few hours ago, I had entered with no idea how much danger I'd put myself in by coming here.

"Someone needs to tell Justin's family that he's dead." She closes her eyes, her body sagging in what to me seems like relief.

Phan stays close to Olivia but focuses on Ava. "You're all safe now." Then she looks at Olivia. "I'd like you to sit there"—she gestures to the bottom step of the stairs—"and not move. Can you do that?"

Olivia obeys.

With one eye on Olivia, Phan directs her attention to Raquel. "Is it okay if I ask a few questions before you transport the victims to the hospital?"

Raquel nods. "Yes. Briefly, please. I'll document everything while you do that."

Phan pulls out a pen and a small spiral notebook, which she flips open. "Why were you both here today?" She directs the question to me.

"It's my fault." Tears run down Ava's cheeks.

Ava does not cry easily. I don't actually think she's cried in front of me in years. Now, all her anger, pain, and sorrow pour out, and I inhale it all into me. I reach out to stroke her fingers. It's the only part of her I can touch.

"I'm right here, honey. I love you more than anything, no matter what. Tell Detective Phan everything."

Her eyes swollen, she sobs, "I'm so sorry, Mommy. I saw all your messages and"—she shudders—"photos you exchanged with him when you and Dad came to the dorm after I got caught partying."

The *Mommy* sets off a flood of my own tears. I can't remember the last time Ava called me that. But it's crucial she tell the detective, and me, everything she can before it gets lost in the pain and recovery that is to come. "You went into my phone?"

"You left your purse on my desk when you and Dad went into the hall to talk about me. And you were acting all weird. Sweaty and edgy, and you kept checking your phone."

Utterly drained, I struggle to recall Saturday. It feels like years ago. "Why didn't you ask me about it?"

Ava makes a sound that might be a sarcastic laugh. Any other time, I'd be annoyed. Now I'm just grateful she's still my Ava. "Sure, Mom. Like we ever talk about that stuff. I only looked at your phone because I failed some assignments in music theory and philosophy. I was scared my adviser had emailed you. I wanted to check. But then I found the messages and thought Justin was why you and Dad separated. You act like you're perfect and never do anything wrong, but you sent an almost-naked selfie!"

My tears soak into the silky top I'd worn for my fake date with Justin. I want to burn everything on me.

I run my thumb across her fingers—fingers that Dave and I created, that strum a guitar so exquisitely. "So you catfished the man you thought I'd betrayed your father with?"

"Kind of. After I read your messages, I went to the ARC, this alternative rock club at school, to hang out and couldn't believe it when I saw his photo with his loser band on the wall, like he was some big star. I was so angry that this was the guy you wanted instead of Dad. He was so gross. I assumed Dad never told me the actual reason he left because he was protecting you." Her hand flexes. "And I knew Justin was playing you. I had to do something to get him away from you, so you and Dad could, I don't know, start over."

"It wasn't Justin messaging me. It was his wife." I gesture to Olivia, who's now silently watching us from the bottom step of the stairs, her eyes drinking us in.

Ava opens her mouth.

Before she can add anything, I have something to say. "Ava, honey, your business is mine, at least some of it. But mine isn't yours. I'm your mother, an adult, and your father and I weren't together. As painful as that is, it's reality." I bring her hand to my lips and kiss it. "None of that is important right now, though. But why Madison?"

A tiny smile plays at the corners of Ava's lips. "It's the first name of the girl in my dorm who narked on me for the party in my room."

"Oh, Ava." I sigh sadly. "All I care about is that you're okay. The rest we'll deal with later."

Detective Lieutenant Phan has been listening and taking notes. Now she asks Ava, "Did Justin Ward hurt you in any way other than the physical assault?"

I'm scared to hear the answer.

Ava vehemently says no. I let out a loud exhale. "No. He never touched me. It was all texts." She shudders again. "I knew right away that he wouldn't care that I'm seventeen and he'd message me just like he did to my mom. So, I wanted to catch him in the act."

Raquel interrupts. "I think that's enough for right now. We really need to get them to the hospital."

Phan nods. "Just one more question for Ms. Miller. Why did you come here today?"

Ava blushes. "When I spoke to my dad this morning, he was really scared and really mad that I'd turned off my phone and slept at my friend's. My girlfriend's. Lara." Another tiny smile appears. "He told me my mom went to a friend from college's house to ask for help looking for me, then to a hotel to get some rest." She moves her eyes toward me. "I lied to Dad and said I was going back to my dorm. I knew the friend must be Justin, so I found his address online in the white pages." She winces. "Then I came here to confront Justin and record him. But when I saw your car parked at the curb, I thought I'd be able to do it in front of you. You weren't here, though, or I didn't think you were, so I decided to also blackmail him for my Les Paul."

Phan looks confused for a moment, so I help out. "It's a kind of guitar."

Ava half smiles at me. It's the best thing I've ever seen.

"Your mother is a very good person. I want to be more like her." Olivia's voice, suddenly strong and clear, surprises us all. And her words help soothe my wounded soul a little bit. I'm far from perfect, but I am a good person.

While we've been up here, there have been voices from the team in the basement. Still, a bang startles all of us then Phan's radio bursts to life. I make out, "Male. Justin Ward. Vital signs absent. Termination of resuscitation. Dead on scene. Also skeletal remains encased in plastic sheeting in a chest freezer. Need the coroner and CSI."

Phan raises her eyebrows at me.

I gesture at Olivia. "It's her story to tell."

Phan nods. "She can tell it at the station." She walks toward Olivia. "Olivia Ward, please rise and place your hands behind your back."

Olivia does, and handcuffs snap onto her wrists.

Phan says, "There is reasonable cause to place you under arrest on suspicion of kidnapping a minor, kidnapping an adult, forcible confinement, indignity to a dead body, obstruction of justice, and voluntary manslaughter."

Phan reads Olivia her rights, then leads her to the door. But before they make it, Olivia stops. "Wait."

The detective grips her arm more tightly. "What is it, Mrs. Ward?"

Looking over her shoulder, Olivia holds my eyes with hers. "Eden, I'm very sorry I hurt you. I really am. The tiger eye pendant. I want you to have it."

The detective shakes her head. "No. It's evidence."

Olivia's face falls for a moment, then something strange but almost angelic happens. A faint rosy blush spreads across her cheeks, and she smiles. "That's okay. She doesn't need it."

With my hand in Ava's, I watch Olivia be taken from her home, no longer a prisoner here, but hopefully she will never be free to hurt anyone again.

When Phan opens the front door, I see that the rain has stopped. The sun has come out. The door slams shut. I focus solely on Ava.

"You're a badass, Mom."

I laugh sadly, lay my fingers on the inside of her wrist, and breathe deeply as her pulse beats against my skin.

CHAPTER TWENTY-THREE

OLIVIA

Six Months Later

Though Olivia had feared being locked up more than anything, removed from society like a pariah as her brother had been, she likes her cozy cell in the mental health unit at the women's correctional facility. The tiny room, with only a bed and steel door, keeps her safe. The small space reminds her of the pantry. Sometimes she dreams about dying so she can join Alistair, but most of the time Olivia is afraid to die because she might end up wherever Justin is, bound to him for eternity.

And if she dies, she'll never see Eden again.

Through therapy, Olivia's learned that she has borderline personality disorder, which helps her understand why Alistair hated medication and the dulling of all his senses. Olivia feels the same way. And because she's trying so hard to be good—volunteering in the library and following every rule set out for her—no one suspects she's hiding her pills between her tongue and cheek every dosage time. Olivia doesn't need medication, like her mother did. She needs to be sharp.

Olivia learned a lot about how to charm people from Justin. And she has a new friend in prison. Penny, a guard, has become Olivia's confidante, and Olivia is hers. Sometimes, Penny gives Olivia access to a cell phone. It's their little secret. Olivia has her own secret to tell, but not to Penny. She told Justin, in his truck, with Tyler dead in the back, because she thought he was her twin flame. But he was her captor. It's Eden, selfless and good, the very best person Olivia knows, who is the mirror of everything Olivia can be. But not yet. First, she needs to set herself free from the deepest darkness inside her and tell it to the person she betrayed the most.

It's rest time in the dialectical behavior unit, so Olivia uncaps the pen she's allowed to have, now that she's proved she's not a risk to herself or anyone else, along with the journal Penny gave her.

And she writes:

Dear Ally,

I lied to you. I lied to Dad. I lied to everyone. You didn't cause Mom's death. I did.

Everything that happened to you was my fault. I was the one who took you to the basement that day so we could sneak ice cream sandwiches from the freezer when Mom was resting and Dad was working. I was the one who insisted we play hide-and-seek. And I was the one who abandoned you in the basement, told you to count to one hundred, didn't worry soon enough when it took you longer than usual to find me.

You never told anyone the truth. Then you started to believe what Dad had assumed—that you'd gone down to the basement by yourself and left the trap-door open. You got sicker because you protected me by hurting yourself. I was your big sister and should have protected you.

Everything you've suffered was my fault. I was so scared of Dad, so frightened not to be his princess anymore, because he'd spank and slap us every time we did something wrong. I was afraid he wouldn't love me anymore. I let you take the blame when you were the only person who truly loved me.

I am so deeply sorry. I hope you can forgive me, because I'm trying to be a better person. I saved Eden's life. Maybe you can see me, even though I can't hear you anymore. But if you don't know, I gave her a broken piece of your urn so she could cut through the ropes, tear the duct tape from her mouth, and get out of the basement.

I've been punished. I never had children. I was abused, assaulted, used, and held captive for almost my whole life. It was what I deserved. You deserved better than me.

I'm going to try to be a better friend than I was a sister to you. I love you forever.

Always,

Your Olly

Olivia quietly, slowly tears the paper from the journal, crumples it into the tiniest ball possible, and swallows it. It grates against her throat when it goes down. She won't leave any evidence behind this time.

The recording Justin made of her confession has never been found, but the police did, of course, find her silver Mazda with the dented fender and broken headlight parked in the garage, adding charges of a hit-and-run and vehicular assault against Dave.

There's a knock on her cell door.

"Liv, it's exercise hour in five minutes," Penny calls out.

She likes the name she's given herself, a mix of Olivia and Lila. Liv Walker is what everyone here calls her. One day, Eden will too. It's also Penny's signal that Olivia has five minutes left to use the contraband cell phone.

That's all the time she needs. Olivia scrolls and taps. Then she smiles.

Twin flames might smolder, but they never extinguish.

CHAPTER TWENTY-FOUR

EDEN

I arch my back, moaning loudly with pleasure, sliding myself down so I can feel the man inside me as deeply as possible. I then lean forward and wrap my hands around his wrists, pressing them against the headboard.

"Say my name," I command, nipping my teeth along his neck.

In response, he makes a sound of pure ecstasy. "Eden."

I let go of his wrists. "Pull my hair," I instruct.

He places one hand under my hairline, stroking with sure fingers, and tugs the hair on my scalp with just the right amount of force and pressure. We collapse on the bed, and we laugh.

We've come a long way, my estranged husband and me.

It hasn't been an easy six months. There's been a lot of communication, tears, and healing for all of us.

Once Dave was discharged from the hospital, Natalie and Jenna brought him to Ann Arbor, to the hospital where I was being treated for dehydration and shock and where Ava spent two weeks recovering from a concussion, a broken cheekbone, and broken ribs.

When Ava was released from the hospital, Dave and I took her home to Grosse Pointe. Together we all stayed in the house on Ivy Court for a month. Dave and I slept in the same bed for comfort, talking all night long, because we both had so much to say to each other before we were ready to be together romantically again. U-M gave Ava the time she needed to recover from her recurrent headaches and fogginess and get caught up with her courses and for the three of us to begin family counseling. It's been gut wrenching, eye opening, and ultimately cathartic.

"It was a good session yesterday with Dr. Alohi," Dave says, referring to the couples therapist we see once a week. "I like her suggestion that we write notes to each other like my parents did. Have our own private space to express our needs and wants if verbalizing them is hard for us." He pulls me down so I'm lying flat again, and I rest my head on his shoulder.

I poke him in the ribs. "Brush up on your dirty talk. I have plenty to write about my fantasy next week."

Sometimes the fantasy is nothing like the reality. Unless it's with someone who will protect your whole heart and who is, at their core, a good person. Neither Dave nor I know where this new sexual exploration will lead us. But we want to take the journey together.

"I like this Eden and Dave 2.0." I flip onto my stomach, sliding my hand under the covers.

He strokes my hair, which I've cut into a shag I love. "You're going to kill me."

I giggle. "Maybe the wrong choice of words."

I can only laugh about my traumatic experience when I'm with Dave. He is my best friend, my coparent, and a man I trust to protect my body, heart, and soul.

I sit up, the sheet pulled to my waist, and look in the mirror across from Dave's king-size bed in his condo, where I now sleep a couple of nights a week. I smile at the rosy flush on my skin and my mussed hair. Then I move my gaze to the photo he's recently hung of me, him, and Ava. Our strong, resilient, brave daughter has the Les Paul that we'd finally bought her slung over her shoulder, a huge grin on her gorgeous face. But her mischievous smirk is there too.

Going into my phone then planning to set up a grown man to get her parents back together was so impetuous and dangerous. But Ava isn't perfect. I don't ever want her to feel like she even has to try. But now at eighteen, she's beginning to, if not understand, then accept that her mother and father's relationship is separate from our parenting of her, like Dave had to learn.

While Ava was craftier than we realized—she admitted she'd been the one who'd opened the basement window; it was how she snuck in and out of the house without Dave or I ever knowing—she's also more self-aware than either of us gave her credit for. No one's judgment or opinion of her has ever or will ever stop her from being completely herself. She's taught both her parents a lot about self-love.

She's also kept me apprised of all the social media posts and videos about Justin and his family, who have been bombarded by the press. Once she was physically and mentally stronger and ready to return to U-M, Dave and I drove her there. After kisses goodbye, which she initiated, he and I went to visit Tyler's parents. They'd called me after the news broke and his bones were identified through dental records. They thanked me for bringing their son home to them. When they hugged me, I held them tightly. They'll never stop grieving, but perhaps they can find some peace finally knowing what happened to their kind, loving, courageous son.

If not for Tyler, I don't know if Dave and I would be together.

"I should go home and get changed for work," I tell Dave, kissing his cheek and swinging my legs out of the bed. I reach for my phone next to my pillow, but he holds my arm.

"Or we can both play hooky and spend all day in bed? It's one of the perks of being the boss."

Sylvie welcomed me back to Greenwood Realty, after Olivia confessed that she'd been the one to report my indiscretion to prove to me how Justin was ruining my life. But I was ready to soar on my own.

In February, after passing the Michigan Real Estate Broker License exam, I used my share of the proceeds from the sale of our house to open my own brokerage and rent a one-bedroom condo. Dave and I haven't yet made set plans to live together again, but it's what we're working toward.

I snuggle back into him, trailing my fingers over his chest. "I'll stay, but I have to be at Nat's restaurant at six for Jenna's birthday."

My experience inspired Natalie to follow her passion. She quit her decades-long position as the in-house accountant for a marketing firm and opened her own Indian restaurant. And Jenna started a campaign with other doctors to offer free GHB test kits to college students. Once my story was in the media, ten other women came forward, asserting that Justin had drugged them too. All but Jenna and I had been sexually assaulted. The women hadn't put it together until the news came out. Neither did Jenna.

That day on the Diag during homecoming, when I first saw Justin, Jenna told me he'd hit on her at a bar. It never occurred to her to mention that he'd tried to buy her a drink, because it didn't seem significant at the time. She'd declined, dodging a bullet, intuitively knowing that Justin was a predator.

My phone pings on the bed. The sound always makes me jump a little. It's a trauma response, Nancy's told me. I went back to therapy with her on my own, because I was ready to talk openly about all the uncomfortable, raw, private parts of myself.

And I'm healing from what Olivia did to me, relieved that she's getting help and is behind bars in Ann Arbor.

There was no trial. She pleaded guilty to all the charges Detective Lieutenant Phan arrested her for, plus admitting to a whole host of other offenses: stalking, theft—she had stolen and copied the key from under the cushion on our porch swing—and entering our house and turning on the stove while I slept. She had been behind every strange thing that was happening in my life. She's incarcerated for the next twenty-five years, with the possibility of parole, because her court-appointed attorney argued battered woman syndrome, which she suffered for decades.

Everyone is moving forward.

Dave's phone had pinged too. He checks it and grins. "Ava in our group text."

I leave my phone where it is and look at his screen.

Ava: Do you guys want to come visit this weekend? I'm doing an open mic night at Benny's. But no PDA. ☺

I laugh and Dave blushes, still my awkward, nerdy partner-in-life. Then he removes his glasses and wipes them with the bedsheet, which is twisted from our energetic adventures last night and this morning.

He texts Ava a thumbs-up emoji, which earns him an eye-roll emoji back.

I laugh, get my own phone, and send Dave a text.

I'm up for some more under-the-covers affection if you are.

He tosses his glasses onto the nightstand and dives under the duvet.

I don't know what the future holds for us. Losing my marriage, my daughter, my job, my whole self—all of this has taught me that truly experiencing life means letting go of the "supposed to" and embracing the what-ifs.

I'm in love with the real Dave for the first time. It's never too late to start over.

There's another ping on my phone. Expecting it to be Ava, I quickly glance at the screen. It's a text from a private caller.

When the time is right, we'll meet again.

I freeze.

Then Dave presses his mouth to my skin. I block the number, and gripping the covers, I close my eyes and fall, unafraid, into the moment.

ACKNOWLEDGMENTS

All I've truly ever wanted has been to write and have my work published. It didn't happen for me until *Woman on the Edge* was released when I was forty-six years old. I will be fifty when you hold *A Friend in the Dark* in your hands, and I might never fully believe that I'm fortunate enough to live my passion every day. My ultimate goal with every book I write is to push myself outside my comfort zone and create the best work I can.

All my books are the culmination of not only my own efforts but also the efforts of the outstanding community of dedicated, hardworking, talented people I have supporting and believing in me.

If it weren't for my exceptional agent, Jenny Bent, my decades-held goals would not have been realized, and she keeps making them happen for me. I am the luckiest author in the world to have had Jenny in my corner for ten years. And as well, Victoria Cappello and the Bent Agency team, who do so much for me.

Megha Parekh, my phenomenal, insightful, brilliant editor at Thomas & Mercer, read the proposal and first three chapters of *A Friend in the Dark* and changed my life. Working with Megha; my extraordinary developmental editor, Heather Lazare; fantastic production manager, Miranda Gardner; my sharp-eyed copy editor, Anna Barnes; keen-sighted proofreader, Jenna Justice; and the entire team at Amazon Publishing has been a beautiful experience. And the moment I saw the cover for this book (the pink!), I was madly in love. Huge thanks to

Mumtaz Mustafa and the design team for such creative, gorgeous art. As well, the Amazon Publishing authors are so warm and welcoming and have brought me into their family with open arms.

I'm indebted to the experts who so generously give of their time and knowledge to ensure my books are as accurate as possible. Any errors are my own and/or artistic license. I'm grateful to Steve Urszenyi—author of *Perfect Shot* and former paramedic, tactical medic, and commander of the Ontario Emergency Medical Assistance Team—who spent hours answering my medical / crime scene questions and obtained the information I needed from the Ann Arbor EMS. A massive thank you to psychotherapist Mitch Smolkin, my go-to for all strange and uncomfortable questions about the human psyche, and to author, teacher, and musician Dave Drew Maze for his consulting help.

I'm honored to participate every year in the annual Authors for Voices of Color, founded by Andrea Bartz and Jennifer Keishin Armstrong, in support of We Need Diverse Books. This past year, I auctioned off the opportunity to name a character in my book to benefit internship grants that support underrepresented college students and professional development for midlevel diverse employees. The winning bidder was Bookstagrammer Ali Hird (@my_year.in_books). The name of Alistair "Ally" Walker is in tribute to her late uncle, Alistair Walker Hird. While Alistair's name is real, the character is entirely fictional.

Music is a vital part of my writing process. I make carefully curated playlists and listen to songs to motivate, inspire, and help me better access my characters' mindsets. Since the early '90s, the Watchmen have been one of my favorite bands, and I had their music playing on repeat while writing this book. It's such a privilege for me to include a portion of the lyrics from "Run & Hide" in my epigraph. I'm so thankful to songwriter and guitarist Joey Serlin, for his generosity in allowing me to use his stunning words; Sammy Kohn for his kindness; and to the entire band, including Daniel Greaves and Ken Tizzard, for creating music that fuels my work and brings me so much joy.

The author community is my family. To thank everyone would require enough pages to fill another book. I do have to give special thanks to the people who over the last year or so have gone above and beyond: May Cobb, Vanessa Lillie, Danielle Girard, Robyn Harding, Christina McDonald, Roz Nay, Dara Levan, Lauri Schoenfeld, Lisa Barr, Rochelle Weinstein, Barbara Conrey, Lindsay Cameron, Georgina Cross, Hannah Mary McKinnon, Hank Phillippi Ryan, Jennifer Hillier, Laurie Elizabeth Flynn, Samantha Downing, Damyanti Biswas, Jaime Lynn Hendricks, Heather Levy, Tessa Wegert, Elle Marr, Darby Kane, Jon Lindstrom, Don Bentley, Jeneva Rose, Daniel Kalla, Sheena Kamal, Ghabiba Weston, Bianca Marais, Cecilia Lyra, Lydia Laceby, Maggie Giles, Jessica Hamilton, Suzanne Dugard, and Eden Boudreau.

I'm very thankful for all the Bookstagrammers, booksellers, librarians, BookTokkers, and every single person who helps me promote my work, fills me with happiness and confidence, and works tirelessly to give authors a stage simply because they love words. I would not have been able to achieve any of what I have without you, with shout-outs to Matt of Matty and the Books, Laurie of the Baking Bookworm, Jenna from Flowers Favourite Fiction, Blair at Books and Bevies, Katie of the Insta Bookworm, Jenn at Burlington Biblio, Erin of Girl Well Read, Stephanie Likes Books, Ashleigh of Teatime with a Book, Sonica at the Reading Beauty, Dasha Book Girl, Jennie Shaw, all the Canadian Book Enablers, Dana Orgnero of Danish Mustard Reads, Susie Pasquariello at SusieQPasq, Carrie Shields of Carrie Reads Them All, Jamie of Beauty and the Book, Robyn at Robyn Reads 1, Sara DiVello of Mystery and Thriller Mavens, Tonya Cornish of Blonde Thriller Book Lover and her amazing team, Gare Billings and Kate Hergott of the *Killing the Tea* podcast, Abby from Crime by the Book, Carey Calvert of Supalovacreads, Alicia at Thriller Chick, and also Joe Shwartz and Jen Jumba.

My friends are everything to me. I'm incredibly lucky to have them to lean on and laugh with. Miko, Nicole, Michael, Cheryl, Rachel Y., Deb, Lisa G., Helen, Val, Karen J., Jessica, Beth, Frances, Maggie, Lesley, Catherine M., Hugh, Lisa B., Kathy, Simone, Jenny, Adam,

Sylwia, Karen R., Idan, and Christopher; my godkids, Zackary and Zoe; and every single person who cares for me, I can't imagine doing life without you. And to the late Audrey Spence-Thomas, beautiful, brilliant, sassy, and classy, I think of you every day.

My Beach Babes, to whom this book is dedicated, are the group of female authors who have been there for all the highs and lows over the last twelve years. For nine years, the seven of us have convened in a beach house for one glorious week a year. Meredith Schorr, my critique partner extraordinaire; Francine LaSala, an eagle-eyed editor and a supreme chef; Josie Brown, who has the best snort-laugh I've ever heard; Julie Valerie, my angel; Eileen Goudge, who gives the best foot rubs; and Jen Tucker, whose heart is more golden than the sun, are my soul sisters.

My family has always inspired me to go after everything I want and embrace every second that I'm given. My parents, Celia and Michael; my brother, Jonah; my sister-in-law, Perlita; Mommy- and Daddy-in-law, Eileen and Ron; sisters-in-law Lori and Lindsay; brothers-in-law Todd and Scott; and nieces and nephews Hannah, Brynna, Mikey, Felix, Bassie, and Owen, I love you.

To the late Ron Mintz, who was like my second father; was also my teacher, high school principal, guide, and mentor; was one of the kindest, most loving people; and who made such a significant impact, you will live in my heart forever.

Brent, Spencer, Chloe, and my little dog, Jasper, I know that living with an author can be challenging, especially when I'm on a deadline or staring into space, conjuring up wicked plots. Without you, my world wouldn't turn and my heart wouldn't beat. I love you so very much.

And to my readers, I cannot thank you enough for the unbelievable love and support you've given me and for taking a chance on me. It motivates me every time I sit down to work. I write because I want to entertain you, make you think and feel, and yes, be scared. Because of all of you, I get to live my dream.

ABOUT THE AUTHOR

Photo © 2018 Dahlia Katz Photography

Samantha M. Bailey is the *USA Today* and #1 international best-selling author of *Woman on the Edge* and *Watch Out for Her*. Her books have sold in eleven countries. She lives in Toronto, where she can usually be found tapping away at her computer or curled up on her couch with a book. Connect with her on Instagram @SBaileyBooks and Facebook @SamanthaBaileyAuthor, and visit her website at SamanthaMBailey.com.